Blackburn entered the stateroom slowly and saw the woman.

Perhaps "mutilated" wasn't the proper word for the condition of the body. If it weren't, Blackburn thought, it would serve until someone looked up a better one on the hypercom. The woman's death-contorted remains were recognizable—just—but the face was another proposition altogether. Somebody had pointed a low-powered force projector at the bridge of her nose and pulled the trigger.

Fifteen or sixteen times.

THE WARDOVE

L. NEIL SMITH

BERKLEY BOOKS, NEW YORK

THE WARDOVE

A Berkley Book/published by arrangement with
the author

PRINTING HISTORY
Berkley edition/October 1986

ISBN: 0-425-09207-0

A BERKLEY BOOK® TM 757,375
Berkley Books are published by The Berkley Publishing Group,
200 Madison Avenue, New York, N.Y. 10016.
The name "BERKLEY" and the stylized "B" with design are trademarks
belonging to Berkley Publishing Corporation.

PRINTED IN THE UNITED STATES OF AMERICA

PERMISSIONS

The author gratefully acknowledges Professor Peter Shickele, of the University of Southern North Dakota at Hoople, without whose world-renowned musicological scholarship Chapters XXI and XXII wouldn't have had titles.

Something nice ought to be said, as well, about Frank Zappa and his never-ending struggle against the evil forces of M.A.F.I.A.

This book is dedicated to the heroes on both sides, who, with courage and distinction, fought an ugly little war in the jungles and mountains of southeast Asia or, with equal integrity, fought it in the streets and classrooms of Amerika.

Also to Martha, Nina, J.J., Mark, and Alan, for providing "reason to live despite news of botched world."

CONTENTS

THE WARDOVE

PART ONE
15 JUL 3008

Oh little terr, he is a bother, 'cause he'd really never rather
 Stand up an' fight a real God-given war.
So we denounce his acts as heinous, an' intended justa pain us—
 An' we're right, 'cause that's exackly what they're for.

Here we're goin' t'all the pains, a-buyin' missiles, ships, an' planes,
 While little terr just builds a bomb or lights a fire.
He's found a way that he can play agin the richer kids; but they
 Won't never praise 'im. Wiseguys just stir up their ire.

> —Anonymous First Skirmish Veteran
> circa 2951

I

Benjamin Parkinson

I'm no lonelier now than I was before you left me.
I felt my life begin again when you walked out that
*   door.*
I'm no lonelier now than I was before you left me.
You finally reach a point where hurting don't hurt any-
*   more.*

Sun broiled the back of his neck as he climbed out of the car.

Settling on its deflated skirt, the battered old Frontenac steamer sighed, sheet metal ticking in the heat. It had taken him more than an hour, trying to find the right berth in this line of moorings that stretched along the western "shore" of Mare Tranquillitatus nearly to the sad, weather-eroded Apollo Shrine.

Chelsie Bradford was dead. The old *Benjamin Parkinson* was about to be broken up for scrap. And the only person in the great glaring galaxy for whom the two events were inevitably associated was an unemployed hero who'd been drinking too much for a dozen years.

Chelsie Bradford was dead. In Archimedes, center of the human entertainment industry since mankind had once again had time to think about such things, a million individuals of every species would put in a bereaved appearance when they laid Chelsie in the ground. Maybe as many as ten million.

A hundred billion more would catch it on the hype. She'd had that kind of personality, all right, persuading each and every watcher that she was singing just for him. Maybe that's why she'd lasted longer than the usual pop-star.

> *The question isn't "Am I lonely now?"*
> *I don't like it but I get along somehow.*
> *I'm not saying these aren't teardrops in my eyes,*
> *But it should come to you as no surprise . . .*
>
> *That I'm no lonelier now than I was before you left me.*
> *My life was empty long before you said that we were*
>   *through.*
> *I'm no lonelier now than I was before you left me.*
> *There's just one difference—you're not here while I am*
>   *missing you.*

Chelsie Bradford was dead. A lot of speeches—one would be too many—too little music, then they'd slowly lower her pale body into a dark rectangular hole, bury it beneath damp Mare Imbrium dust and a snowy mountain of flowers. Camera shutters by the thousands would chatter, making their peculiar, insane, insectile racket. Maybe the people with their fingers on the buttons would even catch themselves shedding a genuine tear, their own lives forever dimmed because her special magic was gone in a way no holo could ever bring back.

Ever, ever again.

For him, it had been gone for twelve long years, which is why he was attending his own private memorial, half a hemisphere away, clattering over a tarnished metal boarding plank—heat-waves shimmered up from its sun-cooked surface—into the peeling gray labyrinth of an ancient decommissioned military starship.

Over his left shoulder, not far from the misty, jungle-fringed Lunar horizon, mocking the clean, if merciless, warmth of the sun overhead, dead Earth shone with the internal, sickly light of a moldering phosphorescent skull, the same funeral-shrouded radioactive cauldron it had been for a thousand years.

I asked so many questions, but the answers never came.
Our lives together running out like sand,
While all along you swore to me that things were still
the same.
So now I guess that you will understand . . .

Chelsie Bradford was dead. In here, inside the *Benjamin Parkinson*, it was cool, humid, a little musty-smelling. Just like his memories. Of all the places for a special magic to linger, it couldn't be anyplace but here. Not for him.

I'm no lonelier now than I was before you left me.
I wish I knew how many times I wanted you to care.
But I'm no lonelier now than I was before you left me.
How can you miss somebody who was never really
there . . .
How can you miss somebody who was never really
there?

PART TWO
10 NOV 2996

People may die for love, but they seldom
kill for it. By the time they're ready, it's
usually turned to something else.

—Captain-Inspector Nathaniel H. Blackburn

II

The War Against the Powers

Grey-eyed angel, princess of the plains,
Are you happy, or are you feeling pain?
Are you crying, or is it just that high-plains wind
Brings those teardrops and dries them up again?
Brings your teardrops and dries them up again?

Rain beat down the back of his neck.

The C.A.F. *Benjamin Parkinson* hadn't been new even the first time he'd clumped aboard, in a furious Tranquillitatus summer downpour. No crew had ever had reason to love her.

She'd been slapped together in a desperate hurry, two generations before, to fight an earlier war, one of a rare handful to survive the famous First Skirmish with the Clusterian Powers and come back in one piece. Transport starships a mile long aren't made for interstellar combat. They hadn't known that at the time.

Wishing he'd had five minutes for another drink to warm him, he hefted the large gray soft-sided bag he carried, stenciled in black with his name reversed, rank, and former unit designation. He tugged at his weather-soaked civilian cape where it bunched at his shoulder beneath the luggage-strap, and limped out of the elevator.

FRESH BLOOD WAR-FUND TOUR
starring *Fresh Blood*, with Chelsie Bradford
and introducing *Frog Strangler*

He blinked.

The giant banner assailed his senses even through the rain, composed, as it was, of thousands upon thousands of low-powered laser cells strung in acres of netting covering the side of the starship. The shade-shifting glare it threw was garish, deceptive where the footing, precarious or not, at least seemed so.

Rather than risk wedging the plastic tip of his cane in the open metal meshwork of the platform, he tucked it under his other arm, leaning hard on the rain-slick rail, keeping his eyes focused straight ahead. He refused to look down into the harrowing chasm between starship and boarding gantry, the depths blurred and exaggerated by the steady, falling rain. That kind of sight had always been a weakness with him. It wasn't going to get any better on *this* job.

He'd listened to the audio on the long drive to Tranquility from the Escarpment. The war news wasn't good. It hadn't been, not from the beginning. Clusterian Powerist forces were mopping up out on Aeri. The Central Rim remained the problem it had been for half a century, thanks to its unfortunate proximity to the Cluster. There'd been another messy pull-out from Lohua Fihr.

Heavy casualties.

He shuddered suddenly at unbidden memories of Osnoh B'nubo: a world of eternal snow, hurricane-swept glaciers, punctuated lately by charred machinery, mutilated bodies, quick-congealed pools of scarlet, green, and gold. "Military service builds men," the colorful recruiting posters had proclaimed. Broken men, he argued wordlessly and from experience. Men with memories they can never put away, of humiliation—the survivors had been forced to use the gloating propaganda broadcasts of the enemy as a beacon to follow home—of bitter retreat, and of pain, unrelenting and indescribable. His "foot" had begun throbbing again. The flask inside his travel bag seemed a million miles away.

Back home, here on Luna, they were having another spy-scare.

Along the busy concourse at the bottom of the gantry, he'd invested in a hype-print, not knowing what information services would be available aboard ship. He might as well have saved the copper. He'd learned five minutes later that the Arm Force had outfitted the old gray troopship like a luxury yacht, a hypercom in every stateroom. As an unsatisfying alternative to digging the flask out of his bag, he'd leafed through the print during the endless elevator ride.

More of the same. The espionage-hysteria was nothing extraordinary, just extraordinarily depressing. It was what had brought him here, although even now he wasn't sure . . .

A flash of light and movement caught his eye. Precarious upon a long, narrow platform, suspended on invisible force beams a few yards forward of the midships boarding-hatch, half a dozen workbeings struggled against wind and weather to weld a house-sized thermopatch onto the dull gray surface of the elderly starship's hull. He didn't envy them their job. The wind brought an eye-watering stench of scorched adhesive to his nostrils. Their heat-guns pulsed, glowing a dull, threatening red as they ran them along the edges of the repair.

A man had died in this place. That, too, was what had brought him here. Fifty square yards, he thought, of Arm Force gray sheet-plastic made a piss-poor headstone.

The little ensign bobbing shoulder-height at the dry end of the starship's boarding-ramp saluted him, requested, through the thin-film synthesizer plastered on her ventral tympanum, to see his credentials. He looked her over.

More than anything, she resembled, as every member of her species did, a translucent, helium-filled umbrella. Hydrogen, actually, a byproduct of her metabolism, rendered inflammable by a fraction of the other gas which was, to her kind, an all-important metabolic trace-element. The resemblance was complete, even to the sinuous "handle" which she'd uncurled toward him, expecting to receive his papers.

Even at this moment, late in the war, rear-echelon Arm Force officers were still ad-libbing their own uniforms. Hers was a beaut, a basic charcoal drapery of netting, with enough gold braid, scrambled eggs, and red spaghetti to set some civvie tailor up for life. An ornate, jeweled force-projector in a brass-bound velvet-covered scabbard swung nearly to the tip of her manipulator from a fine golden chain fastened in two places at the rim of her flotation canopy. He tried hard, as he always did, not thinking in stereotypes about the aesthetic sensibilities of the Ogat—which is what the little ensign happened to be—then gave it up. They were all *born* colorblind.

There was some shelter to be had here, as long as the wind didn't gust. On either side of the open hatchway, the starship's leaden flanks stretched into hazy infinity. Setting the bag on the perforated walkway of stamped titanium, he switched his cane to the other hand, reached into his sporran, extracted a palm-sized piece of officially embossed plastic, half expecting from the way she was dressed that the ensign would tear it in half and hand it back to him:

Captain-Inspector NATHANIEL H. BLACKBURN
Coordinated Arm Force
23 Aldrin Parkway, Altai Escarpment, Luna
(Hypercom) ALTai 5-2525

She didn't ask inspector of what. The *Benjamin Parkinson* was an unhappy ship. Somebody was taking all the fun out of what had been meant to be an essentially cheerful mission. Instead, she swiped with bad humor at the half-dozen droplets of wind-driven rain her expensively manicured canopy had accumulated, then drifted inboard, turned left toward the bow, conducting him down a dim corridor toward what Blackburn had expected would be the bridge or the captain's cabin.

At one badly lit corner, they had a mishap. A lime-green fire extinguisher suddenly crashed from its chromium-plated bracket just as they passed, missing his already-ruined leg by the barest fraction of a centimeter. If he'd ever been inclined to believe omens, that would have been the one to pay attention to.

The ensign apologized as if it had been her fault, or perhaps for the fact that, as an Ogat, she lacked the weight and strength to do anything about the fallen fixture, which must have outweighed her by a dozen kilograms. He set his bag down, grunted against the precarious support of his cane, picked up the heavy extinguisher, and helped her clamp it back into place on the slate-colored bulkhead.

There was something else. More than merely colorblind, perhaps: in the poor light, the little Ogat didn't seem to notice a length of hair-fine transparent monofilament knotted to the extinguisher's fastener-toggle. Blackburn didn't have more than a moment to glance across the dingy corridor, but he was sure he saw another piece just like it, wrapped around a brass door handle, the end curled back upon itself with relieved stress. He'd broken the invisible diagonal barrier passing through it, but it had done its job, freeing the extinguisher.

He filed the incident away for the moment, picked up his bag again to follow, his cane making tapping noises he couldn't avoid on the painted metal flooring. Somebody aboard this ship was a practical joker, with no sense of proportion.

He sniffed. This place didn't smell any too good, either, not after forty-odd years of frightened combatants, dreary mess-hall cooking, odd peacetime jobs everywhere from the Centaurus System to the Galactic Rim. Plastic permapanels, fastened at every seam with aluminum rivets, were slathered over with a dismal shade of military paint which had indiscriminately absorbed the odors of fuel and fertilizer, food and pheromones, and were now generously giving them back to the atmosphere inside the ship.

When the ugliness had been just a couple of coats deep, tens of thousands of young holiday-soldiers in their *own* custom-designed *Student Prince* outfits, had gaily trooped aboard, looking forward to a madcap weekend or two of hunting down villainous Clusterians. It hadn't quite turned out that way. One ship like this in twenty had survived what later came, inadequately, to be called the "First Skirmish." The sentient casualties, human and otherwise, had been far worse.

But they'd beaten the most professional soldiers in the human-occupied sector of the galaxy. In the wake of victory, a wave of joyful anarchistic chaos had swept the Outer Arm, no longer under the thumb of the Clusterian Powers, overturning the aristocratic status quo of friend and enemy nation alike. Too bad, he thought, conscious again of the constant pain which he was sometimes able to ignore, that the tide had shoaled out somewhere between there and the Cluster itself.

Blackburn's escort interrupted his ruminations with what passed for a polite cough. It turned out they'd been headed for passenger country. The little Ogat curled her dangling manipulator and rapped an oval door in the bulkhead before them.

A moment, then another young female officer, human this

time, in an even gaudier uniform, saluted them in, while letting herself out. Not for the first time did it strike him as ironic—or at least reasonably silly—that the exigencies of war had put the Arm's men in kilts and its women in trousers.

For a few heartbeats, the little Ogat wanted to argue with Blackburn about his bag, insisting she lived only to drag it wherever they planned to park him. Not wanting to point out that the thing outweighed her by an order of magnitude, he objected on grounds he'd done without a valet all his life and didn't intend changing now. Grumbling in Ogatik, she drifted away. Maybe he should have given her a tip. He shook his head. She'd just have spent it on more gold braid.

Inside the stateroom, dreary shades of gun-metal gray gave way to warmer pink and ivory, as the old ship's musty dampness surrendered to the aroma of strawberries and vanilla. He lit a cigar. He still wanted a drink—his body ached for it in every cell—but, he thought, that could be arranged presently.

Somebody made a throat-clearing noise.

He looked around. A colorful group we have here, Blackburn thought. Half a dozen assorted individuals, variously standing or seated about the stateroom.

To the inspector's left, an older, dark blue Ewon with silver *bohnous*—captain's—stripes and a matching prosthetic tentacle had assumed an uneasy Ewonese parade-rest as Blackburn entered. The Ewon's resemblance to an overmuscular starfish might have been remarked, had that Earth-evolved animal been the size of a small hovercraft. And had starfish not been thoroughly extinct for the past nine hundred years. The old Ewon, visibly embarrassed in that unreconstructedly civilian setting, shifted the heavy military force-projector he carried diagonally across his ample central hump to a more comfortable angle.

Nearby, a tall, skinny individual in coal-black civvies looked more to Blackburn like a mortician than a performer. *The* Bandell Brackenridge, he realized. Blackburn had recognized him by the mop of premature grizzle that had made the leader of *Fresh Blood* famous—or the other way around. The tiny black and silver shock-knife velcroed around his left forearm would have served him better as a guitar pick, Blackburn thought, than as an instrument of self-defense. Something about the man gave him the impression—which he instantly suppressed—that he was the sort to play dangerous jokes with fire extinguishers.

The performers' plump, ruddy-faced manager and agent, Scotty Moctesuma, with whom Blackburn had already spoken on the hype—noticing then what he noticed again now, that the man's right arm was in a sling—occupied one end of a large couch on the right wall of the stateroom. A gasketed oval door through that, and another like it in the opposite wall—featuring, incredibly, either a fireplace or a good, convincing fake—led, he assumed, to adjoining rooms.

A pair of women he couldn't place, one of them small, overripe, dark-haired, and orchid-eyed, the other a sallow blonde who seemed familiar in a vague way, were settled behind drinks in chairs anchored against the accidental failure of ship's power, across the room from Blackburn, against the porthole wall.

Blackburn filed them all away, exactly like the sabotaged fire extinguisher, in an unconscious mind well-trained never to forget. This time, however, he had to make a conscious effort, deliberately fix all of them in his memory for the record because, from the instant he had stepped over the stateroom's riveted threshold, the only person he could see—or cared to —was Chelsie Bradford.

The effect wasn't precisely unplanned, but the inspector couldn't bring himself to object to that much. It was the singer's calling card, her personal stock-in-trade. She was— well, he thought to himself, observing that Chelsie Bradford was decorative was like saying Osnoh B'nubo is frosty: accurate, but hardly adequate. Not much over five feet tall—a statistic never apparent in her hypercom appearances—she affected the eight-inch platform heels in vogue that year. They'd always be called for where she was concerned. Fair, inhumanly slender, with an avalanche of wavy platinum cascading to her milky shoulders, it was a tossup, he thought, whether she was better in profile—she had the profile for it: uptilted nose, a good chin, well-proportioned alabaster brow—or full-on, where you could wander around inside those sad, innocent eyes for what seemed a lifetime. She somehow gave the impression of a princess someone had been just a little too late rescuing, an impression underlined by the expensive snow-white tatters floating about her body.

Scotty Moctesuma blinked. "Captain Blackburn?"

Reluctantly forcing his attention around, Blackburn realized that the rock band's agent was in fact the only pink thing in a room he'd first absorbed as pink and white. The man's blushing scalp radiated through an otherwise full head of sandy hair, matching the flush of his shiny, overstuffed chipmunk cheeks. They clashed with the poppy-colored tartan of the suit he wore, the pleated trousers bloused over two-tone boots in which he'd tucked a pair of short, no-nonsense T-handled push-daggers. Everything clashed with the Arm Force camouflage of his sling. The arm inside was, as far as Blackburn could see, neither bandaged nor in a cast. Moctesuma had a carroty walrus moustache, and when the Age of Decision had arrived for him half a century before, as it must for all men, he'd apparently decided to wear *his* stomach *below* the belt.

"Let's make it 'Inspector,'" Blackburn answered, "or there'll be one too many captains aboard."

"A point well taken, sir." Moctesuma indicated the elderly Ewon. "This is Captain Luswe Ofabthosrah." The manager nodded toward Blackburn. "Captain, Inspector Blackburn." He swung his good hand, plump and pink, toward the orchid-eyed woman seated across the room. "And Miss Edith Lenox, here, represents the Galactic Coordinator."

III

A Miscreant Collector

Toying idly with the small gas-dirk she wore angled at her right hip, Edith Lenox, the darker of the pair of unfamiliar women, dressed in violet, tossed Nathaniel Blackburn a speculative glance that could have meant anything.

Moctesuma pointed out the cadaverous young man in sable. "I'm certain you've already recognized Bandell Brackenridge, leader of *Fresh Blood*, Inspector Blackburn. And this is his associate, Sabina Neville"—with a nod he indicated the sallow, wry-faced blonde—"and, of course ... Chelsie Bradford."

He put it that way, like a stage emcee, complete with the breathless little pause to build it up. Show-biz. That was just fine, Blackburn thought to himself. The thoroughly phony feeling to the whole production touched off certain of his professional alarms, allowing him to get his brains back in gear.

"*Bohnous* Ofabthosrah," he nodded, pronouncing the Ewonese words carefully, "Brackenridge, Miss Lenox, Miss Neville, and, of course ... Miss Bradford. I'm Nate Blackburn." He resisted the urge to shake hands all around. It might have been very nice winding up in physical contact with Chel-

sie Bradford, but the preliminaries would have been awkward.
Instead, he wrenched his eyes back to Moctesuma, his mind
back to business. "Now what can I do you for?"

Moctesuma crimsoned. He adjusted his sling, looking for
something, first to the captain, then to the Coordinator's representative, to Chelsie Bradford, Sabina Neville, even to Brackenridge—with a grim little shudder—sudden uncertainty
brushing his flamingo-colored face. After further thought, he
even managed to clear his throat.

"*Tell* him, Scotty." Seated on a bleached suede hassock to
Blackburn's right, Chelsie Bradford used the same growly
whisper she sang with, dispirited now, tired instead of ener-
getic. Forearms resting on her thighs, she had a cigarette in
her hand. An ashtry at her elbow overflowed with used ones.
She sighed. "One of us has died already, Scotty. *Please* tell
him now, and get it over with."

Blackburn suppressed several remarks that occurred to him
in the silence that followed. Moctesuma had been glib and
persuasive enough on the hype. Why was he hesitating now?

"B-but, my dear—"

"Hey, man . . ." It was the band leader who sneered. He
pointed an instrument-calloused finger—he was of the middle-
finger–pointing type Blackburn had never much liked—at
Moctesuma, slopping the rim of the glass he held in the same
hand. He took a huge gulp from the glass. "This was your
dumbshit idea in the first place, man, calling in a shamus like
in the flicks."

Something kept telling Blackburn that he wasn't going to
like this Bandell Brackenridge, no matter how hard he tried
for professional neutrality, just as he was beginning to feel an
involuntary bias in favor of Chelsie Bradford. To begin with,
the band leader wasn't clean. At six foot four or five, on a
good day he'd have tipped the scales at a hundred fifty—if
he'd carried his double-necked guitar with him. He hid his
face behind some scruffy something that hadn't yet decided
whether it was a beard. Dressed from head to toe in ebon-
stained leather, he squeaked when he moved. His small eyes
glittered down at Moctesuma like lumps of anthracite through
a sooty thatch.

Brackenridge took another big drink, tossing his hair from
his eyes with a jerk of his neck and addressing Blackburn.

"Look, man, this is a murder. You can't do anything for us, dig, except cause us all a lot of trouble. Like, you people in the Arm Force—"

"Er—" Strapped around one of his four good arms, Ofabthosrah's human speech synthesizer had started a syllable. Before he got a whole word out, Lenox interrupted.

"Inspector Blackburn is technically on recuperative leave from the Arm Force." She gave him an oversweet, commiserative smile. "Murder or not—and that hasn't even been substantiated yet—the Arm Force is not officially empowered to do anything infringing upon the rights of civilians. The Coordinator says—"

"Does she say what this is all about?" Blackburn had the feeling, not unusual in his profession, that he'd come in at the middle of a movie. "Or is *that* what I'm supposed to detect?"

Curling back thick protective lips of mottled, bumpy skin to expose a leathery face—an uninjured Ewon possessed five, one at the end of each arm, with its own pair of eyes, ears, mouth, and single nostril—the elderly captain addressed the inspector in a rumbling bass. "Just how old are you, anyway, son?"

"Fine," Blackburn answered, "it was bound to come up sooner or later. Let's get it over with now. I'll be nineteen next May twelfth, old enough to get shot at and shoot back. I've earned a living wage since I was eleven. I was Assistant Brigade Manager with the First Nectaris Volunteers on Osnoh B'nubo. I've seen the elephant, the *adzudyzh*, the *h'foni*, and the Loch Ness monster. I currently support, besides myself, a house, a suite of not-too-terribly-expensive offices, and one third of secretary-receptionist in the Altai Escarpment. Anything else?"

"A survivor of the march from Uthaboh to Lohua Fihr, I understand." The former had been a human colony on the frozen planet Osnoh B'nubo before being overwhelmed by Clusterians. The latter colony was Ewonese. Glancing down at Blackburn's right leg, bare between kilt hem and stocking-covered dressing, the captain regarded his own missing arm. "A war hero, then. Kill anybody out there, son?"

"On our side? No."

The old Ewon gave an agreeably startled grunt, shook the head he was using at the moment, then, apparently satisfied with Blackburn's answer, turned it away from the inspector, gave his pistol webbing an adjustive jerk, and stared at the wall.

Blackburn turned from the Ewon and the Coordinator's flunky, back to Scotty Moctesuma. "Okay, friend, give. You interrupted half a dozen other cases I've been assigned while 'technically' on leave, got me up here in a doubletime-hurry, claiming this was a matter of life and death. Okay, before it really gets to that, give me the straight story. Right now. I don't like heights. I don't like space-travel. And I *especially* don't like standing around soaking wet!"

"Great merciful heavens—I didn't..." Like big pink birds, Moctesuma's fleshy hands, even the one hanging before his chest in its green, brown, yellow, and black wrapper, were all aflutter. "We're so... Here, dear fellow, let me take your cloak." He addressed the younger man over his shoulder. "Bandell, mix the inspector a drink. What would you like, Inspector Blackburn?"

"The truth—" He paused briefly. At the mention of a drink, relief had swept through Blackburn's body like injected Demerol, numbing the ache where his right foot should have been. "—and about four fingers of Mellow Meltdown."

He shrugged the steaming cape off, flopping it over his equally damp travel bag, found the upholstered chair nearest Chelsie Bradford, lowered himself into it, and sat with both hands on the crook of his cane, watching Brackenridge's spidery fingers skittering around with the plasticware on a bar over by the left wall. When Brackenridge had finally finished with it, Moctesuma walked the drink over to the inspector, lit a nervous cigarette of his own, then resumed holding up a mantelpiece of which the wet-bar was an extension.

"Well?" Blackburn asked at last over the polished rim of the container he'd been handed. Attempting to restrain himself in front of company, he took a sip. Not Mellow Meltdown, but something about five times as expensive. It tasted terrible.

"Well..." Once again, Moctesuma looked from one of his companions to each of the others. They all looked back. Nobody offered him any help. Blackburn couldn't tell whether his sunburned color was embarrassment or healthy circulation.

"Well..." Bandell Brackenridge whined through his knife-edged nose, mocking him.

Lenox spoke again, "Well, Inspector Blackburn..." She

rose, began pacing the center of the room, her eyes fastened
on the carpet. Blackburn felt one of his unavoidable first impressions forming of the woman, and it wasn't, he knew,
going to be particularly favorable. "We have reason to believe
that . . . that someone aboard this vessel has violent intentions
toward the *Fresh Blood* Tour."

She stopped, turned to face him, spreading her hands, "He
—or she—has demonstrated them, graphically"—she locked
her hands together in a supplicative gesture before her ample
bosom—"repeatedly." She dropped her hands to her sides. "I
don't think you can ask for it to be put more plainly than that,
do you?"

When he failed to answer, she asked, "Are you aware of
the purpose of this tour?"

Blackburn didn't know why certain people brought out the
urge in him to bait them, he just knew that Lenox was going
to be one of them. He lifted his shoulders. "How in hell's
name could I miss it? Every time I open a can of *voez* and
beans there's an ad on the underside of the lid." Leaning back,
he focused on the singer in an effort to moderate the immediate, inexplicable dislike he'd taken to the Coordinator's representative, while continuing to address Lenox. " 'Fresh Blood
War-Fund Tour, starring Chelsie Bradford. And introducing
Frog Strangler,' whoever the crap they might be. You're—
rather, Miss Bradford, here, her group, are raising money so
the Arm Force can fight Clusterians."

"The Clusterian Powers," insisted Chelsie Bradford with
surprising quiet vehemence. Her eyes stayed fixed on the carpet, "not the Clusterians themselves."

"Quite correct." Lenox had glanced sharply at the singer, a
tight, unreadable expression on her face. Blackburn sensed
something tense and hungry about the woman as she resumed
pacing, her hands locked behind her back. She wore a deep
violet business suit over a high-necked pale burgundy blouse.
"To every appearance, Inspector, somebody's willing to kill to
keep that money from being raised."

Abruptly, she cleared her throat, "You know, of course,
that the Powers have certain, um . . . pragmatic advantages in
this conflict. Out of popularly held sentiment, which Miss
Bradford has articulated, the Coordinated Arm, the Arm Force
itself, considers the use of indiscriminately destructive
weapons—thermonukes, for example—to be unethical, while

the Cluster recognizes no such limitation. Likewise, the Powers get all the support they require from taxation, while we—"

"The Coordinator," the inspector nodded, flicking ashes into Chelsie Bradford's well-used tray, "doesn't want to join the Banishment belatedly." Once again, he struggled to bring himself up short, control his belligerent impulses toward the woman. This was no way to begin an investigation. "What's happened with the tour so far?"

Scotty Moctesuma had at last found his voice. He straightened, stubbed out his half-finished cigarette. "To begin with, a week ago, Chelsie had an accident—"

Bandell Brackenridge emitted something low and dirty-sounding, halfway between a laugh and a snort. Moctesuma looked up, scowled at the younger man, but went on.

"The tour began a week ago yesterday, October twenty-third, in Tsiolkovskii, with a big Backside Banishment Day sendoff. The idea was to zigzag around Luna, doing concerts until we jumped off into the Arm around the beginning of November. At the first stop, Fermi, a portable stage suspended from the side of the ship collapsed, dropping Chelsie nearly thirty meters into the banked amplifiers."

Chelsie Bradford slumped, put her face, chalky at the mention of the accident, into even chalkier hands. Suddenly she caught herself, sat up straight, and lit another cigarette. She didn't say anything. Watching her silent struggle with unbearable memory, Blackburn thought that if he'd been Moctesuma, he'd have crossed the room, put a hand on her shoulder. Moctesuma didn't. Nobody did.

"Luckily, a single assembly bolt kept the stage from falling ten times that distance, and somehow she hung on." A sour look crossed the agent's florid face. "We all wrote it off as an unfortunate accident. At least we did until yesterday, when Zibu Zytvod, our keyboard artist and technician, came close to being killed himself—with a short-circuited microphone. Instead, he . . ."

Blackburn gave him a questioning look.

"He's in his cabin, recovering. You can talk to him later. As soon as he regained consciousness—the ship's medics labored over him at least two hours—the poor fellow insisted on examining the faulty microphone, naturally far beyond repair—"

"Good thing Zib wasn't in the same shape," Brackenridge offered. His back was to the rest of them as he mixed himself another drink. "Without a synthesizer, we'd be S.O.L.!"

Chelsie Bradford shook her head as if she couldn't believe what she was hearing—or was about to say. She cleared her throat, "Zibu says the mike had been sabotaged."

Blackburn grunted. "Whereupon it suddenly occurred to some genius among you to examine what was left of the collapsed stage—which also turned out to have been tampered with."

Brackenridge whirled to face him. "Say, you *are* a detective, aren't you?"

Blackburn fired a warning look into the skinny band leader's beady eyes. Brackenridge gulped, took a startled step backward. Blackburn shrugged to himself. It was a knack.

Irritation wrinkled Scotty Moctesuma's pink-scrubbed complexion. "Bandell, you're not helping things any." He turned to Blackburn. "The bolts that keep the stage assembled had apparently been placed half in, half out of a powerful ultrasonic cleaning bath until they crystallized along the line of liquid."

"How do you know that?" Blackburn asked, half admiring some unknown criminal's inventiveness.

"I hyped Security Assurance in Mare Crisium," Lenox answered, "The incident occurred as Miss Bradford was rehearsing for her appearance there." She glanced upward, in the direction of the starship's docking bay. "They flew in an expert from Maskelyne University." She took a step closer. "But that's not the worst of it, I'm afraid. Very early this morning, shortly before we landed here, Victor Baldwin, *Fresh Blood*'s public relations representative, and the tour's liaison with the Coordinator's office, disappeared—"

"Yeah—" The noise Brackenridge emitted couldn't have been described as anything but a snigger. "Like through a big hole in the side of the ship! Disappeared, my bleeding ass, you Durationite lickspittle! Baldwin's dead as dirtside, and we all know it!"

There was a long, embarrassed silence. Brackenridge turned his back again. Edith Lenox had gone white, her already tight-looking mouth drawn into an even tighter line, hands curled into trembling fists at her sides. Moctesuma coughed.

Blackburn tapped his cigar on the edge of the ashtray. "How about your arm, was that another of these 'accidents'?"

The manager shook his head, "That was a little traffic mishap I survived, the day before the tour started. Entirely my own fault, and nothing at all to do with—"

"So you've got the Arm Force," the detective interrupted, "the Coordinated Arm's biggest private security outfit, and a flock of tame scientists working on this." He shook his head. "Tell me, what do you expect *me* to contribute?"

"Keep it from happening again," Lenox answered.

Moctesuma added, "Find out who—"

"Hold on," the inspector interrupted, "Are you looking for a bodyguard or a bounty hunter? Make up your minds, because the two jobs just aren't compatible." Whiskey warming every part of him by now, he smiled at Chelsie Bradford's puzzled expression. "One assignment calls for me to spend all my time with the customer, the other for wandering around collecting miscreants. If there's a choice—and you're the customer, Miss Bradford—I'll take the former. I don't even collect stamps."

She smiled back. Very beautiful, he thought, in need of help, and pretty brave, all things considered. It hadn't been much of a smile, but then it hadn't been much of a joke. Under the circumstances, he gave them both a passing grade.

The silence was longer this time. His cigar was cold. Nobody offered him another drink. After a while they all decided they wanted to talk it over some more. He told them they could do that a lot better without his help. Meanwhile he'd get billeted and start poking around. As he endured the pain of rising from the chair—the nice warm buzz he'd begun building vanished in a wash of adrenaline—gathered up his bag and cloak, he resigned himself. He'd wind up collecting miscreants, all right. No one had mentioned the obvious way to guarantee *Fresh Blood*'s—and Chelsie Bradford's—continued well-being.

Canceling the tour.

IV

Runaway Grandmothers

Sometimes, Nathaniel Blackburn thought to himself with a shudder, there was no good way to start.

The *Benjamin Parkinson*'s main portside boarding hatch was flanked by a pair of suiting-up rooms, one forward and one aft of a thick-doored airlock the size of a handball court.

The old-fashioned armor-jointed spacesuits, with the bright, reflective finish that period video directors were so fond of featuring, were long gone, of course, probably to some museum or a patriotic scrap-drive. But the two tiers of heavily spring-loaded stainless steel clasps they had once hung from, one set for the shoulders, one for the booted feet, still marched down the inboard wall of each enclosure in orderly rows. That was the only thing orderly about either room.

On this trip—and for the last several hundred, the inspector judged by the cluttered and dirty appearance of the still-intact aftermost chamber—no vacuum-dancing of any kind had been anticipated, either in free-fall or even across some airless planetary surface. Both suiting rooms had devolved, over the weary decades, into catchalls for worn-out equipment, extra baggage, and incidental cargo.

And one had become the perfect place for a murder. There had either been a bomb here—a big one—waiting for Victor Baldwin, or someone had brought it especially for the occasion. Some of the forensics—particles of expensive and exotic leather sand-blasted into the walls, and which might have come from a gentlebeing's briefcase (Baldwin's couldn't be accounted for) indicated that maybe the publicity manager had somehow been conned into bringing the bomb himself.

The midships hatchway area was one of the strongest structures in the hull. (And a good thing, it had turned out, for the rest of the ship's occupants.) Nevertheless, the explosion had not only holed the outer skin, it had noticeably bulged two of the other walls, the ceiling, and the floor. The only partition left relatively intact lay between the suiting room and the airlock itself, intentionally built to withstand a direct H.E. hit (though presumably arriving, Blackburn thought, from outside the ship), or simply decade after decade of the endlessly repeated stresses of evacuation and repressurization.

As far as any investigation might be concerned, there hadn't been much to see. The hull had been opened outward, in a ragged twelve-foot circle, something like a peeled banana skin. But most of the damage had been repaired by the time Blackburn had come aboard. Some of the smudges on the walls, he had been informed via hypercom by Security Assurance, were traces of the explosive, a cheap and ordinary agricultural plastique, available anywhere. Others were traces of its victim, and, of course, what they thought was vaporized briefcase. The contents of the room had been ejected outward over the sparsely populated Lunar countryside, looking as if they'd been cranked through a giant food processor.

The only convincing argument—although it was a good one—that a murder had been committed here at all was a solitary two-toned shoe, the right one, which, with its mate, Sabina Neville had testified she had helped Victor Baldwin pick out in a shopping mall only the week before. Spared by some quirk of the explosion, the foot was still neatly velcroed inside it, an oddly obscene reversal, Blackburn thought, of the injury he himself had suffered on Osnoh B'nubo.

Now, sitting on the edge of his bunk, Blackburn pulled down his right stocking, exposing the gold foil wrappings, which reached from high on his ankle to where his toes should have been. He took a long drink from the flat plastic bottle he'd just unpacked. Somewhere down inside that foil-wrapped mess, the tender, microscopic buds of a new foot were supposedly being encouraged by nutrients and electronic current. The technique was new, accelerated by the war, prolonged and very painful. A panel inset on the side of the calf displayed a dozen tiny lights, all of which were green at present, and an inscription:

WARNING: DO NOT TAMPER—
CONTAINS NO USER-REPAIRABLE PARTS

Chilled by his memories, he took another drink.

When it's 130 below outside, a force-projection, however small, through any part of a spacesuit—altered in haste for cold-world assault operations—is an invitation to terminal frostbite. After the ambush which had wiped out nine-tenths of his unit during the long trek back to what passed for civilization in Lohua Fihr, his pitiful attempts at first aid had only made things worse. Anyway, that's what the surgeons had told him afterward. Maybe when he'd signed up, they should have tattooed the same non-user-repairable warning on his hide somewhere.

Suppressing a sigh, he rolled up his stocking, stowed his bag under the bunk, then pulled the hypercom across it on its swinging arm, and punched the number he knew best.

"Captain Nathaniel H. Blackburn's office." The high-pitched, nonhuman voice was rendered even tinnier by the compact, inexpensive hype. "Inspec—oh, it's you, Boss. How have they been treating you up there in the Big Footprint?"

"Take an ordinary plastic kitchen scrubber," he told the image in the screen, "use it for a whole year on the greasiest, most disgusting jobs you can think of. Never, never rinse it out. Then retire it to the back of the sink where it can stay nice and moist—say for another six months. Now take a good deep whiff."

"Disgusting," the voice answered him, "but is it relevant?"

He grinned back at the three-dimensional picture for lack of a more appropriate way to arrange his features. "Unfortunately so. I'm afraid that's how the cabin they've assigned me smells. Or would, if there were room to inhale."

It wasn't *Bohnous* Ofabthosrah's fault, or that of his crew.

You can only do so much with the materials available. Nor was the *Parkinson* herself to blame. He explained those facts of life to the image before him on the hyperscreen.

"I looked it up," he finished. "Forty-three years is just too long to ask a starship to keep torching. Forget that. Anything interesting going on where you are, Mallie?"

A thin stream of mirror-shiny bubbles drifted upward in the screen. Their source was the blowhole of the female *Tursiops truncatus,* Malilu Ackackack Seeng, whose secretary-receptionist services he shared with several of the other tenants in the suite of offices he occupied in the Altai Escarpment.

In the background he could hear music, as usual, some old ditty from Before the Day After. Something about "I wanna hold your ha-a-a-a-and"—she was always listening to classical stuff like that. Personally, he could take it or leave it alone.

"An elderly couple called first thing this morning. Menopause parents, I'd guess, very upset and wanting someone to look for their fourteen-year-old runaway."

"I don't do divorce work. There's no lower age limit on Arm Force enlistment, and they should know it. Out of my bailiwick. Anything break on the Hodgson case?"

Somebody had hijacked one of the antique aerocraft from an old lady's collection. She was hopping mad, suspecting a Powerist plot. With something resembling a sense of humor, the local peacekeepers had kicked it over onto Arm Force turf, and, like it or not, he was stuck with it. Not wanting to monopolize Mallie's time, he'd coupled his office computer to a voice stress evaluator before he left the Escarpment, had it make a routine series of calls to all the sales lots.

"No soap, Boss. Not even any bubbles. They're all liars, of course, but not about that. Three or four routine matters coming down from on high—Arm Force headquarters. I told them you were busy and referred them to the Coordinator's office. That was fun. Nothing new on the missing grandmother thing, either."

He laughed. "At least Chelsie Bradford's breaking my streak of cases involving elderly females. Listen, I only had time for a quick glance at the news on the way up—"

"It's still bad," she told him. "The Coordinator's announced another series of meetings with the Uthabohn refugees—the news media are really eating them up—along with delegates from other colonies on Osnoh B'nubo. There's been a Clusterian attempt to infiltrate the non-terraformed colony on Sonofabitch, the one the Coordinator visited with all that fanfare a couple of years ago? Those colonists took the saboteurs for a walk outdoors"—she gave him an evil chuckle she hadn't learned growing up among her own species—"without their spacesuits!"

By nature far less bloodthirsty than any porpoise, Blackburn shook his head, seeing both sides of that particular proposition at once, a habit he increasingly regarded as unfortunate. He didn't need any hypercom, computer, or sanguinely patriotic assistant, however, to appreciate the overall situation. The starting point of the matter, the basic fact, with some nine hundred years' perspective to trim off the ragged edges, was that, following Earth's destruction by a couple of "superpowers" the entire galaxy was much better off without, the few thousand surviving Lunar colonists had found themselves divided.

One group had pointed to the hundreds of conflicting governments which had ruled Earth, saying that, from now on, mankind had to have a single, unquestionable unitizing authority to prevent such tragedies in future. Another, much smaller, number of individuals maintained that the tragedy would never have occurred without the existence of such authority in the first place.

It never came to a vote. The smaller group was faster on the draw—proving the principle they operated under had a point—and discovered a practical use for the prototype stardrive most had been stationed on Earth's moon to develop in the first place. The "Powerists" were bundled up in the middle of one long Lunar night—"Banished" was the historical term for it, settled upon much later—and sent off under the unquestionable unitizing authority of a locked-down autopilot, toward a tight-knit faraway Cluster of stars, where it was considered reasonably likely there were habitable planets to be found.

Perhaps it had been another case of the round-worlders shoving the flat-worlders off the edge. That's what the departing Powerists had complained, loudly and bitterly, until their angry signals had faded against the celestial background noise, and generations of Left- and Right-revisionist historians agreed with them. That it was an overly merciful act which billions, a millennium later, would have substantial cause to regret, no one else would now dispute. It was inevitable that, after the passage of nine centuries, the hammering of Luna into a decent place to live, and the creation of agreeable partnerships with alien races—the Ogat and the Ewon—mankind had met while exploring this galactic Arm, that they would once again encounter their Clusterian outcasts.

It was equally inevitable that the encounter would take the mutually destructive form it had.

Mallie's old-fashioned stereo was playing another track now, a piece he vaguely recognized. "A Little Help from My Friends" he thought it was called. That was exactly what he needed now—if he'd had any friends. Well, the chorus's second line contained a bit of good advice. Blackburn shook his head and took another drink.

At least visiting with his part-time assistant never failed to cheer him. In addition to her perpetual *Tursiops* grin, she made a hobby of collecting and emulating human conversational rhythms, tones, and slang. Among the surviving members of her own abstractly intellectual people, long friendly to the human race, but often lofty and disdainful of them as well—especially in light of Earth's destruction—she was probably regarded as a harmless psychopath.

Works for the right guy, he thought to himself.

"On the local front," he told her, "I've begun setting up appointments with passengers and crew. Damn few of the latter. This ship's ninety-nine percent automated, a klick and a half long, with only ten or eleven beings to run it."

"Well," Mallie said, "that narrows things down a bit. What about the passengers?"

He grunted. "Things look pretty bleak all around. Half my suspects were alone, sawing logs, when Baldwin got it. A good fraction of whoever wasn't, isn't going to want to admit it. That sort of thing isn't going to solve this case, anyway. My only hope's that the background check will turn up something."

"You realize," the porpoise suggested, "you're dealing with show-biz. When it comes to documenting whatever they say, you're going to run into a stone wall of privacy seals."

"Yeah." He emitted a sound halfway between a groan and a sigh. "I've been looking forward to that. Thanks for reminding me."

Seals of privacy, never much at odds with Banisher philosophy in any case, had been initiated when social engineers, who never failed to omit the human factor from their careful, foolproof plans, were appalled that "vat babies"—those whose conception and gestation had been carried out in an artificial laboratory environment in order to supplement humanity's depleted population—were being discriminated against, at first by playmates and peers, later by neighbors, coworkers, and employers, for no better reason than that they were "different."

In fact, they weren't different at all, just ordinary human individuals who had been created in an extraordinary manner—and didn't much like being picked on for it. The idea of sealing their irrelevant pasts against public and private scrutiny soon found other, more general application in post-Blowup culture, and had spread.

An economic history instructor of Blackburn's had once joked that it was like having an unlisted Social Security number. Nobody in the class had laughed at the instructor's joke. They hadn't gotten to the section in the texttape about pyramid schemes.

"Anyway, I've confirmed Security Assurance's diagnosis on the tampered stage-assembly bolts. The ends look like pyrite. And the recorded blood-type and HLA factors match what's left of Victor Baldwin, so we've got a body—after a manner of speaking—and what couldn't be much of anything except a murder."

He explained in full about the "accidents" afflicting the *Fresh Blood* tour, seasoned with a dangerous undertow of emotional crosscurrents he'd felt even during his brief exposure in Chelsie Bradford's stateroom. He didn't relish jumping in feet first, as he'd have to do. Mallie loyally cluck-clucked in all the right places.

"There's a rumor going the rounds that, despite her support for the tour, the Coordinator isn't too appreciative of 'modern music'—"

"That's funny," Mallie interrupted, "since so much of it is a revival of pre-Blowup music."

"Yeah, well, whatever it is, she thinks it's 'depraved'—and, I gather, the Coordinator's opinion of Edith Lenox approximates her opinion of modern music."

"Oh, dear."

"I even checked," he finished at length, "with the Backside

road company where Moctesuma had his little wipe out, day before Banishment Day. It's written up as an ordinary traffic accident, equipment failure compounded by driver error. S.A.'s covered the ground here, in ways that go far beyond my resources. Their specialty's hardware. They can make it sit up and tell stories even when it isn't programmed to. My specialty, if any, is people, innocent or otherwise."

"The trick, of course," the porpoise offered, "lies in telling one from the other."

"Yeah, that's always the trick, all right. I'll be in touch. Don't take any wooden mackerel."

"You bet, Boss. Talk to you later." Her image dimmed and began shrinking to a pinpoint.

"Right," Blackburn told the empty screen.

He hadn't bothered telling Mallie about the extra little surprise he'd found waiting for him in the stateroom, lying smack in the middle of the freshly made-up cot. It would probably have been slipped under the door if this had been a cheap hotel instead of a worn-out starship. When he'd unfolded the plain slip of white plastic, all that had been written inside—in the odd, contorted lettering of the Clusterian alphabet—was PAUL IS DEAD.

There didn't happen to *be* any "Paul" aboard the *Parkinson* on this trip.

And why Clusterian?

And what the hell did it mean?

V

Warriors' Peace

Bluegrass, that's all she ever knew.
She kind of wished that he would play it too.
Bluegrass, she'd sing a country song.
She always wished he'd sit by her and try to sing along.

Nathaniel Blackburn thought that Starship Captain Luswe Ofabthosrah would have been the blue-jawed Mediterranean type who gets five o'clock shadow fifteen minutes after shaving—on his forehead—if only he'd been born human.

As it was, his skin was a bumpy indigo-black, indicating late middle age among his kind, maybe a bit premature in his case. His eyes, unusual for an Ewon, were the ferocious azure of a gas flame. The massive prosthetic he wore in place of one arm—unlike Blackburn's, it looked permanent—may have had something to do with the fact that he wasn't in combat. All he lacked to complete the portrait taking form in the detective's mind was an eye patch and a parrot. Blackburn figured maybe he'd gotten thrown out of the war for unnecessary roughness.

"I'll tell once only, kid, I don't have time for this *fonth-dun!*"

Ofabthosrah glared at a hype-screen checklist dancing in the air before him, doing things with the light-pen he held in one mouth. "I have to get this antiquated lumbering behemoth underway in half an hour! *Half an hour!* Nectaris City, New Wichita, Hipparchus, Armadillo, then off into the Wild Black Yonder! Who in the name of *fonthdun* ever thought of using a *starship* for a concert tour?"

Blackburn had attempted to open polite conversation with a question about the PR man, Victor Baldwin, disappearing through a hole in the side of the ship. Ofabthosrah had answered curtly that, if such was the case, hunting dogs would find more of his remains among the Tranquility foothills than anyone would aboard his ship, and in any event, it wasn't his *fonthdun* department.

Now he looked up. "Son, I'm busy. Do you have any idea how much effort it takes to get this galvanized salami stopped and started again without breaking her in half?"

Modern vessels plying *commercial* space were twice the *Parkinson*'s size, named after the sectors and systems they served, not heroes of the Banishment. They *never* entered atmosphere, taking on passengers and cargo in orbit from smaller shuttle craft rising to meet them. Blackburn had a suspicion that, if they'd been underway, *Bohnous* Ofabthosrah would have been a happier individual. And he—Blackburn— would have been even *less* welcome on the bridge of the *Benjamin Parkinson*.

Outside, it was still precipitating. The big-paned windows, with their absurdly antique centrifugal wiper-sections, afforded a view of a break in the rain-soaked foothills. Through them, the muddy refueling village of Hulme's Folly could be seen, site of an ill-starred attempt, in the early years of terraforming Luna, to supply the protein needs of a new world by raising giant rabbits. The all-devouring two-meter mutants had finally been wiped out by a contingent from an Australian research station, and the incident had become a part of Lunar folklore.

Captain Ofabthosrah had every reason to be unhappy, like a man who'd been asked to undertake a sponge-diving expedition with an aircraft carrier. Trying to get some weight off his bad leg, Blackburn took a jumpseat opposite an old-fashioned video display.

On the console before him stood a fist-sized Ronson table-model cigarette lighter, circa 1950, seventy-three years pre-Blowup, a genuine Recovered Artifact—at least that's what it said on the metallic label sticking to the underside—retrieved by some foolhardy adventurer from one of the "cooler" regions of Dead Earth.

Grave robbery, even on a grand scale, failed to appeal to him. There were lots of risks Blackburn could imagine himself taking before he'd voluntarily burn down into that perpetually roiled atmosphere in a cheap, expendable ship, instruments blinded by radioactivity and the shielding it necessitated, groping around in the dust-filled, deadly darkness in an armored suit, just to bring back an age-darkened soft-drink bottle or a rusty license plate.

Such items weren't rare. Blackburn possessed two or three; they were a common gift item. But he'd never have purchased one himself, regarding it as ghoulish. They were expensive. Most were either certified non-radioactive, or sealed with some metal-bearing plastic which would protect the owner and his offspring—especially his unborn offspring. The captain's lighter, owing to the expectation that someone would actually be *inhaling* its output, must have been *very* expensive.

Blackburn shrugged. Earth was dead and gone, the galaxy's biggest graveyard, best forgotten by those of her children who'd managed to survive her. They'd built something—he thought in moments when he wasn't thinking about the present insanity—that was probably better, or at least worth the trade. Maybe lots of good things were buried on Earth, but there were a million years of mistakes buried there, as well.

He chewed a cigar without lighting it, staring out through rain-streaming plastic.

When the pain had faded a little, he spoke.

"Captain, my heart bleeds for you. I won't even say we each have our jobs to do. But there's been a killing, and there's still an important load of talent back there—"

The captain's dark skin puckered. "I'm tone deaf! Bah!"

> *He was ragtime man, his syncopated hand*
> *Would play an old guitar, he went from bar to bar,*
> *He played a thousand things upon those light-gauge*
> *   strings*
> *And made the people cheer just to have him there*

For when he began to play,
All the people there just had to say
"Gee, I'm glad it's ragtime once again!"

Bluegrass, he left her all alone.
She gave up hope that he was coming home.
Bluegrass, her lonely heart would cry,
And secretly she wished that she could find someplace
to die.

Bah? He was the only person Blackburn had ever heard use the word. Nor did the inspector believe the rest of it. Upon meeting mankind, the Ewon had taken to human music, Scott Joplin's ragtime, for instance—information collected in Luna's computers before the End, perhaps the total of accumulated human knowledge, had become the race's first item of trade—as if they had invented it themselves. Blackburn was sure he'd heard the syncopated tinkle of recorded ivories —"The Cascades," he thought it was—just before being ordered gruffly to "Come in, goddammit!"

"You're not blind," he answered. "Take Chelsie Bradford. She seems to be a decent enough person. You want to see her, or anybody else, killed aboard *your* ship?"

Bohnous Ofabthosrah finished the computer list he'd been working on, picked up the intertalkie mike, held it to the synthesizer on his next leg as he issued commands—not a one of them containing an obscenity in Ewonese or English—then punched buttons on the console to cue up a new list of chores. He rummaged around in a webbing pocket, produced a battered pipe, and filled it. Blackburn thought he was softening.

"Son, I've got problems of my own. This neutron-powered rhinoceros was built for a single—count 'em—one-way trip, over forty standard years ago. She's been retrofitted for a dozen different purposes, not always very skillfully. She's *old*. We just may be the proud, foolish owners of the last spaceborne fusion engines in existence. Sloppy, jackleg inertial shielding I don't dare enter atmosphere with, powered up. Every time she stops and starts, the strain on her hull-members—"

He interrupted himself with a deep torso-born sigh. Rubbing the back of a pipe-filled tentacle across his dorsal hump, he blew air out through his one visible nostril.

"All right, son, so I'm the one who said it. You've got your problems, I've got mine. What *do* you want?"

"To ask you and your people a lot of tiresome questions." Blackburn spread his hands. "The run of the entire ship to poke my nose into a thousand places it doesn't belong. Little things like that. I promise I won't ruin anything important."

The *Parkinson*'s crew had been especially assembled for this trip—probably another thing the captain didn't like about it—of disabled veterans and rescued prisoners of war. Living examples, no one said aloud, to a public being asked for money, of what this war was costing others. Blackburn, a disabled vet himself, who had only narrowly escaped becoming a POW, thought that was ghoulish, too. But, while it didn't remove crew altogether from the focus of his investigation, it did allow him to set them aside for the time being as second-string suspects.

He didn't think he had to point out to the captain, either, that he was under no compulsion to ask nicely. His commission from Coordinated Arm Force Intelligence—as far as noncivilians were concerned, at least—was absolute (he wasn't sure that he approved of that much authority, himself), and, had he required it, could be backed by the Coordinator's office in five minutes. All it would take—he shuddered at the thought—would be to spend that five minutes with Edith Lenox.

Edith Lenox. Sometime in the last few hours, he realized in that moment, he'd finally hit upon the reason for the instant dislike he'd taken to the woman, an emotional reaction the suddenness and strength of which had puzzled and disturbed him.

Edith Lenox. Aboard the *Parkinson*, she was the government—what little government the people of the Arm would willingly lay claim to—and, somewhere not very deep inside him, he blamed the government for the war, for all the misery he'd suffered on Osnoh B'nubo and would continue to suffer perhaps the rest of his life, for the indignities and injuries (he wasn't certain which was worse) it had inflicted upon countless other decent individuals.

Edith Lenox. It was her fault. Government was supposed to prevent war, that was one of the few excuses offered for its existence. Whenever it failed, and it seemed to fail more often than not, innocent men and women—combatant and noncombatant alike—got their futures viciously truncated, while political predators like Lenox stayed safe at home and made excuses. And more politics.

Unaware of Blackburn's ruminations, the Ewon grinned, exposing serried pseudoteeth, "Fair enough, fair enough. Where were you between 25:63 and 25:64 on the night of Septober forty-first, all that sort of detecting palaver, is that it? Well, my dear Mr. Holmes, when you get around to me—as I'm certain you will—I'll tell you that I was right here, in the same *fonthdun* place, doing the same *fonthdun* thing I'm doing now, and will be for the rest of my *fonthdun* life!"

He slapped the huge force-projector, an L.A.R. 2000, the inspector noted, fitted with Ewonese grip-plates, lying across his hump. "Now I'll ask you one. Where's your sidearm?"

Blackburn pulled the front of his recently dried cape to one side. The weapon's floorplate showed at his waist where he wore it with the butt reversed like the old-time movie cavalry. "An Ingersoll 291," he admitted, "the smallest weapon I could dig up on short notice. Not too long on stopping power, but they tell me it's a faux pas to make holes in the starship I'm riding in."

Ofabthosrah didn't say anything.

Blackburn added, "I'll try not to have to use it—unless you're threatening now to take it into custody."

It would have been the usual shipboard precaution, asking the inspector to check his piece with the purser, and well within a ship captain's technical rights, although another conference with the Coordinator's representative might have complicated matters a bit more than that. Traditionally, nothing could part the people of the Arm from their weapons—that was one of the things the Banishment, and this War with the Clusterian Powers had started over. But, for the sake of not ruining the starship, civilians aboard the *Parkinson* seemed to be favoring cutlery. Even without falling back on his borrowed authority, Blackburn could afford to offer Ofabthosrah his force projector.

He had another, exactly like it, in the bag under his bunk.

Ofabthosrah frowned for a long moment, looking the man up and down. He shook his mottled hump, tugged at his massive harness, ran a dark arm over his central mass, then relit his pipe with a kitchen match scratched on the console.

"Our shielding may fit a little loose, son, but it works just fine when there's enough vacuum around it. At least we're safe on that account. That's one reason the *BP*'s such an awkward, wallowing *th'fusa*—takes a sizeable generator to build a field she wasn't designed for. What do you usually carry?"

Surprised, Blackburn raised an inquiring eyebrow. "Is that important? A Browning 680."

A blue trickle of smoke rose from the corner of Ofabthosrah's mouth. Somehow it made Blackburn think of an ancient gruff but friendly dragon. "Just say I have my own peculiar ways of judging character. A big-stick man who thought that far ahead? All right, then, keep it. And like you say, try not to use it."

> They went their separate ways, it was a thousand days
> Before they met again, they didn't know it then
> That their two songs would blend, the lonely years
>   would mend
> Her broken country heart, she'd take an alto part
> While his light-gauge strings would sing
> About the happiness the years could bring.
> Their country rag would sound throughout the land.

Blackburn nodded, rose stiffly from the jumpseat, and leaned heavily on his cane, giving his own prosthetic a few moments to adjust to the unpleasant fact that it was going to have to start carrying his weight around again. Against his will, he felt his face begin falling back into the same familiar creases of long-borne pain he was so weary of looking at in the mirror. Character. Ofabthosrah didn't seem to see it, already back to concentrating on the hype-screen.

Then he lifted a tentacle. "And kid?"

Pausing in the bulkhead door to lean against the frame, Blackburn answered, "Yes, *Bohnous?*"

The old Ewon's eyes, cornflower now, but showing much of what Blackburn himself felt about life, twinkled back at the inspector. "You can keep the extra 'jector in your suitcase, too."

Blackburn left the control room shaking his head, and didn't remember until later that he hadn't thought to ask the captain if he knew who "Paul" was.

*Bluegrass—he'd rag it at the end for his long-lost
　　friend.*
She'd sing it in a voice so pure and sweet . . .
*Bluegrass—said he was coming home, never more to
　　roam.*
*Together they'd grow old, his silver strings
　　and golden bluegrass country song.*

VI

A Shocking Experience

"The door's open!"

Zibu Zytvod was occupied with peeling a tangerine when Nathaniel Blackburn went to see him, recovering since he'd crisped his canopy about 230 volts' worth and thereby gained a certain grudging respect for wartime technology.

"A Nolan-Travis cell, they call the dadblamed thing. A big fat revoltin' surprise, I call it, when you grab onto it, expectin' somethin' else altogether!"

The Ogat half floated in the wall-mounted bunk with a tray swung across it on a hinged arm. The human glanced around. The Ogat don't take up much room, he thought, or rather, capable of employing its entire volume, they make much better use of it than groundbound creatures. There were shelves up the entire wall-height, and small hooks on the ceiling held more of the being's possessions. Zytvod's cabin was about the same size as his own, decorated a bright reddish-yellow.

It smelled better.

In addition to a bowl of apricots and peaches, the tray across the bunk held the fused remains of an expensive-looking wireless microphone, and a roll of delicate Ogatik tools.

"*S'posed* t'be a friggin' one-point-five volt nickel-cadmium battery, it was," the Ogat complained. "Some demented genius somehow managed t'cram in about a hundred an' fifty times that much power. Wrapped my little grabber around the thing, pushed the slide-switch, an' I'm here to tell you that's the last I 'member till I came to an' saw Chelsie hangin' over me, administerin' CPR."

Blackburn shook his head, indicating sympathy. In a purely Ogatik gesture of pain and frustration familiar to the inspector, the nonhuman looped his single manipulator into a loose overhand knot at its base near his dorsal tympanum, then let the knot ripple down the length of the appendage until it untied itself at the end. Blackburn noticed that Zytvod wore no speech-synthesizer. It wasn't unheard-of to run across an Ogat who could imitate human speech with his own unaided speaking-tympanum, but it wasn't exactly common, either.

"They tell me I lit up just like a gall-blasted Chinese lantern! She sure did a good job, though. It still hurts whenever I laugh—or try t'breathe!"

Blackburn grinned, shaking his head. "I know a lot of people who might think it was worth some pain to get mouth-to-mouth resuscitation from Chelsie Bradford." He levered the plastic bottle he'd brought with him out of his sporran. "Can I offer you a little convalescent care?" Without waiting for an answer, he unscrewed the lid.

Zytvod bobbed his canopy. "Plastic cups in the bathroom dispenser—that's right, on the wall beside the mirror. An' it wasn't just 'some' pain, amigo. But it was worth it t'wake up an' find myself still alive. Chelsie's about the nicest *rivet* I know, Inspector, a good friend. 'Side from that, she ain't my type. Wrong pheromones." He mused. "Other hand, I guess that wouldn't stop some people . . ."

Everybody knows about leading questions, Blackburn thought. But there were leading answers, too. Over his shoulder from the head, two paces away, he asked, "Like for instance?"

"Like for instance Xev Kypud, our rhythm bandolarist." Zytvod's voice carried a hint of disgust. "He's . . . well . . . forget I mentioned it, okay? Scruples, at my age. I guess I been in the business too long t'tell tales outa school. You understand."

Returning with two small cups, Blackburn set them on the

tray. He poured. "I understand that I'm trying to keep Chelsie Bradford, among others, from getting killed. I want you to understand it, too. Murder is a pretty personal thing, after all. Information about relationships could turn out helpful."

Zytvod hesitated a long while. Blackburn lit the cigar he hadn't used up on the bridge and kept his mouth shut, giving the keyboardist plenty of time. He considered the ability to do that—and to know when to do it—his chief asset as a criminal investigator.

"Me, I hadda start gossipin' with a damned shamus." Zytvod extended his manipulator, picked up the plastic cup, and played with it. "All right, then, have it your way, just so long as we both understand it don't go any further than—"

"Zibu, you know I can't promise that, not if it has any bearing on the case. You could have figured that out for yourself." He drank his drink. It burned, the way Mellow Meltdown was supposed to. "Look," he offered, "I certainly won't go out of my way to spill anything sensitive—not unless I have to. In this job, discretion had better be a part of the inventory, or you don't work for long."

Zytvod considered it, still not emptying his own cup. Blackburn swallowed his impatience, waggled the bottle at the Ogat, along with his eyebrows.

"All right, then, blast that alleycat Sabina Neville an' every other female like her, Homo sap or otherwise! If you really gotta know, she used t'sing lead for *Fresh Blood* till Chelsie come along. Now she yodels backup, sees a deal more of Xevroid Kypud than her seed-parents—or mine—woulda considered decent, and plays bass theramin." He held his cup out for a refill.

Blackburn obliged. "How happy is she about being replaced by an outsider?"

Zibu Zytvod thought it through for a while. It was hard to tell whether he was looking straight at Blackburn. An ancient saying, shared by all three cultures, had it that humans hide their genitals, Ewon their appetites, and the Ogat their eyes.

"Well, she ain't exactly ecstatic about it, lemme tell you. But she keeps it pretty much to herself—say, Inspector, you got another one of them stogies? They're lookin' out for my health, here, and it's killin' me. Thanks." He tucked the freshly lit cigar somewhere up under his canopy. Smoke rolled out around its edges. "Guess I would, too, in her place—keep it to myself, that is. We're all makin' about ten times as much as we were before Bandell signed Chelsie on."

Together, they nursed their second drinks in silence for a moment. In this tiny cabin, the inspector thought, two cigars added a nice coordinated ocher fug to the general decor. When the ashes grew to an appropriate length, Zytvod offered Blackburn an unused bedpan for an ashtray. At least Blackburn hoped it was unused.

"I think I see," he replied, after the minor ceremony with the ashes was complete. "Leaving all that aside, what do you know about the stage accident last week?"

Zytvod took a deep drag. He winced. The loose curve of his tympanum taughtened as pain stiffened his manipulator. "Everything there is t'know," he answered, "meanin' nothin'. *I* put that stage together, Inspector Blackburn, with this very manipulator." He held it up, bandaged. "Shoulda guessed somethin' was wrong. One of the damn bolt-heads twisted off when I put the wrench to it a mite. Didn't think. Just tossed it away, and got another one."

Blackburn nodded toward a huge vase of marigolds with a card. "Saving Chelsie's life in the process. Those are from her, aren't they? I take it that was an airborne concert, held at the mooring gantry in Fermi. She would've fallen a thousand feet if the one good bolt hadn't slowed the collapse."

Zytvod sipped his Mellow Meltdown. "Well, hell. I can't take any credit."

"You'd be the best judge of that, I suppose. Tell me, where did the bolts come from? The originals, not the replacement. That one came from ship's stores, didn't it?"

Zytvod bobbed affirmative. Blackburn offered to fill the Ogat's cup a third time. Zytvod held his empty manipulator out to say he'd had enough. Shrugging, Blackburn left the bottle on the tray. There was plenty to spare. Another one was keeping his spare Ingersoll force projector company in the bag, back in the Moldy Sponge Suite. Blackburn used the medical ashtray, so did Zytvod.

Finally: "'Bout four dozen of 'em in a plastic bag tied t'one legga the disassembled stage."

"Which was kept," the inspector repeated what he'd just learned from Security Assurance, "with no particular precautions, in the hold with the rest of the equipment." He pointed his cigar upward toward the starship's cargo area.

Zytvod bobbed again. "Why'd anybody thinka standin' guard over a quarter ton of pipe and sheet metal? Say, that's why the killer—if that's what was s'posed t'happen—thought of it!"

Blackburn nodded.

"Sounds sensible enough," the Ogat went on, "and those crystallized bolts coulda been prepared well in advance, brought aboard ship and swapped for the originals any old time."

"Well," Blackburn grinned, "that seems to take care of my plan to detail-search the ship from bow to stern for an ultra-sonic cleaner big enough to do the job."

Zytvod laughed—and winced again, then poured himself another drink, after all. This time, with a rapidly thickening buzz which threatened to impair his judgment, it was Blackburn who refrained. "Too bad, Inspector, woulda been a spectacular piece of smugglin'."

"It would at that. What about the microphone? How much trouble would it have been to sabotage that?"

He shrugged, then waved his injured manipulator over the tray. "Not all that much. A standard nickel-cadmium torch battery, and this Nolan-Travis thing, they're close to the same size. Bad engineerin'. Nolan-Travis cells are somethin' new, somethin' about drawin' power directly outa the structure of space. They're usin' 'em in Osnoh B'nubo for weapons, this and that, runnin' vehicles."

"And heating spacesuits." Blackburn shuddered with the bitter memory, hoping the Ogat wouldn't notice. "Tell me something. I've been out of circulation a while. Is something like that particularly hard to get on the home market?"

The Ogat slewed his canopy side to side. "Not at all. Hell, I was plannin' t'convert all our own equipment next tour—that is, if there *is* a next tour."

"I see." Parking his cigar on the broad stainless lip of the bedpan, Blackburn took out his notebook. "*Fresh Blood* consists of Bandell Brackenridge himself, playing slide guitar, Chelsie Bradford as lead singer. Bass theramin is Sabina Neville, her boyfriend Xevroid Kypud on rhythm bandolar, and you, Zibu Zytvod, on the synthesizer." He looked up. "I've seen your records, of course, isn't that complement a bit thin for such a big sound?"

"Just our tourin' band." Zytvod drew on his cigar, pain

again visible in his motions. "Back home in the studio, we'd have a coupla hired piconetists, somebody on saxonelle—that's an alto saxonet—maybe a clarolo, a harmonicorn, an obophone, a pialele. Throw in a flocka violars, a few trombets—"

Blackburn grinned. "Which is a tenor tromboon, a reed instrument with a slide."

"Say, you sure do your homewor—" He started coughing, an activity which consisted, among the Ogat, of a series of contractions—and even more alarming expansions—of his flotation canopy. He quieted down after another application of medicinal ethanol.

Blackburn shook his head. "Like the captain, I'm tone deaf. But I know what I like. I take it that you stand in for most of this army with your synthesizer." He changed his expression. "You're indispensable. If the idea was to wreck the tour, slipping that Nolan-Travis cell to you could have done it, ever consider that?"

The idea sobered Zibu Zytvod and shut him up. Less patient, after all, than he gave himself credit for being, Blackburn waited with concealed ill humor through a long silence, then decided he was going to have to start all over again.

"Speaking of Ofabthosrah, what's he got against Chelsie Bradford, aside from this tour, which he swears is bringing his noble steed to an early grave?"

Zytvod upended his cigar, grinding it out. He crumpled his cup, then added it to the wreckage in the bedpan. "I'm just a passenger. How the hell should I know?"

"I've got a guess or two. I'm interested in yours. C'mon, Zib, this is for Chelsie, remember?"

Zytvod sighed. "Shucks, I'm ex–Arm Force, myself, Inspector. First Skirmish. That's right. I'm a touch older'n I look, and I lied about my age when I signed up in the first place. Shipboard scuttlebutt has it that the *bohnous* lost that limb in the Vytpukav ad Regey last year. He's gonna be a long painful time growin' a new one, if ever."

The injured Ogat was silent for a while, partly in apparent sympathy for the captain, but mostly, Blackburn thought, as if considering his next words carefully.

Then he added, "Also heard around somewhere that the poor old schmo had a brand-new daughter—or a sister—at the Vytpukav Spaceport when the Clusterian fleet . . ."

"It amounts to the same thing when you reproduce by fission. What's that got to do with Chelsie Bradford?"

"Not too much—except that her cardiovascular system ain't exactly in the glorious Coordinated war effort. She's more for love and peace, you see. Can't say I blame her there. So am I. War I've seen. She's only doin' the tour 'cause Scotty talked her into it." He stopped, then floated closer to Blackburn and lowered his voice. "That ain't s'posed t'be general knowledge, by the way. Bad publicity."

"I told you, Zib, that I'm the very soul of discretion." He didn't bother to add that some special individuals, most of them currently under heavy restitution bond to their former victims, had a lot more reason to believe he was the heel. "I noticed Moctesuma's wearing a sling on his arm. You think that might be connected with these other things that have been happening to the rest of you?"

The Ogat came as close to a snort as his species could manage. "Y'know, I wondered about that, m'self, kinda in retrospect. Turns out it's connected more with too much t'drink the day before Banishment Day, an' a fella who's too cheap t'rent a hovercraft from Number One or even the folks who Try Harder. Saw it m'self. The car, I mean, afterward. Threw an impeller blade, an' he lost control. Lucky t'be alive, but nothin' t'do with any of these other shenanigans."

"Tell me about Vic Baldwin, then. What did Paul think of him?"

"Paul? Paul who?"

Was that alarm he heard in the Ogat's voice, or merely a detective's wishful thinking. Blackburn shrugged. "I don't know, I could have gotten the name wrong. What I really care about is your opinion, anyway. What was it about Baldwin that got him killed?"

"There's one I can't figure, Inspector. Can't say I was overfonda Vic myself. But he got along right well with pret'near everybody. He was the kinda guy whose motto is 'Them's my principles, and if you don't like 'em—I'll change 'em.'" The Ogat swung his canopy again in a human gesture of negation. "His gettin' himself macerated an' all sure won't make things any easier on this trip."

"How's that?"

"Lemme tell you, it's gonna add considerable to the coefficient of friction around here. Y'see, Vic handled that Coordinatin' lady real smooth for Scotty, who's up to a lotta things, but sure as shootin' wasn't up t'that. Overly impressed by her authority, I guess—either that or by her generous frontal whatchamacallits. Hear tell they're already havin' trouble decidin' between 'em who's runnin' the tour."

Blackburn nodded. He'd gotten much the same impression, himself. "One more thing, Zib, one more question, and then I'll leave you alone to rest: you have any purely personal guesses as to who might be behind these 'accidents'?"

He slewed his canopy from side to side again. "I sure wish I knew, Inspector Blackburn, and that's a solemn fact." He curled and uncurled his manipulator. "Hell, I'd strangle 'em myself, soon as the bandages come off. I know for damn sure it ain't me."

Leaving the bottle after all, Blackburn got up, thinking he wished he knew, himself. He didn't know anything except that his leg hurt, he'd already had too much to drink and the day was barely started, and he didn't have enough evidence—any evidence at all—to eliminate anybody, not even Chelsie Bradford.

But he didn't tell Zibu Zytvod that.

VII

Mixed Singles

She's my part-time woman, hard to understand
How I can hold her and then let her go.
Ain't no other woman who is sweeter than
The girl who loves me and leaves me, I know.

Unlike Zibu Zytvod, Mellow Meltdown wasn't good enough
for Sabina Neville. Neither was the higher-priced substitute
available in Chelsie Bradford's suite, or anything else you
could pour into a glass. Her tastes ran to a dampish, aromatic,
light brown powder containing no intoxicant ever developed
by any purely human civilization—and to jaundiced opinions
disguised as something else.

"Are you joking, darling?" The expression on the woman's
face was one of genuine disbelief. Nathaniel Blackburn had to
remind himself that all of these people were entertainers—
actors of a kind—dissimulators by profession. "Why should *I*
bear Chelsie any ill will? She's the best friend a girl ever had.
Before she came along, I was a second-rate canary in a third-
rate band."

She laughed at the surprise which her open frankness had

painted on the young inspector's face. Stretching luxuriantly on the sofa she occupied—her dagger, an old-fashioned, unpowered, stainless Gerber, and the belt that carried it, were draped over the back—she curled a lock of butter-colored hair around one index finger, thought for a moment, then reached for a transparent plastic shaker on the end table, sprinkled Ogatik *vedyzhiete* powder onto the tender skin inside her elbow, and folded her arm tightly. Eyes closed in a kind of benediction, she inhaled deeply once or twice and went on.

"And I'll tell you something else, darling. Those stories about her are just so many donkey-muffins, so don't go spreading any lies that other people tell you."

Standing, as he had been since first entering the room, Blackburn hung his cane over a wrist and thrust his hands into the kilt's side pockets which were the military garment's only concession to a civilian-soldier more accustomed to—and much more comfortable—wearing trousers. "Just spread the lies that *you* tell me, right?"

She smiled. "Right."

Blackburn had already learned from Mallie that the band's first—pre-Chelsie—album, *Shoot to Maim,* had only been a moderate success. That hadn't been the case with *Oversaxed* (its jacket covered with saxophones), *Undersaxed* (Sherlock Holmes smoking a tiny saxophone), or *Aural Sax* (a naked girl—not Chelsie or Sabina—in a birdcage playing a strategically placed saxophone through the bars). The album just released was *Sax and Violins.* He'd been interested to discover there was no saxophone in the band.

To be sociable, Blackburn lit the third cigar he'd smoked aboard the ship so far this morning. If this business went on too long, he was going to have to put in an expense voucher for a new pair of lungs. Well, he thought, at least his liver was getting a temporary respite with Sabina Neville. Her remark about a third-rate band—the one she still worked in—he passed up for the present, at least verbally. There was nothing in it for his purposes. He also refrained from asking her "what stories." He knew her type. She'd tell him.

Instead, he asked, "Those are scenes from *The Mikado,* aren't they, and *The Pirates of Penzance*?" Raising an eyebrow, she nodded, and he nodded back. He'd referred to the matted brightly colored posters she'd put up all over the walls, sulphur yellow in this stateroom; not much of an improvement, he thought, over the battleship gray outside. "A bit out of your line, isn't it, Gilbert and Sullivan?"

She shrugged, pulling the long hem of her shiny saffron dressing gown down around her knees. "Business is one thing, darling," she answered amiably. "We all have to eat, don't we? The nonhuman Arm is greedy, it appears, to experience every facet of the mysterious alien culture of poor, dead Earth. A little ghoulish of them, I've always thought, considering the circumstances." She paused. "But if you made nothing but neowestern shoot-'em-ups all the time, maybe what you'd like to see in your off-hours is bedroom farces."

"Or detective stories," he replied. Setting the end of his cane on the floor again, he put both hands on the grip, leaning hard on it. "Miss Neville, I just got finished talking to Zibu Zytvod. Let's start by tackling the same question he finished with. Who do you personally think might be trying to wreck this tour?"

"Powerist spies, darling, isn't that what Scotty told you? It's what Her Extreme Officiousness Miss Edith Lenox thinks. And the captain, too. Why should I be different?"

He shrugged, accustomed to evasion. "Okay, if you prefer it that way, then let's make the question 'who do you think is the Powerist spy trying to wreck this tour?'"

"Ah, persistence." She pulled the big sleeve of her dressing gown up under her nose, peered at him over it. "How about me? Don't I look like a spy to you?" Grinning wasn't called for here, even though he felt a bit like it. The trouble was, he was beginning to like Sabina Neville. He tended to like everyone—with the odd exceptions: Lenox, Brackenridge—which made him, in his own estimation, a terrible detective. He controlled the grin.

Sabina would have been considered quite attractive in almost any company but Chelsie Bradford's. In her middle thirties, the lines beginning to form in her face, from the inside corners of her eyes to the outside corners of her mouth, were impossible to overlook, but she was constructed in a generous manner pleasing to many, and wore a citron perfume that wasn't overdone. Her eyes, heavy-lidded and full of shrewd humor, were of a color difficult (maybe even intriguing) to attempt describing.

But, where Chelsie was—a what, he mused, an apple blossom?—Sabina Neville was ... a dandelion. Even worse, she knew it. She'd always known it. For the sake of the small fortune she and the others of *Fresh Blood* were making on account of Chelsie, she'd had to stick around anyway, and pretend it didn't matter. But it was audible in every lemony-sweet syllable she used to describe her "best friend."

He put all of that to one side for the moment.

"How about letting me pick my own suspects, will you? Tell me everything you think is important about Victor Baldwin. Or better yet, let's start with Paul."

"Paul? Oh, dear," Sabina answered, putting a finger to an imaginary dimple and rolling her eyes upward as if trying to recall. "Are we speaking now of yet another of my indiscretions? Paul who? I *must* learn to keep better records!"

"You don't know anybody by that name?"

"I didn't say that, darling, but there isn't any Paul in *Fresh Blood,* and most of the ship's crew are nonhuman."

"All right, how about Xevroid Kypud, then, your outfit's bandolarist: I haven't had a chance to talk to him yet. How does he look as a spy—or a murderer?"

She laughed. "You've been talking to Zib, all right! That limp-tentacled, stiff-skinned, balloon-headed, Ogatier-than-thou prig! Don't worry, darling, I'll never tell him you told me. Besides, you could have learned it from anybody. We don't make a particular secret of it." From the end table beside her, she picked up a framed holo of an Ogat. "Xev won't do as a suspect: he hates the Powerists almost as much as they hate any Ogat who considers himself the equal of us *rivet.* Leave him to it, he'd be using this old scow to lob incendiary bombs into the Cluster, instead of benefit concerts into the Arm."

Blackburn raised his eyebrows, offering no other answer.

Sabina Neville changed the subject. "But I haven't asked you to sit down, yet. And you sure don't look like the *vedyzhiete* type. What would you like to drink?"

"Nothing at all, not at the moment, thanks." Despite his pain and fatigue, he remained on his feet. It was less trouble than sitting down, allowing the injured limb to freeze in that position, then enduring the agony of getting upright once again. "If you don't like Kypud as a suspect, then how about the three you named. Moctesuma. Lenox. The captain. It certainly wouldn't be the first time that the guilty party was forced for appearance's sake to call in the detective."

"You'd know a lot more about that sort of thing than I would, Inspector. Scotty wouldn't harm a hair on Chelsie's profitable little head—even though she successfully refused to be inducted into the band in the time-honored and traditional manner..."

"You're saying Scotty's a dirty old man?"

"I'm saying he was a dirty young one, just like his—" She stopped again, thought a moment, then went on. "Captain Luswe I don't know about. He's just the bus driver, though he seems like a nice enough old grouch. Somebody said he lost that leg in the war. Maybe he knows about Chelsie's opinions of same. That's no motive for murder, since she's helping fight it, despite her opinions."

He shrugged. "Edith Lenox?"

"Wouldn't that be too much? She's bad enough as it stands now. The war's terrific news for her—it always is for politicians, isn't it? I'll bet you she wouldn't mind acquiring a martyr to liven up the headlines: 'Chelsie Bradford Killed While Serving Her Species.' That would get recruitment up."

Blackburn asked, "Just like his—what?"

"What?"

"You were saying that Scotty Moctesuma was a dirty young man just like his—who?"

"'Whom.' Just like the rest of his profession. Chelsie was too good for that, though, she turned him down flat. She's a chaste abstemious virginal high priestess. So Scotty, who isn't altogether stupid, advised Bandell to hire her anyway. Audiences like her. Maybe because she's a chaste abstemious virginal high priestess."

"Quite a tribute."

She laughed. "From Scotty and Bandell? You bet your sweet residuals it is, honey, coming from those two."

"Just like Bandell, then? Is that who you meant? He looks more like the celibate type to me than—"

"You've got a one-track mind, haven't you—and it's laid right through the gutter, darling. Sure he's the celibate type, the son of a bitch, at home. I ought to know. I had the misfortune to be married to him for three years."

As always, witnesses tended to contradict one another. Some people were liars, some were mistaken, some were both. There were two basic approaches to this kind of thing: getting opinions about everybody from one person; getting opinions about one person from everybody else. Whichever he chose, Blackburn expected to continue getting conflicting reports on Brackenridge, Chelsie, everybody and everything else. Already he'd heard that Brackenridge was a lecher who couldn't leave the little female fans alone, that Brackenridge had a wife and kids on Luna, that Brackenridge was a homosexual who'd played at being an Experimentalist in his younger days. Now this: a philandering eunuch.

Sabina got up from where she was sitting, and stretched. She was taller than he'd expected, and clearly would have shoved her hands into her pants pockets if she'd had any.

"You sure you don't want a drink?"

"Lady, I have never been surer of anything in my entire life. Married to him, were you? You know, it's hard to get that kind of information. All of you *Fresh Blood* people have privacy seals on your personal records that I haven't had time yet to—"

"It would be the same with any other group. Show business is like that. It's a matter of self-defense. Otherwise we'd be up to our lead-sheets with solicitous fans and inquiring reporters. Too bad more journalists aren't paper-trained."

He laughed this time. "It's too bad, Miss Neville, that, considering wartime scarcities and the advance of technology, that joke will be obsolete in another—"

The cabin door opened.

Sabina turned toward it. Xevroid Kypud drifted in, broad for an Ogat, with a dark, translucent canopy. He wore moss-colored civilian draping, with an eighteen-inch whip-slim smallsword hung high behind his manipulator. He carried with him an electronic musical instrument of lightweight Ogatik manufacture which he let down carefully onto the floor, leaning it against a table near the door.

He floated over to the center of the room, placed himself beside Sabina Neville, gently took the *vedyzhiete* shaker from her hand, and used it on the lower third of his manipulator. "I heard you were talking with the captain-inspector, Sabina. I never saw a real detective work before, so thought I'd look in."

"Don't go on trying to keep up appearances, Xevroid darling." The woman fluttered her eyelashes and gave a deep, dramatic sigh. "I greatly fear that Inspector Blackburn has ferreted out our secret. Who do you know by the name of Paul?"

"Paul?" The alien assumed a startled posture, then relaxed. "I see. Fat for a ferret, isn't he?"

Sabina considered that hilarious. "We're playing 'Who's the Spy.' We'd ruled you out on account of your prejudices. We were just discussing our glorious leader when you interrupted. As a forfeit, you have to state your opinion."

Kypud gave an Ogatik snort. "Vic Baldwin may have slept with everyone, male or female, human or otherwise, aboard this barge and everywhere else—or he may not have, you know how rumors are—but he was all right. He didn't deserve—"

Sabina laughed. "Wrong glorious leader, sweetie."

Kypud rotated toward her, perhaps a little confused, then turned back to Blackburn. "All right, but if I stated my personal opinion of Scotty Moctesuma in public—"

"*Bandell*, darling Oggie, we were discussing Bandell."

"Why," Blackburn suddenly asked, "aren't you out fighting Clusterians if you hate them so much?"

If he was confused before, the Ogat wasn't caught off-guard by the abrupt change of subject. He raised his manipulator, curled into the semblance of a fist. "Inspector, it's true, I could kill a few Clusterians with this." He drifted toward his instrument propped on one end, picked it up, and played a few quiet bars.

> *"When she isn't near I always think of her name.*
> *Though she doesn't hear, I know she's doing the same,*
> *'Cause she's my part-time woman, chains no one can see*
> *Will keep her coming to her part-time man . . ."*

He stopped. "But on this tour, Captain-Inspector Nathaniel H. Blackburn, with words and music alone—ideas, you see—I can kill a billion of the bastards."

"Entirely by remote-control." Blackburn nodded. "And taking none of the risk yourself."

Kypud laughed. "Considering what became of poor old Vic, what happened to Zib, and what almost happened to Chelsie—maybe even what happened to Scotty on the highway, the day before the tour—that sure isn't the way it looks right now, is it?

> *"Because a part-time woman,*
> *You know a part-time woman,*
> *A part-time woman needs her part-time man."*

Sabina Neville giggled.

VIII

"Do Not Remove This Tag"

"While lying in my bed, obliviously asleep,
A tiny, tickling thread over my moustache did creep.
I woke up with a snap and traced it to its source,
A little linen scrap with the following discourse . . .

"I like it in here," Chelsie Bradford sighed, interrupting the
line of melody she'd been humming under her breath. The
intervals formed minor chords, less sad than comically dramatic. She ran a slim white finger along a metal shelf piled
with mysteriously shaped objects and even more mysterious
boxes. "It's cool and quiet, and, for once in a very great
while, I can be alone. In here."

His right hand still wrapped around the outer doordog, Nathaniel Blackburn retreated an awkward step toward the corridor outside, his breathing suddenly irregular, almost painful.

"Pardon me all t-to hell," he stammered, not at all intending the sarcasm those words ordinarily conveyed, and intending even less to stammer. His tongue seemed to belong to
someone else, and, for once, he really felt nineteen. Whatever

57

this black magic was that Chelsie Bradford worked on him (and the rest of the civilized galaxy, he admitted grudgingly to himself), it was embarrassing. "I, uh, I didn't realize I was intruding, Miss Bradford. I'll—"

"No, please, I—" She stretched a hand out, the same one she'd run along the shelving, then pulled it back, almost stopping to examine it as it came to her breast, as if surprised it had a will of its own. Her voice was low and husky, almost hoarse; but, then, he thought, it always was. "It's all right, Captain-Inspector Blackburn, please stay a while. You wanted to ask me some questions?"

He nodded, grateful to her, although he didn't know what for, desperately struggling to regain control of the conversation—and of his uncooperative metabolism. "The same as I have everybody else aboard." He added lamely, "It's what I do."

"Well," she smiled, "go right ahead."

There was a long, awkward, agonizing silence, during which Blackburn ceased to feel nineteen, and began to feel ninety—and senile. He opened his mouth. Words refused to come out until she nodded encouragingly. An odd corner of his mind realized that she must have to suffer through a lot of this sort of thing.

"Okay, for starters, who do you know named Paul?"

"Paul?" She wrinkled her brow, and he was alarmed to find himself thinking it the most beautiful brow, with the most beautiful wrinkles he'd seen in his life. "Paul. Why, I know several men named Paul. I have a brother whose name is *Powell*."

In addition to all of his other miseries at present, an anticipatory chill began its spidery run up Blackburn's spine—in the purportedly phonetic alphabet of the Clusterians, the two names could well be interchangeable—but, before it could complete the voyage to the nape of his neck, she went on.

"He's a stockbroker over in Langrenus. In fact, he called me on the hype, not fifteen minutes ago, just to wish me luck out in the Arm. Why do you ask?"

"Because—" It emerged as an unintelligible croak, and he cleared his throat and started it again as carefully as he could manage under the circumstances. "Because I found a note in my cabin when I came aboard that said that Paul is dead."

He could see her reaction, a violent, shaken start, when he pronounced that final—and very final-sounding—word, *dead*. Then she asked, "When did you say this was?"

"I didn't say—oh, yes, I see what you mean: when did I find the note? This morning when I came aboard. Which means that your brother should be safe. That is, if you just heard from him." Almost against his will, he added an inane, "There's lots more Pauls in the galaxy than Powells," and immediately felt like an idiot.

"I certainly hope so—if that's an appropriate response." He watched her go through the process of regaining her own poise. Somewhere inside him, the fact that she had to do it at all made him feel a bit less like a dolt himself. His reaction to that realization was both complicated and contradictory. "You know," she told him, "you should be more careful, scaring people that way."

On the infrequent self-examinatory occasions when he made such judgments, he had come to think of himself as a weary, prematurely hardboiled figure. Was it possible that, like a schoolboy, overly impressed with images splashed at him by the mass media, he was falling in love with this woman? What had happened to the comfortable self-righteous cynicism he'd brought aboard with him, about life in general, and about what she and her friends did for a living, in particular?

What was happening to him?

"I try to be, Miss Bradford." His voice was a little stronger now, his intonation a bit more certain. "But I can't be a detective if I don't do any detecting. I've seen the captain, and Miss Neville, and Xevroid Kypud, and Zibu Zytvod . . ."

Had he also detected a frown beginning to form at his mention of Sabina Neville's name? Was it on account of her bizarre relationship with the Ogat musician, or simply on some unspecified general principles? Whatever it was, she had transformed it into something else by the time he allowed the sentence to taper off.

"Zib's a dear, really. It was terrible what happened to him. I'm glad he's feeling better."

Blackburn shrugged. "So is he, I imagine. I, er, stopped at your stateroom and they told me you were on your way to the rehearsal hall—which this doesn't look much like, by the way—and when I asked somebody in the corridor for about my twelfth set of directions, they said they'd seen you coming here."

She smiled vaguely, indicating a dim corner where brooms and mops and buckets had been clamped against the wall. Some of them were still there, along with other janitorial supplies, leftover furniture, and old-fashioned corded lamps, probably stuck there when more sophisticated cordless units which drew their power from nearby walls by induction had come into fashion—about thirty years before.

Incredibly—or maybe not so incredibly in this ancient, much-rebuilt and overly refitted vessel—there was also a small porthole in the wall, which, at present, gave them a limited view of the rural Lunar countryside, soggy-looking under a sky which had remained overcast for days. Any trace of brilliance the scene might have offered derived as an accidental side effect, a byproduct of the starship's idling inertial fields.

"This is just a storeroom. The *Fresh Blood* tour is using it, for the time being. They gave it to us, the Arm Force, for some of our extra equipment. I like looking at it sometimes— the equipment, I mean—when it's gathered together like this, like a jumble of odd toys in an overcrowded secondhand store. I enjoy thinking about all the music it can make when it isn't piled on a shelf."

"Odd is right—the toys, I mean," Blackburn agreed, inwardly annoyed that he had begun unconsciously to imitate her speech patterns and choice of words. He attempted to stop. "What the devil is that thing, anyway?" He pointed to a battered and grotesquely shaped leathery-plastic case lying on an eye-level shelf, its lid down but unlatched.

She lifted the top.

It hinged backward until it was restrained at a slightly obtuse angle by a ribbon of fabric. From the case itself, lined like an expensive coffin with plushed-up fabric the same color as the satiny ribbon, she took a long-necked musical instrument, much like the one he'd seen Xevroid Kypud carrying with him.

> " 'Do Not Remove This Tag! Under Penalty of Law!'
> So said that little rag and filled my heart with awe.

Its gumption made me gag, it stuck right in my craw.
So read my battle flag: 'Do Not Remove This Tag!'

"A funny song," she mused, quieting the strings with a soft white palm and holding it out to him, "Zib wrote it. I like funny songs, too, but I can't carry them off onstage. Bad for the image, anyway; that's what Scotty tells me." She sighed, then took a deep breath, straightening her spine. "This is a rhythm bandolar. A semi-acoustic Cardenas, one of our spares, basically a twelve-stringed fretted banjo." Abruptly, she held it out toward him. "Here."

For a moment only measurable in microseconds—or in eons—their fingers brushed.

The bandolar turned out to be much heavier than it had looked, another way, Blackburn thought, with Xevroid Kypud on his mind and the billions he intended killing with ideas, in which it was like a weapon. The investigator's arm dipped with the sudden unexpected weight, and he gave the frail-looking singer a surprised and suspicious look. Kypud, too, must be much stronger than he appeared.

Once the instrument had been turned face-toward him, Blackburn had recognized it. Like most nonmusicians, he had never seen a rhythm bandolar this close before, let alone handled a specimen. He didn't know how, and he was self-consciously certain that it showed. He finally settled for grasping it like a two-handed force projector, one hand under the drum-shaped body, the other stretched out along the neck, which was inlaid in dots with some pearlescent synthetic.

The wide brass-fretted finger-board held a dozen strings, grouped in pairs. He imagined, correctly, as it happened, that the player would mash them down to the frets as one. Most of the pairs consisted of a relatively thick wirewound cable and a single steel monofilament, which looked like it could cut flesh. At the end of the neck, geared, chrome-plated thumb-screws stamped with the tradename GROVER anchored the strings. At the other end, a membrane-covered rim, where they crossed a small plastic bridge—a wire for the amplifier trailed from beneath it—they were fastened to a fan-shaped metal clamp.

He ran a thumb across the strings and winced at the chord-less racket they produced in the tiny slick-walled room. "Not my cup of tea," he said. "What else you got?"

Returning the bandolar to its case, the girl reached to a higher shelf, briefly lifting another drum-headed instrument. "Well, there's the bandolin—some people call it a manjo, about the same difference between a fiddle and a violin. It's eight-stringed and fretless, and I think you'd like it even less than the bandolar."

> *"I looked at it askance, it made me really sore.*
> *Without a further glance, I ripped and pulled and tore.*
> *I proved I was a man and preserved the American way.*
> *As it lay there in my hand in vain the tag did say...*
>
> *"'Do Not Remove This Tag! Under Penalty of Law!'*
> *So said that little rag and filled my heart with awe.*
> *Its gumption made me gag, it stuck right in my craw.*
> *So read my battle flag: 'Do Not Remove This Tag!'"*

The noise it made was heartbreakingly sweet—despite the comic subject matter—like a thousand tiny chimes. Still humming, she let the instrument fall gently back into its own smaller case, and selected another from beside it on the same shelf.

"Try this one."

Something he recognized, at last. He took the slide guitar, like Bandell Brackenridge's, much like an ordinary guitar, flat-bodied and clumsy-feeling to him, only with a built-in nickel-plated slide-bar on the ebony-veneered neck, and no frets. A long, subtly curved and similarly plated lever traveled from a complicated-looking bridge toward the pick-guard. He held the instrument and strummed it briefly with what he imagined were disastrous consequences.

He realized, embarrassed, that he couldn't even tell if the goddamned thing had been tuned correctly.

In quick succession, he also tried the ukelin and the violar, four-stringed and six-stringed fretted instruments, both played with bows, before finally turning to the obophone, a sort of woodwind tuba—he'd had some short-lived musical instruction in school and was slightly more in his element with wind instruments—the piconet, a soprano clarinet, the tromboon, a ridiculous-sounding reed instrument with a slide, and the trombet, a tenor tromboon.

"To rid me of my fears, as darkness turned to dawn,
I diced that tag with shears and flushed it down the
*   john.*
Although it has been years the warning haunts my
*   dreams,*
And drives me into tears as through my head it
*   screams . . .*

" 'Do Not Remove This Tag! Under Penalty of Law!'
So said that little rag and filled my heart with awe.
Its gumption made me gag, it stuck right in my craw.
So read my battle flag: 'Do Not Remove This Tag!' "

She sang the words as he tried vainly to keep up with her, more, he thought, torturing the instruments than playing them. "Well," he shook his head at last, placing the tubular metal reed cover back over the trombet's double-reeded mouthpiece, "I'm sure glad there isn't any ASPCI. Guess I won't give up my day job—I was thrown out of my high school band for violating the Geneva Convention. And I haven't even gotten to the bass theramin, the clarolo, the harmonicorn, or the pialele. Have you got a triangle, or some woodblocks on those shelves?"

He'd also noticed a half-used roll of silvery tape, thinking it part of the janitorial inventory—until he realized that duct tape was the only thing keeping most of the instrument cases together.

Chelsie Bradford laughed softly. "Yes, along with tambourines, cowbells, sheepbells, fire and police sirens, boat-, train-, and slide-whistles, air-raid klaxons, reindeer jinglebells"—she waved a hand over a jumbled box of objects which looked like white-enameled road-construction cones—"and assorted mutes."

"That's my instrument," he exclaimed, feeling comfortable at last, and proud of himself for overcoming his initial awkwardness. "I'm a natural. I'll learn to play the mute!"

Oh now I am a bum, and I seek forgetfulness
In whiskey, gin, and rum. My conscience is a mess.
I'll never be the same, I might as well be dead.
And to think that all this came from a little tag that
*   said . . .*

"Do Not Remove This Tag! Under Penalty of Law!"
So said that little rag and filled my heart with awe.
Its gumption made me gag, it stuck right in my craw.
So read my battle flag: "Do Not Remove This Tag!"

It didn't strike him until hours afterward, that, aside from one or two brief and uninformative words about "Paul," he'd forgotten to ask Chelsie Bradford a single question.

IX

"The Music in My Head"

I've written songs for enemies, I've written songs for
*   friends.*
I've written songs to say that I was trying to make
*   amends.*
I've written songs about injustice, suffering and pain,
And there was a time I thought that I would never write
*   again . . .*
There was a time I thought that I would never write
*   again.*

The sacrificial lamb was ready at the appointed hour.

Flying by the seat of one's instincts is fine, up to a limit. Nathaniel Blackburn had needed a feel for the personal histories and relationships among the *Fresh Blood* troupe.

But rather than spend the rest of his "day"—an arbitrary period mandated by a biology which had evolved elsewhere than on the small globe they now occupied, with its 672-hour rotation—interviewing subjects off the cuff, he'd opted, after his strange nonconversation with Chelsie Bradford and a brief, unappetizing sandwich in his cabin, to undertake the "legwork" which Arm Force intelligence hadn't given him a chance to do before he'd started this job.

Now his fingers were sore from pushing hype buttons.

He'd talked shop electronically with Security Assurance once again, encountering no fundamental disagreement with what Zibu Zytvod had told him about the collapsing stage and the microphone with a sadistic sense of humor. They regarded the eccentric Ogat as a competent technician. That was going some distance for them. They didn't render Blackburn an opinion on his musical abilities.

As he'd told Sabina, once he'd begun gathering data on each of the principals—credit references, usually registered facts such as births, education, declarations of majority, marriages, divorces, wills—he'd have a better picture of what he was up against. But "better" is a relative expression: there wasn't an individual aboard, crew excepted, who hadn't purchased an expensive seal of privacy on his—or her—affairs. Worse, they had a reason so plausible that, in their place, he'd have done the same. Maybe none had any documentable reason for wanting to see the sweet and popular Chelsie Bradford dead, dead, dead. Maybe all of them had. He was beginning to think he'd never know.

He'd punched out a chart, as he'd been instructed in Intelligence School, entering the putative whereabouts of every passenger and crew-being aboard the *Parkinson* at the moment Victor Baldwin had been killed. Naturally, everybody had been somewhere else at the time. Considering the evidence, that Baldwin had carried the bomb to the airlock himself, he was inclined to believe them. He gave it up after a while. This wasn't a matter for deductive genius, even if he'd possessed it, but for rather different talents. What Edison had said about inspiration and perspiration applied to other fields besides invention. By the time evening had rolled around (or the *Parkinson* had rolled around to evening) he'd resigned himself. He was going to have to grill the weenies, one by one, after all.

> But the music in my head is always playing.
> It follows me, it's there when I arrive.
> It's something that I do instead of praying.
> Sometimes I think it's the only thing that's keeping me
>   alive . . .

Sometimes I think it's the only thing that's keeping me alive.

Concerts on the terminator were always the most popular, with performers and customers alike, and brought the highest ticket prices, as well. The agencies, mass media, ticket offices, and scalpers had done their job tonight. The audience was packed in, shoulder to shoulder. He'd read somewhere that the expression "scalper" came from a time, shortly before the Blowup, when this sort of merchant had been persecuted. Even given the degree of economic illiteracy governments had encouraged in those days, it was difficult to understand why.

The scalper took an entrepreneurial risk, like any jobber or wholesaler—"middlemen" whose market role was also often misunderstood—except that he bought tickets at the retail price, assuring a sold-out concert, a profit for performers and their associates. Later, he assured a full house, providing an otherwise unobtainable commodity to those who decided at the last minute they must attend at any price. It was that scarcity which determined what the traffic would bear, natural rationing which meant even the most negligent customers could have what they wanted and were willing to pay for. And, of course, if such demand failed to develop, then the scalper took a loss for which no one would compensate him.

It was for this, taking a risk to provide a needed service, that he was persecuted. But Earth had always persecuted anyone who demonstrated intelligence and gumption, systematically punishing success and rewarding failure—then putting the human results of that process of "unnatural selection" in charge of nuclear explosives.

Blackburn shuddered but, then, it was beginning to get chilly.

Earlier, before the concert had really started, there had been a good deal of noise at the back of the waiting crowd, lasting through the first couple of numbers *Frog Strangler* had performed.

It was a delegation from "Mothers Against Freedom in the Arm," a splinter, either of the Durationites or the Experimentalists—Blackburn wasn't sure which, and wasn't sure it mattered—denouncing lyrics, costumes, and album covers used to promote popular music, along with the alleged lifestyles of its performers.

Blackburn shook his head sadly. Almost as soon as the most recent revival of pre-Blowup culture had gotten underway, there had been someone to complain about it, crawling out of the woodwork to cite what they regarded as the vulgar, licentious, seditious, or occult content in rock music. M.A.F.I.A. was simply the most militantly stupid of the lot. The detective wondered if they appreciated the historic reputation of the acronym they had adopted, or if it was just a matter of being fully as ignorant about history as they were about everything else.

The only media representatives giving them any coverage at all—Blackburn had seen the camera lights and reporters draped with hype equipment—were from the *Lunar Enquirer*, which somehow seemed appropriate, since that's where M.A.F.I.A.'s "facts" about the entertainment industry had come from in the first place. At their not-so-subtle urging—protesters merely marching in circles with picket signs was much too boring—the noise had turned to shoving, and local peacekeepers had been called in to deal with it.

Tomorrow's hype headlines, on one news service, anyway, would feature armed and uniformed thugs brutalizing helpless women whose only heartfelt desire was a legitimate one—to use the law to beat up and kill anyone they disapproved of.

He shook his head again. For *this* he had fought, and damned near died, on Osnoh B'nubo?

Stepping into darkness, he watched some of the evening's performance. Earthlight on the silvery hull of the *Parkinson*. The stage unfolded alongside the mile-long starship, as it must have been when Chelsie had her fall, a thousand feet above the audience. The spotlights slammed down on Chelsie—softer on Bandell Brackenridge and his troops—as she alternately raged at the microphone and wept into it.

The ship hung before a terrace at the lip of the Altai Escarpment, the wild, rugged countryside, the jagged peaks and dizzying clefts reduced to a mere backdrop for the mesmerizing performance she gave that night. It was cold—at that altitude it gets that way at sundown—but Chelsie didn't seem to notice.

There always seems to be a song a-playing deep inside.
It pesters and it nags at me no matter how I hide.

I've been in love and out of love, I've wished that I were
      dead,
But somehow it never seemed to stop the music in my
      head . . .
Somehow it never seemed to stop the music in my head.

'Cause the music in my head is always playing.
It follows me, it's there when I arrive.
It's something that I do instead of praying.
Sometimes I think it's the only thing that's keeping me
      alive . . .
Sometimes I think it's the only thing that's keeping me
      alive.

She'd started with "The Music in My Head," a subdued
choice for an opener, he thought. But of course she—or
somebody—had known exactly what she was doing. A
hundred thousand upturned faces identified with the experience of being followed by a line of melody from cradle to
grave, the torment and warm familiarity of wandering through
life making your own background music. They were on her
side from the beginning, and stayed that way as she sang and
danced in place before the microphone all through the long
"evening."

Ironic, he thought—or perhaps it wasn't—that, at a moment in history when all humanity (excepting, presumably, the
Clusterians), indeed, all of the sentient life in the known galaxy, stood united in a single purpose, to defeat the Powers,
that was the very moment when individuals felt the loneliest.
Twenty songs: "Being Alone Ain't the Same as Being Free,"
"I'm No Lonelier Now," "All We Ever Love Are Shadows"—
everything that had ever been felt about being left to yourself
and not liking it much—finishing with "Grey-Eyed Angel,"
sort of a theme with her, and a great favorite with her lis-
teners.

Grey-eyed angel: he thought back to their odd conversation
earlier that day in the storeroom. "I guess," she'd told him,
cradling one of the smaller stringed instruments in her arms as
if it were a child, "that the average person would say we're a
rock band."

He'd nodded politely, much more interested in the strange

way she gazed down so intently at the instrument she held. It was a mandolar, a stringless "stringed" device, entirely electronic, which had buttons instead of frets. Curious vanes or ribs along the body which were strummed like strings. *Fresh Blood* never used a mandolar, and this one, through the neck, had been broken and reglued half a dozen times until it was obviously beyond repair. She held it, almost cooing to it, like a precious, injured child. What, if anything, did that mean?

"But you know," she'd gone on, oblivious to his polite response or to much of anything else, "that isn't true at all—at least historically speaking."

He'd blinked. "Yeah? What do you mean?"

She'd looked up. "Our people, the people of Earth, invented many kinds of music, over thousands of years. Thousands of varieties, maybe more than that. Rock just happened to be the most widespread and popular variety when the End came."

"I follow you. And so . . ."

"And so," she'd sighed, "to the majority of our audiences, our paying customers, the nonhuman people of the Arm, the terms 'Earth music' and 'rock music' came to be interchangeable. But they aren't, not really. It would be like saying 'Ewonese food' or 'Ogatik food,' when in fact thousands of different cuisines arose on Ewonatha and Ogatravo and their colonies in the Arm."

"I see. So, just as you can't say there's any one kind of Ewonese or Ogatik food . . ."

"There isn't any one kind of Earth music, even though plenty of humans believe it, too, after a thousand years, the destruction of our native planet, a dark age here on Luna, and the effort of rebuilding. It's like we've had three or four centuries edited out of our tape. There were five or six billion people down there. Every one of them liked something just a little different from his neighbor. What we do—*Fresh Blood*, I mean—is, well, it wouldn't be accurate to say it's a *lot* closer to anything else than to rock. But its roots, melodically, harmonically, in terms of lyric content, can be found more easily in a form called 'country' before the Blowup, than in rock."

Blackburn had grinned. "Nevertheless, to the people of the Arm, 'Earth music' means rock."

"Yes. And that's another tag that can never be removed. If

it hadn't been for our music and our plays and our movies, things like that, we'd have had nothing of value—we poor, self-orphaned humans—to trade when we met the Ewon and the Ogat. So the tag stays on, because the customer is always right."

"Except sometimes," he'd said, "it's a curious universe."

To Blackburn, the most curious thing now was that she seemed as hypnotized by the crowd as they were by her. The phenomenon might be a common one among these music people, but it was quite new to him, and not a little frightening.

Brackenridge's group took breaks while *Frog Strangler,* the Uthabohn refugee warm-up band, a striking trio outfitted in eerie, hand-painted air filtration masks, filled in. Sharp and strident compared to *Fresh Blood,* they provided precisely the right contrast to keep the evening fresh. Chelsie sat behind a scrim with a glass of water in her hand and a store-mannequin expression on her face, not saying a word to anyone, not noticing anything going on around her.

People noticed her, all right. Plenty of them. Someone would brush her golden hair, wipe perspiration off her pale face (the music business consumed more fresh towels than a bathhouse, he observed), fluff up the billowy white dress she wore, or help her with a costume switch as if she were a child's foam-and-plastic plaything being given a change of doll clothes. She stayed in her trance until the time arrived once more to go out and face the beast with a million eyes.

Then she came alive again, all smiles and tears.

> *No matter where I go I know that it will be the same:*
> *That it will be my company through joy and fear and*
> *   shame.*
> *The music is my enemy, my lover, and my friend,*
> *The only thing I have that didn't leave me in the end . . .*
> *The only thing I have that didn't leave me in the end.*
>
> *The music in my head is always playing.*
> *It follows me, it's there when I arrive.*
> *It's something that I do instead of praying.*
> *Sometimes I think it's the only thing that's keeping me*
> *   alive . . .*
> *Sometimes I think it's the only thing that's keeping me*
> *   alive.*

Blackburn had other, less disturbing, but less pleasant business to attend to—the appointed hour had arrived, he repeated to himself, the sacrificial lamb couldn't put it off any longer —and only stayed for half the concert.

X

"Ruffles and Flourishes"

He'd previously shaved and showered—before the concert and the appointment he was dreading afterward—put on clean Arm Force issue tunic and kilt, even given his boots a perfunctory wipe with a pair of dirty socks. No Archibald Leach, he observed in the tiny scrap of bathroom mirror he'd been allotted, but then he'd always considered himself more the Marion Michael Morrison type, anyway.

To the sound of night-throbbing music filtering in from outside, he traced an uncertain pathway through the dim, twisted maze which constituted the insides of the C.A.F. *Benjamin Parkinson,* eventually found a stateroom three doors down from Chelsie Bradford's, and rapped with the backs of his knuckles on the magnesium panel.

"Come in, sweetie!"

The voice was a bit more muffled than it ought to have been, even more saccharine than he'd remembered it. For the briefest moment, the edema-swollen, blotchy image of his mother's face flashed inside of Blackburn's head, wheedling him drunkenly for whatever it was she always wanted. He'd formally divorced her and his father—both had died not long afterward, smearing their car into an overpass abutment in an alcoholic haze—as soon as the idea had occurred to him and he could find a lawyer. Now, he wiped the disgusted—and possibly unjustified—reaction off his face, took a deep breath, trying not to let it out in a dispirited sigh, then turned the dog and let himself in.

"Make yourself at home!"

Never in a million years.

It's easier than one might think, Blackburn thought to himself, assessing someone's character from a temporary lodging. Unlike the misleading, random clutter of a home, the contents of a hotel suite or a starship stateroom represent a concise statement. Travel forces people to take along with them just what they consider important. Apparently to this specimen, it was hardcopies—political journals and news magazines for the most part—and an enormous freestanding hypercom. No doubt for conferring with the Coordinator—in code, judging from the keyboard—when inspiration on the job was lacking.

The voice came again, sickly sweet, from the adjoining room. "I'll be right out!"

The place had been as overdone as the rest of the luxury quarters aboard ship—too bad they hadn't lavished some attention on the companionways—some Arm Force decorator's idea of what civilian VIPs would want. This one was the same shade of violet that some species of mildew turn when they sit in a half-full coffee cup for a week. Blackburn's accommodations, half a mile away as the worm burrows, and despite the way they smelled, were a combination of pastels he wouldn't even have tried describing to his finny assistant, Mallie.

Edith Lenox swooshed out toward him from the single bedroom, a lacy, fringe-bordered wrap draped over one bare, dimpled arm, both plump hands held up to one ear, fastening an overly large earring. Amethyst. She smelled, Blackburn noticed, of three or four preparatory drinks, clothing packed inside a suitcase for too long, and of a lilac perfume which farmers could have used for crop-dusting.

"Captain-Inspector Blackburn—Nattie—you wouldn't like to help me with this, would you?"

She was right: he wouldn't, but he did, giving her unnecessary—and unnecessarily intimate—assistance until she was

satisfied that the jewelry was in its proper place, and believed
he was, too. She was well upholstered for a woman her size.
Her décolletage resembled a pair of starships jostling for
mooring space.

They broke contact.

"Thanks ever so." She smoothed the orchid-colored dress
over her ample contours. "Would you like a drink, Nattie?"
Without waiting for an answer, she turned to the bar, which
seemed to be a feature of every room aboard this ship except
the engine-room.

"Sure, why not, since you're having one." Or nine, he
muttered to himself. "Looks like you've got plans for the evening. Don't worry, I won't interrupt them. I'm just here to ask
a few questions. It won't take us long at all."

"That's really too bad . . ." She made noises with glasses,
then turned back to face Blackburn, handing him a tall one.
". . . are you talking to anybody else this evening?"

He took a sip. "Just myself, and I can do that any old
time."

"*Splendid!*" She crossed the room, tossed the wrap down,
then sat on something that looked like a giant bilious caterpil-
lar, arranged her plump legs, and patted the seat, not a fraction plumper, beside her. "Then we have all the time in the
galaxy, don't we? Come. Sit. Ask me absolutely anything you
want."

Strong liquor is a wonderful thing, Blackburn thought. You
take a gulp, make a face, and everyone imagines it's the
drink. Ignoring her invitation, he lowered himself into a
plum-colored chair at a right angle to her end of the matching
couch. Lighting a cigar, he asked, "How long have you
known Miss Bradford?"

Her turn for the hasty gulp and the nasty look. "Chelsie?
Not very long at all, not really. The Coordinator introduced us
only a couple of days before the tour began—of course I'd
been preparing assiduously for weeks before . . ."

Changing the subject: "How is it that you came to work for
Anastasia Wheeler, anyway? To the extent that I follow current events, I understand you and the Coordinator are on opposite sides of a pretty tall political fence, aren't you?"

"You certainly do your homework, don't you, dumpling?
Though I suppose it's common knowledge. You're quite cor-

rect, of course. Anastasia belongs—reactionary heart and nonexistent soul—to the Banishers."

Blackburn raised his eyebrows. "You could say there's a war on, I suppose, that we've all got to lay our partisan squabbles aside and work together."

"But the truth," Lenox sighed, "is that she only keeps poor little old me around because I'm awfully good at what I do—which is public relations, but you know that, of course—and, just incidentally, to keep a predatory eye on my side of that political fence you mentioned . . ."

Watching for his reaction—Blackburn was careful not to display any—she swished the ice in her glass, took a long drink, gave him another arch expression from underneath a half pound of purple eye shadow. After a few seconds had passed and he hadn't said anything, she added, ". . . while we keep an eye on her."

" 'We'?"

She shrugged. "The Durationite faction, if that's at all pertinent to your assignment."

He nodded. A last "respectable" remnant of a moderate anti-Banishment group, which had somehow managed to remain on Luna when the rest were ejected, the Durationites had for centuries paid a certain prudent lip service to the Banishers' philosophy of individual rights above all else. But these days they mostly concentrated on the individual right to make contracts—lucrative ones—with more government than most of the Coordinated Arm was willing to tolerate.

Whenever a social problem arose, their answer, proclaimed through a press mostly sympathetic to their views, was another committee, another law, another branch of authority, created, of course, "only for the duration of this unfortunate conflict."

No wonder, Blackburn thought, that the Coordinator wanted to keep an eye on them. Reportedly, they'd been instrumental in turning what had begun as a minor territorial dispute—over colonies on Osnoh B'nubo—with the Clusterian Powers, into a full-blown war. And for no better reason, according to the less-numerous anti-Durationite media, than that war was good for their kind of business.

"Guess I should have stayed in school," he answered at last. He'd long since forced into the back of his mind the

Durationite role in creating the mess which had cost him his foot. At least for the time being, feeling it was better left there, he forced it right back again. "You're the second person today who admires my homework." Switching subjects, he gave her a meaningless look. "And what do you think of her?"

"The legendary superwoman, Anastasia Wheeler, our dearly beloved Coordinator? Well, Nattie, I certainly wouldn't want to—oh!—but of course you mean little Chelsie, don't you?" She paused, took another big gulp of her drink, swallowed it whole, inhaled, and exhaled again. "Strictly off the record, Nattie, I personally think she's an awfully spoiled, terribly naive, horribly ungrateful little brat who doesn't have the foggiest notion at all of what the universe is really like outside the warm, safe confines of the Coordinated Arm."

"Hmm. Remind me to ask for your *frank* opinion sometime." He leaned closer to her than he wanted to, and arranged his features to simulate surprised admiration. "You know, you're pretty straightforward for a PR lady. Maybe a little too straightforward. And all this rancor, simply because she's not enthusiastic about the war effort? Why, I hear that even the Grand Duchess herself—"

Edith Lenox raised both hands, palms outward, a look of genuine alarm on her face. *"Please!* Nattie, we never, *never* refer to the Coordinator that way, whatever those horrible media people say. It's true, of course, that Anastasia has mixed feelings. She's a Clusterian immigrant, after all, having abandoned her family, title, and position in the Cluster for the privilege. And, aside from the inherently gentle proclivities of the Banishers, who will tolerate any form of nastiness and perversion except for common sense, rational order, social discipline and public decency, how would *you* like to be waging all-out total war against your very own mother polity? That's one reason we don't—"

"Right. And what about Chelsie? Hasn't she got the same right to mixed feelings as—"

"So it's 'Chelsie,' now?" Lenox snorted. "Unlike the Coordinator, darling Captain-Inspector, Chelsie Bradford is completely unappreciative of the awesome sacrifices her forebears made to create this haven—not to mention the terrific professional break the Coordinator's handing her with this tour."

"At least she believes in something," Blackburn answered,

almost to himself. "I think I envy her that."

Lenox snorted again. "'Believing in something' is a common but imperfect substitute for having a personality!"

Blackburn made a show of studying the woman before him. "It's better than having no personality at all. Pardon me all to hell, Miss Coordinator's Representative, ma'am, but haven't I heard somewhere that this 'haven' is principally for the sake of preserving differing opinions? Also that, professional breaks aside, Chelsie Bradford was already the most popular entertainer in the Arm?"

"You heard it, all right—from that lecherous grasping old shit of a manager of hers!"

He threw back his head and laughed, unable to control himself any longer. Lenox got her anger under control, lowered her voice, and once again assumed an expression of Frank Sincerity.

"Do you want to know something? Keep it to yourself, because I heard it—strictly confidentially, you understand—from a lawyer in the Coordinator's office. It's possible Moctesuma thinks Chelsie's records would be more valuable—at least to him—if she weren't around. The girl has no family. Moctesuma's the only beneficiary in her will.

"You're a serviceman, Nattie, a disab—a combat veteran heroically wounded in the act of defending your polity. You've made your sacrifice. Don't you really agree that the general public simply isn't taking this war seriously enough? And that selfish and self-centered disaffection, exactly like Chelsie Bradford's, for the Arm's side, is dangerously contagious? And as for Moctesuma, why he'd cheerfully be running this tour for the *Powers* if they only paid him enough!"

She might have something there. There were stories that Moctesuma needed money badly, having invested his own and the group's heavily in the Vytpukav ad Regey.

No, he didn't agree with her about the public and the war, but he didn't say so. Heroic sacrifice? How about getting hurt simply by being in the wrong place at the wrong time, making it worse through pure stupidity, while doing his ignorant and frightened damnedest to stay alive? War heroes were cartoons for the people back home to write poems—and press releases —about. People like Edith Lenox, who would dirty her underwear just like anybody else the first time she happened to be shot at. The trouble was, dirty underwear, uncontrollable

sphincters, and the poor saps who had to live and die in a real
world, suffering both afflictions, made lousy copy.

Instead of speaking, he let her ramble. It went on like that
for quite a while: "Luswe Ofabthosrah? You can't ever really
tell what people like that are actually thinking, down deep
inside, can you? As if they had real, human emotions. Strictly
between you and me, Nattie, I think the galaxy would be a lot
better off if we hadn't ever messed around with teaching the
Ewon and the Ogat to get along!"

Teaching the Ewon and the Ogat to "get along" had en-
tailed negotiating an end to the ninth interstellar nuclear war
the two species had fought. After a thousand years of destruction, they'd been willing to give it a try. It was only because
they'd been so well spread out among the stars that either race
had survived at all.

Edith Lenox giggled suddenly. "Don't tell anyone I let that
slip, Nattie dear—very bad PR!" She paused, blushing incongruously, looking down at her lap. "Sometimes it's altogether
too easy to tell what they're thinking, *all* the time. Don't you
know how they'd dearly love to get their tentacles on a real
dylos female!"

The real question, Blackburn thought to himself, considering the fact that the Ewon reproduced courtesy of binary fission, was what would they *do* with a real human female?

Another long pause ensued as thoughts appeared to be
pushing their sluggish way through the well-worn gutter of her
mind. They emerged, this time, in a salacious whisper: "You
know, Nattie, dear, I'd never admit this to anybody else, but,
strictly between you and me, I wonder what *that* would be
like."

If you didn't like that, Blackburn thought, then how about:
"Bandell Brackenridge simply gives me the creeps! Nothing
but nasty, dirty, perverted sex on his mind—if he has a mind!
Now if *Bohnous* Ofabthosrah were a real man—even if he is
completely married to this ugly old ship of his. I just *love* a
uniform, don't you? Do you think there might really be something going on between him and that First Officer of his,
whatever they call him? I've heard about sailors before, you
know. All about them. There must be *some* good explanation
why the captain isn't interested in any of his *female* passengers!"

Her speech was becoming slurred. Limited experience,

mostly with Clusterian prisoners, had taught Blackburn that this was the best time to get real information. But it wouldn't last long. Nice of the subject to ply *herself* with liquor, though.

He mused, trying to be casual, "You know, I kind of like Paul as a suspect, if it weren't for the fact that he's dead, too. Paul *is* dead, isn't he?" He ignored the sudden flare of panic he saw in her eyes which contradicted the noncommittal expression on her face. "Or there's always Bandell Brackenridge. They tell me he isn't too crazy about the way his little hired background singer rose to the top, leaving him, and his world-famous band behind. How about you?"

She shook her head as if to clear it, then took another drink to fuzzy it up again. "I like *Chelzie Bradford* azza suspect, that's who I like!" She unfolded the wrap on the couch beside her. It was a shawl the size of a tablecloth, white, with long fringe at the edges, like the ones Chelsie Bradford wore at her performances. Had Lenox been standing it would have reached to the floor. "She gimme this, azza token of 'steem. Looks like it came frommer gran'ma's trunk. You know she won' even cooperate—*co*-operate—to the minimal extenta wearing something . . . well, you know, Nattie-pie, sorta skimpy and 'inspiring'?"

She draped the shawl over her head—white wasn't her color, for a couple of reasons—and began giggling. Then she got herself under control again. "And she posilutively *insists* singin' allat dumbshit garbage she writes with a lotta long words an' ideas—sex! drugs! witchcraft!—steada the patriotic compositions we offered to provide!"

"'We' being the Durationites again—or maybe M.A.F.I.A.?"

No answer.

"Miss Lenox? Edith?"

He shook his head, took the drink from her hand and set it down. He left her snoring, wrapped in Chelsie's shawl and propped up in the corner of the lavender couch.

As he closed the stateroom door behind himself, something made him stay for just a moment with his ear against it. Inside, there was silence, then a mechanical clicking, the sound of fingers racing along the plastic keycaps of a hypercom console.

"Don't give me any of that officious crap!" Edith Lenox

demanded without the slightest trace of an alcoholic slur. "I want to speak to her immediately! That gimp detective she insisted on hiring—over my objections—is doing altogether too good a job!"

They say if you look in the Bible,
The Word, it'll come unto you.
Just ask and your questions are answered
In phrases so perfect and true.

I went to the preacher one Sunday.
A question was troubling me.
But when he heard what I wanted to know,
He got up and walked out on me . . .

>Can you get laid up in heaven?
>It's something I just gotta know.
>Can you get laid up in heaven, my friend?
>If you can't, then I don't wanna go.

Now it may be an asinine question.
It may be it's not very nice.
But when there is something you just gotta know,
You look for the best of advice.

I went to the Salvation Army.
Their kindly assistance is free.
There wasn't no screamin' or leavin' the room,
They simply declared war on me . . .

>Can you get laid up in heaven?
>It's something I just gotta know.
>Can you get laid up in heaven, my friend?
>If you can't, then I don't wanna go.

XI

"Dawn Patrol"

Mornin', darlin', open your eyes.
Let's make breakfast, watch the sunrise.
It's so good to be here alone.
I can't believe it, I'm really home.

Coinciding with the wake-up call Nathaniel Blackburn had programmed into the hype the night before—he'd requested one of the few cheerful songs in Chelsie Bradford's repertoire; still, somehow, it seemed a bit sad, especially with the little bell-like notes at the end of each line—the C.A.F. *Benjamin Parkinson* recrossed the Lunar terminator. The sun appeared to be rising. Artificial dawn seeped through the thick, distorting porthole, damp and gray—as had been the entire week so far—complementing the sour, bad-tasting temperament with which it appeared he was going to face reality over the next several hours.

It's one thing, he thought to himself grimly, to be waking up with a hangover, but when it seems to be in payment for not having done anything much to earn it . . . He seldom suffered nightmares about the war, or even dreamed about it

85

much that he remembered. He—and Mellow Meltdown—
made sure of that. He just woke up every morning thinking
about it, remembering, feeling lousy. Whether that was due to
Mellow Meltdown, too, or to never dreaming, he wasn't sure.
And didn't care.

> *Spent last night just watching you sleep.*
> *Arms around you, breathing so deep.*
> *Been so long, there's so much to say.*
> *I'll never leave again, I'm here to stay.*

His one naked foot on the thin carpet stung with the bite of
cold metal underneath. He found he'd arrived at a decision.
Apparently his unconscious had been doing the thinking for
him overnight again. Usually that process made him feel better the next day, but now the buck had been passed. He, not
his unconscious, was going to have to act, and it didn't look
like it was going to be much fun.

It never is, violating every principle you believe in.

Levering himself to vertical, he stumbled two steps across
the tiny cabin to rummage through his bag. The ancient cooling stacks of Three Mile Island leered at him like a dirty
gesture from the whiskey label. He got even by lowering their
meniscus an inch. In a moment, true to their implicit promise,
the detective's stomach began radiating. The aches and pains
everywhere else went away, as did the aftertaste of the recur-
rent nightmares, which he seldom bothered to remember these
days.

> *There's so much I want to tell you, you were much too*
>   *tired to hear.*
> *So I waited until morning just to whisper to you, dear,*
> *That I hated every lonely mile that kept us far apart,*
> *And how good it is to listen to the beating of your heart.*

Chelsie's song still running through his mind—to his annoyance—he checked the hypercom. The request he'd filed
the day before, through the Coordinator's office, for personal
backgrounding on the *Parkinson*'s passengers was still being
"processed." Privacy, he was reminded by the display-
graphics, was one of the many precious sentient rights this
war was being fought for. Reluctantly, he agreed with the

letters rolling across the little terminal screen. He was resigned to it already, as he was resigned to anything else they tossed his way. Resignation was about the only thing he felt these days. He knew that when the information finally came through to him, if it ever did, it would be "processed" all right. "Sanitized for your protection" would have been a better phrase. Stripped of anything at all useful to him.

To hell with that.

To hell with everything.

He had another drink.

> *Mornin', darlin', open your eyes.*
> *Here's the day we start our new lives.*
> *Here beside you, life seems so fine.*
> *Let's go and meet the dawn, your hand in mine.*

Luxuries available aboard the *Benjamin Parkinson* didn't extend to breakfast in his statecloset. A quick shower and a quicker shave—too many of those in too few hours, his face was beginning to get sore—and he stepped over the little cabin's riveted threshold, cane tapping a rhythm which had become all too familiar on the metal deckplates, into the empty corridor and onward, to see what new trouble his unconscious mind had gotten him into.

> *Last night we both were sleepy when you met me at the plane,*
> *And I didn't really realize that I was home again.*
> *Then this morning I remembered how you wake up with a smile,*
> *And I knew my heart had really crossed its final lonely mile.*

Fumbling through the tangled maze of corridors and the haze inside his head, he got lost and had to ask directions twice before he found the noisy steam- and odor-filled mess room where others of the troupe were finding their own way of dealing with the fact that they hadn't died in their sleep last night and now had another day to confront. From the serving line along one side of the room—Arm Force ratings dishing out scrambled eggs, *kevat*, pancakes, steak, and *faosth*—he took his tray to the table. Chelsie Bradford, Scotty Moctesuma—his sling was gone now, but his arm was moving a bit stiffly—and company seemed to be starting on their second cup of coffee.

He wondered whether there was any point to opening the question of "Paul is dead" again.

"Well, if it ain't Inspector Blackburn himself!" Bandell Brackenridge was up and braying early this morning. The sight and sound of the band leader erased the music from Blackburn's mind. "That what you did last night, man, inspect her blackburn?" To the others: "Our Arm Force *dick* spent the whole night investigating little Edie—all in the line of duty, of course!" He added a guffaw to the bray.

Trying to get entwined in the folding chair without spilling his tray, the investigator wasn't in the mood for breakfast, or for Brackenridge's half-witted innuendo. He had wanted—to the extent that one could be said to want anything at this hour of the morning—to bring up the subject of the personal privacy seals which were inhibiting his investigation. Lenox wasn't there to blush, even if she'd been capable. Her emergency consultation with Madame Coordinator must have kept her up too late. She hadn't looked to Blackburn like the kind to miss breakfast, or any other meal, for any lesser reason.

Moctesuma, with a grim expression on his face, studied the bottom of his coffee cup.

Sabina Neville, sitting next to the spot where her companion Xevroid Kypud hovered, eyed the detective, watching for his reaction to Brackenridge's taunting.

Here we go, the inspector thought wearily, I'm being tested. In all police work, sooner or later, it always comes to this. It's time to see who's top baboon. This, even if his unconscious hadn't come up with a plan, would have made the decision for him.

"Brackenridge," he stage-whispered, perfectly audible to everybody at the table, "I don't like you. I don't like your face. If you had a mind, I wouldn't like that, either. Don't give me another chance to render judgment on your *voice,* or you're going to wind up with a crotchful of scrambled eggs."

The emaciated-looking band leader gulped, blinked, and shut up. It was a corny routine, Blackburn thought, but worth it, at least for the look he saw flicker by on Chelsie Bradford's face. One of the many discouraging facts of life he felt resigned to was the fact that, whatever protestations they might

offer to the contrary, women always enjoyed confrontations—
especially if they came to blows—even more than men
seemed to. On the other hand, it was the first real smile,
however embarrassed and guilty, he'd seen her wear in person.

This morning she had on a white fuzzy sweater, sleeves
shoved up above her elbows, Levis the same color. This must
be formal attire for rehearsal, he thought, since Sabina Neville
wore an indifferent yellow shift, while Scotty Moctesuma affected the same nauseating pink plaid he'd had on the day
before. Brackenridge again dressed all in black. The detective
was almost sorry the band leader had backed down. Scrambled eggs would have looked a lot better on him than on the
Arm Force–embossed metal plate which Blackburn was regarding without enthusiasm—or on the Ogat ensign he'd met
getting aboard this scow.

Xevroid Kypud was shoveling in cornflakes with milk and
sliced bananas, not paying much attention to anybody else. He
wore green again, this time an old Ogatik starship trooper's
canopy dressing (or a good reproduction) from the First Skirmish, which made him the sole individual dressed for the setting. As Blackburn had observed the day before, he was big
for an Ogat, from dorsal canopy-curve to flexible manipulator
tip, almost as tall as the inspector himself. And, the human
had to admit, impressive in all his military regalia. But after
all, he thought, he'd always been a pushover for guys in uniform.

Clearing his throat, Moctesuma shoved a thin sheaf of
hardcopies at the investigator. "Here's our schedule for today,
Blackburn. Rehearsal until lunchtime. *Bohnous* Ofabthosrah's
taking us out in a long loop over the Appenines. Tonight—
ship-time, that is—we'll wind up in Copernicus for another
concert."

Copernicus was three hundred miles east of a line between
Serenity and the Altai Escarpment.

"For the most part," he continued, "we'll spend the after-
noon laying tracks for tomorrow's hype recording. No, that's
over here, on the second sheet."

The detective laid a fork down which he didn't remember
picking up—he'd been hungrier than he'd expected—and
peeled back sheet-plastic on the aluminum clipboard.

"What's all this about airplanes?"

In a reversal of long-standing customs requiring a show to try out in the sticks, *Fresh Blood* was getting its shakedown at the center of human civilization. The real tour would begin once the Lunar tour was ended. Before the starship left the moon for its first interstellar stop in the Centaurus System, the schedule he was looking at called for a rendezvous tomorrow "morning" with elements of the Tranquillitatus Tactical Wing, a volunteer atmospheric fighter-squadron put together in a hurry at the beginning of the war. They'd done pretty well over the Vytpukav, he recalled, but their aircraft weren't fitted, so the hype maintained, for Osnoh B'nubo, where the real fighting was.

Contributions were solicited.

There was a marginal notation that other aerial traffic would be flagged away from the area for whatever time it took to do the recording—up to a limit of twenty minutes.

"We've made a little deal with them," Kypud explained, still paying most of his attention to the Breakfast of Champions—Ogat employed separate orifices for eating and speaking—"They help us tape a spectacular music video, and we split the advance with them against a fifty-fifty cut of the royalties."

"And they get their fighters refitted." The detective nodded. "Sounds fair enough. What passes for spectacular in music videos, these days?" He indicated Kypud's uniform. "They going to buzz the starship while you fight 'em off?"

The Ogat looked up at Moctesuma. "That's not a bad idea. Think we can shoot a bit of that?"

Moctesuma shook his head. "The choreography's already been arranged." He looked at the inspector. "Chelsie's going to fly with them—no, no, not in an airplane—we're going to lower her from the *Benjamin Parkinson* on a cable. The wing's going to fly formation on her." He sat back, pleased with the idea.

The blood vessels in his head beginning to hammer at him once again, Blackburn set his fork down for the second time. "You've lost your goddamned mind."

"I knew you'd be crazy about it!" he laughed. "Everybody will! What a coup! It'll be—"

"It'll be a great chance," Blackburn interrupted, as sick at heart as he was physically, "for whoever's trying to kill Chelsie—Miss Bradford—to finish the job, you idiot!"

Stunned silence all around the breakfast table. One didn't talk that way to the clients.

"Hey, man!" Bandell Brackenridge protested, "butt out! This ain't any of your—"

Finally, the detective thought. He lashed a speed-blurred hand across the table, gathered black-dyed shirt-leather in his fingers, and *pulled*. The musician was even lighter than he looked. With a surprised squawk, and flailing hands, Brackenridge sledded across the food-cluttered table surface toward him, crashing through the dirty dishes and the condiments. All conversation in the mess room ceased. A hundred pairs of eyes turned toward them. Nose to nose with the investigator, Brackenridge opened his mouth to speak—until the detective twisted his lapels, shutting him off like a water tap.

"I'll see you in twenty minutes—before rehearsal—so you can answer questions. Among other things, I want a word with you—and everybody else—about these privacy seals. Until then, shit-for-brains, you'll speak to me when you're spoken to!"

He gave Brackenridge a good, hard shove. With more hand-waving and an inarticulate yell, the musician sailed back through the table garbage to land with spectacular effect on the floor. Two folding chairs teetered and collapsed across him.

Chelsie's face above her snowy turtleneck was as pink as Moctesuma's jumpsuit.

Moctesuma was the color of old walnut, but kept his focus buried in his coffee cup.

Sabina Neville laughed out loud.

Edith Lenox still hadn't shown up.

It's nice to have friends, Blackburn thought, *who're willing to stick up for you.*

> *Mornin', darlin', open your eyes.*
> *Let's make breakfast, watch the sunrise.*
> *It's so good to be here alone.*
> *I can't believe it, I'm really home.*

XII

Good Guy, Bad Guy

An hour later, it still looked like a black day to the detective.

He had a monumental headache starting. Checking the headlines on the hype, shortly after breakfast's contrived altercation with Brackenridge, hadn't helped it much.

The good news, only just released, was that the Arm Force had made a raid the week before on Makmut, a Clusterian system either allied with the Powers or under their oppressive thumb, depending on whose news you listened to. Eight principal cities of the thoroughly Islamic planet had been sprayed, by high altitude tanker-ships normally used for fighting forest fires, with hog urine, pasteurized to avoid propaganda charges of biowar. It sounded like a joke, but was being called "anthropological warfare," using a people's own beliefs against them. Five days' ritual purification would completely foul up the planet's combat and production capabilities, and, on the fifth day, the Arm Force planned doing it again.

Best of all, nobody had died.

Enjoying what Edith Lenox had termed "certain pragmatic advantages in this conflict," the Powers had retaliated by cobalt-bombing the hell out of Linaweaver, a small, but densely inhabited world, surprisingly deep inside territory heretofore considered by the Arm beyond the Clusterians' reach. Five million dead or dying in the wink of an eye, a poisonous wind that would blow around that little world for as close to forever as counted to mere mortal beings, and a new, miniature version of dead Earth to decorate the galaxy.

It was getting so he dreaded looking at the hype, dreaded what he'd see or hear, even what he wouldn't see or hear. More than anything, he dreaded continuing the course of action his unconscious had mapped out for him, but he'd learned the hard way in the past, whenever such a conflict arose, that it was usually right, and he was wrong. His bottle of Mellow Meltdown seemed light-years away through a maze of corridors no laboratory rat would ever figure out.

Backed into a corner, raising his instrument-filled hands defensively before him, Bandell Brackenridge squeaked exactly like that rat. "Forget about it, man! Not after this morning. I've decided I'm not gonna talk to you at all!"

Closing the transparent door behind himself, the inspector leaned on his cane and pointed a thick finger at Brackenridge, directing him to a swivel chair anchored behind the desk which took up most of the room in this enclosure. The band leader flinched as if the finger had been a fully charged force projector, backed up a step, and blinked, close to tears. He ignored the chair.

"Bandell . . ."

Trying not to overdo the sudden switch he planned toward solicitude—there was only one of him, so, when the time arrived to play this ancient policeman's game, he had to play both roles—the detective perched on one corner of the battered desk.

"In that regard, my friend, as in so many others, you're sadly mistaken. You're going to do whatever I want you to, whenever I want you to, exactly as I want you to."

One eye on his suspect, he stopped deliberately for breath. As he expected, Brackenridge opened his mouth to protest. Blackburn put up a hand—the one that held the cane—to stop him, generating another flinch from the musician.

"Concerning what happened at breakfast," the detective said, keeping his voice soft, "I guess you just caught me at a bad time. I've a terrible temper when I first wake up. Absolutely terrible. I suppose I should have warned you."

In the same way someone will test a pressing iron with a

dampened finger—or, perhaps more appropriately, thrust a long-tined fork into the breast of a roasting turkey—he waited for yet another attempt from Brackenridge at a reply which he could interrupt. He received none, and knew things were proceeding properly.

We're all baboons, he thought, and the only question anybody cares about is which one of us is alpha. Gathering his energies for the next move, he shook his head, pasting on a rueful smile. It hurt, but he kept that to himself. Absolutely terrible. He hadn't lied to Brackenridge about his usual state of mind in the morning. Sometimes the bitter-tasting blackness threatened to overwhelm him completely.

"Do we understand each other?"

Brackenridge gulped and nodded with exactly the confused expression on his face which Blackburn had hoped to produce. Lowering the black-enameled slide-guitar he'd raised to ward the detective off, he sat down dispiritedly in the swivel chair.

It creaked.

Blackburn noticed with a concealed grin that he'd changed clothes since breakfast—all black again, something with a surface like felt, a military-cut kilt, a short jacket over a black silk shirt—but had yet to begin rehearsing with the rest of the group. He wasn't going to start now, until the investigator let him.

The plastic-partitioned office was a dust-grimed corner of a cargo hold or hangar in the starship's belly. Hard telling which. Overlapping oil stains of assorted vintages covered the deck. They might have come from aircraft or from heavy machinery being shipped somewhere. Or, for all Blackburn knew, from the miniature tanks they'd ferried over to the front during the First Skirmish.

Outside, on an elevated stage, Zibu Zytvod, his manipulator still bandaged, was warming up the electronics while Xevroid Kypud, Sabina Neville, and Chelsie Bradford went over an arrangement on a hype-screen set up on the stage. God, he found himself thinking, she is beautiful—and about as far-removed a vision from the filthy business which had brought him here to meet her as she could be and still be human. A nervous Scotty Moctesuma paced, glancing back and forth from the office Blackburn and Brackenridge occupied to his watch.

Edith Lenox still hadn't shown up.

The inspector raised his eyebrows, actually soliciting some remark from the musician. It took a while for Brackenridge to realize that, and even longer, after the previous interruptions, for him to gather up the gumption to comply. "Okay, man," Brackenridge told him. "We all have our bad days. Like my crack about Lenox."

More kissy-face, the inspector sneered to himself. "Bandell my friend, it's already forgotten. Don't give it a further thought. Everybody who has to work with anybody else builds up resentments, no matter how much they may actually like one another. Small things add up. I'll tell you what. Let's get this over with as quickly as we can, so you can go do your work and I can get on with mine." He sharpened his voice. "What resentments do you harbor toward Chelsie Bradford?"

Alarmed all over again, the musician raised a protective hand. "Look, man, what is this? I heard you were trying to catch a Powerist spy. I don't want no—"

"How time flies, is it Use Gooder Grammar Week already?" Switching back to the bad-guy role, the detective grinned openly this time. "What do you think excludes you from being the spy, Bandell-baby? You're not too happy with the nasty old war, are you? And while we're at it, what the hell is wrong with something a little less political. Chelsie's a tasty dish, isn't she? How many times has she turned you down, Bandell? Maybe none. Maybe you're a—"

"I'm *not*—I mean, she hasn't—I . . . That's it." Holding his guitar before him like a shield, he rose. "I'm not answering any more stupid questions."

"You'll leave when I'm ready for you to leave!"

Leaning forward, the detective reached around the guitar neck, put a hand on Brackenridge's shoulder, shoved him back into the chair, making sure both the gesture and the shout which had accompanied it were perceivable from outside the office.

"Talk to me, Bandell, or you'll think someone's given you an enema with a chainsaw!"

Brackenridge was having real trouble suppressing tears now. So was Nathaniel Blackburn—somehow his headache had quintupled in the last ten seconds. He lifted his right hand across his chest, nearly touching his left shoulder, as if to backhand the musician. Brackenridge squeaked again. "All right, man, all right! You got it. So maybe I did sort of like put the make on Chelsie a little when she first joined the group. So like maybe it's the custom, dig?"

"I dig, all right," Blackburn answered, lowering his hand. God, he wished he had a drink. *"Droit de singer,* you might call it. Tell me, what did Paul think about that? Did he go along with the custom, or is that maybe why he's dead?"

"What?"

"Never mind," the detective shook his head. It still hurt. Everything hurt. But he'd gotten what he wanted. He hadn't failed to notice Brackenridge's exaggerated reaction to what should have been a silly question. At least Blackburn had felt silly asking it. Someone, at long last, knew something about "Paul"—if you didn't count Edith Lenox. He'd have to go back to her and dig a little deeper. The prospect made his head hurt even worse.

"You were saying. About the custom?"

"Right. Yeah. No, I didn't like it much when she said no, but I took it—like we're making a lot of money, man. And in this business, there's always plenty of other skirt, any way you want it, all the time. As for being a Powerist spy—"

"How'd you like it when Scotty put the make on Chelsie?"

"What?"

"You're starting to repeat yourself. You can do better. Come on, Bandell old buddy, give. I knew Moctesuma was that kind of hairpin before I climbed aboard this beer-barrel. I also know what Chelsie had to do to get a place in your band. Your gripe's that she did it with him, instead of with you, isn't it?"

It was a lie, a shot in the dark taken on the spur of the moment. But Brackenridge was a fair-sized target, vulnerable, and at point-blank range. The band leader sat there as if he were trying to make up his mind. The investigator had rubbed him in six sore places at the same time. Maybe he'd even given him some new disinformation.

Without warning, the detective slapped him. "Come on, Bandell, your mind's wandering!"

A frantic, angry rapping on the plastic distracted them both. Scotty Moctesuma stood outside, looking like an alcohol thermometer ready to burst from overheating.

Blackburn grinned inside himself. Feeling he'd accomplished something, at long last, he swung the door aside, cheer in his voice. "This is Nathaniel H. Blackburn. I'm not in my office right now, but if you'll wait for the tone, you can . . ."

Moctesuma interrupted, missing the joke, what there was of it, completely. "We can't keep this rehearsal waiting any longer, Inspector! We have contracts to fill, and a tight schedule." He tossed a thumb over his shoulder. At the end of an imaginary line between that thumb and the stage outside, faces were turned toward the office, their expressions anxious and expectant. "Bandell, let's go."

"But," answered the detective, letting his lower lip turn downward in an exaggerated pout and altering his tone to go with it, "I'm not finished interviewing him."

His plump face taut with anger, Moctesuma looked toward the same place the investigator was looking, at the hand-shaped red mark pulsing visibly on Brackenridge's otherwise sallow cheek. The individual fingers were distinguishable. "You're finished as far as I'm concerned, you son of a bitch! And maybe for good. We'll see about that, later. I don't much like the way you work!"

Blackburn shot back, "Then fire me, goddammit! I told you before, Mister Entertainment, that I've got other, more important cases which you interrupted!"

Moctesuma trembled in the doorway, fuming for a moment. Then he took four or five deep breaths and his color began to subside. "Just find out who's trying to hurt Chelsie," he replied in a voice which was almost gentle. "With your permission, Captain-Inspector, I need Bandell right now for rehearsal."

Blackburn sighed and nodded agreement. "Well, it's nice to be needed by someone, isn't it, Bandell?" He made a circular gesture with his arm, as if sweeping the other out of the office door. "Run along, we'll continue this later."

Bandell Brackenridge scraped the wall exiting past the detective, trying to stay out of his reach. Oddly, as he left, there seemed to be a new light in his eyes, a gleam of something he liked seeing up ahead. Just when you think you have all the answers, Blackburn thought, wondering what he was up to now. He also wondered precisely what flavor of solicitude Moctesuma's concern for Bandell really—

Behind the inspector, the hypercom chirped for attention.

"Now what the hell do you want?" he demanded of it, not looking up, but turning to rummage, instead, through the

drawers of the dilapidated desk. Maybe some forgetful someone had left a bottle here, sometime back during the First—

"I'm on the bridge."

It was Ofabthosrah's voice. Blackburn looked up at the
screen. There he was, all right, the stiff collar—or cuff, it
amounted to the same thing—of his fresh-pressed uniform
bulging his blue fleshy face coverings out sideways.

"I want you up here in thirty seconds, Inspector."

The screen blanked.

Through the scratched and dirty plastic walls of the transparent office, the detective could see another screen going
blank, outside, the one on the bandstand. Scotty Moctesuma
stood beside it, gloating, with Bandell Brackenridge looking
on.

The detective rubbed his reddened palm where it still stung
from slapping Brackenridge, but he didn't need any reminder
to tell him why the captain wanted to see him. Roughing up
one of his passengers—even a passenger he didn't especially
like, even to apply a gentler pressure on the others—wasn't
anything the *bohnous* could let himself overlook. Not and look
at any of his faces in the mirror.

This, he thought, would call for a stop along the way to the
bridge. He couldn't look at any of the captain's faces, either,
not without some help from Mellow Meltdown. Then he could
go and get the chewing out which even he believed he de-
served.

But Blackburn was wrong.

Ofabthosrah wanted someone to come and take an official
look at another mutilated body.

XIII

Projection of Force

Don't count your chickens until they're hatched,
Or they'll come home to roost.
A tiny little bit of prevention's worth a lot of cure.
If you lock the barn when the horse is gone,
He'll stay on the loose.
I've thought about it just about a million times,
A little bitty pill once a day saves nine . . .

The late Edith Lenox's stateroom door was open a crack when Nathaniel Blackburn finally got there—having become lost in a maze of companionways once more—but the heavily armed pair of Arm Force ratings, a male Ogat and an Ewonese youth, standing in the way would have made unauthorized entry a hazardous proposition.

That leaves only eight, Blackburn thought, or is it nine crewbeings to person the ship. Certainly not enough to watch the companionways around the clock and prevent this sort of thing. Not even enough to monitor them on hype-screens—if the cameras had been permitted to exist in this privacy-obsessed civiliza—*no* (he shook his head, a purely internal

gesture), privacy was one of the things this war was all about
. . . and then he laughed at himself for conducting a one-sided
debate on social ethics on the way to the scene of a murder.

Captain Ofabthosrah was with his people in the corridor,
waiting for the investigator. The expression on his visible face
was worse in person than it had been on the screen.

"Well, Captain-Inspector Blackburn," the old Ewon growled
through his synthesizer, "while you were occupied, brutalizing
one of my passengers, another of them—"

"Yeah, that's right, Captain." *Now* he was defending his
precious passengers. Blackburn put up a hand. "And he sang
like a bird, too—but I'm tone deaf. Bah. Tell me who's been
inside that stateroom, and what did he see? Or she."

"It," Ofabthosrah snarled. "A human cabin-steward, dis-
tributing linens." He consulted the watch built into his synthesizer. "Exactly eleven minutes ago, what's presumed to be the
body of the Coordinator's representative was discovered, lying
on its back in the middle of the sitting-room carpet. The steward got the hell out, called me, and the rest of that time was
spent finding—and waiting for—you."

"I see," Blackburn answered, thumbing toward the pair of
guards. "Call your dogs off, I'm going in."

Using the back of his hand on the hinge side, he pushed the
door all the way open and entered the stateroom. He already
regretted the wisecrack about being tone deaf, but he knew,
too, that it wouldn't be the last. It was the way he always
reacted to situations like this, although he'd tried hard in the
past to resist it. He'd probably try hard again in the future. But
somehow the presence of corpses, of violent death, always
seemed to bring out the comedian in him.

Except for its unusual centerpiece, the room, mostly neat
and orderly, superficially cluttered with books and magazines,
was exactly as Blackburn had last seen it the evening before.
It was too bad, he thought, that the same couldn't be said for
Edith Lenox.

> *You can't erase it, when the moving finger's writ.*
> *Square pegs won't go in round holes, it'll never fit—no*
> *shit.*
> *The world's round, Columbus said.*
> *He felt a little different when he sailed off the edge.*

(Learn something every day!)
He felt a little different when he sailed off the edge.

Perhaps "mutilated" wasn't the proper word for the condition of the body. If it weren't, Blackburn thought, it would serve until someone looked up a better one on the hypercom. Her death-contorted remains were recognizable—just—but the face was another proposition altogether. Somebody had pointed a low-powered force projector at the bridge of her nose and pulled the trigger.

Fifteen or sixteen times.

On the surface, it had produced precisely the same effect as if someone with an exceptionally good arm had worked her over with the rounded end of a ball-peen hammer.

The expensive violet carpet would never be the same.

But Blackburn knew that the damage from two or three hundred foot-pounds of pure, directed kinetic energy, inflicted a dozen times or more, would go much deeper than that. Much deeper. If it had been the massive Ewonese military L.A.R. one-tonner Ofabthosrah carried—was carrying this minute—they'd have had to repair the walls. Even so, inside the dead woman's skull, the results would look like something from a food processor set somewhere between PURÉE and LIQUEFY. There would remain certain characteristic wavefront patterns which could identify the weapon, if it were ever found, provided this many overlapping shots hadn't obscured the evidence beyond retrieval.

For perhaps the ten thousandth time, he wondered whether this was, in fact, as everyone seemed to assume, an act of war. It seemed uncommonly subtle for the Powers—who had recently taken to slipping deep-cover spies aboard Arm warships for the sole purpose of flying them straight into the heart of the nearest star—but perhaps they were learning something from their enemies. Whenever and wherever possible, the Arm—or at least its Coordinator—preferred methods which minimized bloodshed while maximizing *schrecklicheit*.

Take the planet Krain, for instance, which he'd heard about on the hype this morning. Unbeinged solar-powered gliders had been launched from orbit, flying evasive patterns while showering microwaves down on the population. The frequency was one which kept the human brain's sleep center from operating. A week of that and the Clusterians of Krain weren't in much shape to do anything.

The Coordinated Arm Force had then shut the microwaves off, waited four hours, and air-dropped Special Forces into military installations, where they cut the throat of every tenth sleeping soldier, and disappeared into the skies again. There had followed a planetwide mutiny among the Powerist troops, and the expectation was that Krain had taken itself, effectively, out of the war for good.

Shaking his head, he called the captain to the edge of the doorframe, voicing the usual caution about disturbing evidence, asking short-clipped questions of the Ewon and getting answers from him as he knelt to examine the body and its immediate surroundings.

She'd been tripped over, Ofabthosrah told him, by a sleepy steward bringing clean towels and washcloths during his regular rounds, the breakfast hour, when most passengers could be presumed to be elsewhere. Bedding would have been brought later, usually at lunchtime, although the steward had probably been saved the trouble now. An ill wind, Blackburn thought, and so on. The body was dressed. A briefcase, unopened—as he intended to leave it for the time being—lay on the floor beside it, indicating the obvious possibility that Lenox had been just about to go somewhere, when somebody sent her somewhere else.

No more than a possibility, he reminded himself, one that circumstantially seemed to fix the time of death—and with it, as had been the case with Baldwin, obviate any chance that anyone would have a creditable alibi.

That would probably have been sufficient, if this had been a mystery novel or a detective movie. Between what was to be logically expected of people and the protagonist's "feel for phenomena," little else would be required to establish the facts. But real life, the inspector knew, wishing he'd been issued a "feel for phenomena" along with the rest of his investigative gear in Arm Force Intelligence School, wasn't like that. Human beings do a million unobvious things for every obvious thing they do every day. Lenox, perhaps unable to sleep, might have been trying on a new outfit at two in the morning. Or perhaps she always dressed for business when she was by herself.

Perhaps, perhaps, perhaps . . .

The general attitude and position of the body made Blackburn think she hadn't been expecting what she got. Her hands were relaxed, the nails clean and unbroken, and her limbs were straight. She might not even have felt what happened. Not the worst way to go, he thought, if it were absolutely unavoidable.

There was no sign of a struggle, no disruption of the body (aside from the face), the clothing, or, as far as he could see, of the contents of the stateroom. What little daytime jewelry she had worn was still in place. More perhaps. Whoever had done this thing had wanted a dead Edith Lenox and apparently hadn't wanted much of anything else—unless he'd known exactly where it was and had simply gone and gotten it without tearing the place apart.

Reflexively, Blackburn glanced up at the stateroom's thermostat. That was one way of fiddling with a body's cooling rate, and he'd check the little dial for prints as soon as possible. Maybe somewhere aboard this interstellar white elephant some record was kept of each cabin's power draw, and that would be a help.

He wasn't counting on it.

His first rough guess was that she'd been dead no more than two hours, about right if—again, the obvious—she'd been leaving to join everybody else at the breakfast table. While consistent with the steward's story, it might have been exactly what he was *intended* to think. Scientific confirmation of this and of his other guesses would have to wait until he could search the suite's bedroom and get at the investigative gadgets in his bag, back in his own—provided he could ever find it again. And even then, he intended to consult with somebody like Security Assurance, being no forensic man himself.

Aside from the woman's face itself—which was more than enough—there were no additional signs of violence on the frontal or lateral sides of her body. Gulping back his breakfast, which had apparently decided to leave the room without him, he placed a gentle hand on one of the arms, intending to lift the corpse so he could look underneath—

"Captain!"

—he let the dead woman's plump arm fall again, inert, so that it concealed, exactly as it had before, the small, dark, too familiar object which lay there.

There's many a slip twixt the cup and the lip,
And baby, your slip is showing.
The grass is always greener on the other side.
Keep your nose to the grindstone,
And it won't do much growing.
Early to bed and early to rise
Will give you plenty of exercise.

"Yes?" the old Ewonese officer's synthetic voice grumbled from the doorway. Something, either the sinking in of current events, or his impression of the manner in which Blackburn was handling things had softened his tone. "What is it, son?"

"I want you present to witness this officially." The investigator took a breath. "Step inside the room—no, don't come too far, that's right—and watch me."

The Ewon's head shook from side to side. "A lot of damned melodramatic nonsense," he muttered, but his cardiovascular system wasn't really in the complaint, and he complied.

Still kneeling by the body, Blackburn shook his own head. "See if you can get one of your little friends out in the hall to peek around the corner, too. The more eyes, the better. And send the other one after my bag, the one under the bunk in my kennel."

"N'don daoh iey rur?" demanded the captain in what Blackburn recognized as Mid-South Continental, West Plateauland Ewonese. The detective's command of the tongue might have surprised Ofabthosrah. Despite the rather esoteric label it had been assigned in English, by human sentiologists, it was the dominant language of the species. *"Thabes'rth n'duhni us fobb fa, eh fyssh meh uey docha uthoff!"*

It was the first occasion Blackburn had had to hear Ofabthosrah's real, unsynthesized voice, fully as low and rumbling as the electronic one he'd chosen for himself. The bulky, blue-limbed guard grunted an Ewonese *yessir* and departed.

Then, in synthesized Ogatik, the captain issued yet another order: *"Yd doo vet uei yt duvgooxo—tazrytup zaizh!"* The Ogat, having suffered—and, amazingly, survived—ten thousand years of high-tech warfare before getting their act together (first to fight the Ewon, then the Powers) only had one language left.

Rather like Earth's orphaned children.

There was a crisp Ogatik word of acknowledgment. Immediately an additional tentacle joined Ofabthosrah's four larger ones—and the single silvery prosthetic—in the now crowded entryway, this appendage small, brown, and sinuous.

So, thought the human investigator to himself, *an ancient riddle is answered at long last. The Ogat keep their eyes— one of them, at least—in the ends of their manipulators. Now, about Scotsmen's kilts and Santa Claus' beard . . .*

Moving to let his actions be seen from the door, Blackburn rolled the body of the Coordinator's former representative halfway over again. What he'd thought—and feared—he'd seen in his one brief glimpse was what he saw again.

So much for ever being able to find the murder weapon. The killer had been considerate. Beneath the left arm, almost beneath the shoulder-blade, lay a 291 Ingersoll, exactly like the one he was carrying in his holster. Exactly like the extra one he hoped—but didn't believe for a minute—was still nestled securely in the soft-sided bag the Ewonese rating had just gone to his cabin to fetch.

> *A rolling stone will never gather moss.*
> *Judas got his silver, so it wasn't a total loss.*
> *The world's round, Columbus said.*
> *He felt a little different when he sailed off the edge.*
> *(Learn something every day!)*
> *He felt a little different when he sailed off the edge.*

XIV

Hail, Yes!

When in doubt, Nathaniel Blackburn thought, as he had thought many times before since enlisting in the Coordinated Arm Force, call a goddamned meeting.

"All right," he nearly had to shout it over the noise of half a dozen people talking simultaneously. They were all back in Chelsie Bradford's cabin, where the whole dismal thing, at least for him, had begun the previous day. "That's it. By the authority vested in me"—with a stiffened finger, he thumped himself savagely in the chest—"*by me*—the tour's canceled."

Abruptly, Moctesuma stopped his jabbering with Ofabthosrah, Sabina hers with Chelsie. The peculiar ear-grating whine of the Ogatik language—Kypud having some kind of argument with Zytvod—broke off, to Blackburn's relief. It would have been perfect if he could have shut *Frog Strangler* up, as well, but they were in their special staterooms, keeping out of an invisible fog of non-Uthabohn allergens. All heads swiveled—those physically capable of it—toward him.

Both major items of physical evidence, the mutilated (he hadn't had a chance yet to look up a better word) body of the late Edith Lenox and the small 291 Ingersoll force projector which had been used to perform said mutilation (he'd found the time to verify that much, at least), had been left under heavy guard where they lay, still in the process of cooling to room temperature.

What made the force projector really interesting (if that, too, was the correct word) was the fact that it had indeed turned out to be Blackburn's spare, taken from the bag—easy enough, there were no locks on the cabin doors—beneath his stateroom bunk. The mere presence of the thing had not been a hundred percent conclusive. Pure kinetic energy is a lot harder to trace back to its original source than a bullet or a burglar-bar, both of which possess distinguishing tool marks. And there were tens of millions of the little pocket weapons floating around the civilized galaxy. Serial numbers had gone out of fashion about the time of the Banishment. But, setting aside scientific analysis, there could be no doubt about this particular piece, its having been discarded at the scene of the crime, or its ownership.

Moctesuma opened his mouth to speak, couldn't think of a thing to say, and closed it.

"I agree completely with the Inspector," the captain stated, "and lend my authority to his. It's bad enough to have these killings happen here, on Luna, close to civilization; but if this ship were damaged in the middle of a deep-space run . . ."

Bandell Brackenridge snorted. "You're all heart, captain-baby. But I agree with you anyway. I'd rather not become number three on somebody's private hit parade!"

Chelsie Bradford didn't say a word. Sabina Neville laid a comforting hand on her shoulder—that much had changed, at least, although it was a hell of a way to change things.

Each time he spoke, to anyone of anything, Chelsie looked up at him, wide-eyed and with slightly parted lips, as if expecting—or merely hoping desperately—that he was going to do something to wake her from this nightmare. *If he did,* he wondered, *would she*—he brought a mental heel down on the thought until it died unfinished. There was something close to terror in the singer's eyes, but Blackburn, wrapping himself in a comforting and comfortable cynicism, wasn't prepared to say whether it was terror of being murdered like the others, or terror at losing the rest of the tour, and therefore her audience.

Given what he was learning of these "show-biz" people, it could easily have been either.

The captain stiffened, which Blackburn would have thought impossible, considering the posture he'd started from, and added, "I was about to say, young and obnoxious human, that if this ship were damaged in the middle of a deep-space run, there would be precious little hope for the rest of us surviving."

Despite any support they seemed to offer for the position he was taking, Blackburn ignored both beings, Brackenridge and Ofabthosrah, thinking instead about the 291 Ingersoll. With its ergonomically shaped housing removed, a toolless operation requiring less time to perform than to describe, the weapon was essentially a nonferrous metal rod, richly implanted with exotic ions. A triplet of fine-wired Moebius coils was wound tightly at right angles to one another—Blackburn always thought of a "Turk's turban" scout knot—around its back end.

When a trickle from the power cell housed in the grip—a Nolan-Travis retrofit he'd recently had done by an Arm Force armorer who owed him favors—worked its complicated way through the smartpack above it into the mutually interfering coils, they spat out their subatomic frustration in a brief-lived shaft of pure kinetic energy—exactly 291 foot-pounds' worth, owing to some physical constant he didn't know anything more about—in the direction indicated by a small bright scarlet parallel laser, Sir Isaac Newton's equal-but-opposite reaction being regeneratively absorbed by the power supply.

It hadn't been an enjoyable moment in Edith Lenox's stateroom when Blackburn had hinged the trigger-guard away from the frame, the first step in disassembly, watched carefully by the captain and his "men." They'd all seen the initials which a much younger Nathaniel Blackburn had scratched there, **NHB**, on his thirteenth birthday, when, over his parents' whining and ultimately futile objections, his favorite disreputable uncle had presented him with the pair of tiny pistols. The same Uncle Bob, an Arm Force Commander, had bought the farm in deep-space combat, aboard the C.A.F. *Bernie Goetz*, the week before his nephew had enlisted and suffered his own near-miss on Osnoh B'nubo. Either patriotism ran in the family, Blackburn thought now, or stupidity.

"Aside from verifying a match with the wave-front patterns lingering in the, er, remains, which identifies it as the murder weapon, exposure to my instruments betrays no fingerprints or other useful information," Blackburn had told his observers, speaking up for the benefit of the Security Assurance techs listening in by hype. Their own field-people were already on the way. A gruff, badly shaken Luswe Ofabthosrah seemed to hold Blackburn responsible for Lenox's murder. The young inspector, charged with getting to the bottom of this mystery, not helping to deepen it further, felt inclined to share his opinion.

Now, he swore—and until he found the individual who had used his gun to end a somewhat unpleasant, but nonetheless innocent life—he was in the miscreant-collection business in a big way.

"Inspector?"

The chirruping of yet another hypercom brought Blackburn out of his thoughts and back to the meeting. He looked up. Something new had been added to the agitated crowd of human beings, Ogat, and the single Ewon he'd been trying to ignore. A nervous-looking human rating was whispering to the captain, and the captain, betraying a bit of nervousness himself, nodded at the inspector, who stepped, leaning on his cane, toward the stateroom's screen.

"Captain-Inspector Nathaniel Horatius Blackburn," intoned the heavily accented voice, "brevet Battalion Manager, First Nectaris Volunteers. Yes, you do look familiar to me, as they said you would. Did I myself not pin a medal on your chest" —to Blackburn it sounded more like "jezt"—"when you returned from Osnoh B'nubo?"

He nodded at the hype-screen, attempting to keep a neutral expression, "Yes, ma'am. Certainly, ma'am. Whatever it says there in the data-file you're consulting, ma'am."

The Galactic Coordinator made a face. Anastasia Wheeler resembled somebody's kindly old grandmother, Blackburn thought, somebody like Attila the Hun. Tiny and frail-looking, she had unfashionably bobbed silver hair and thick wire-rimmed spectacles; even her accent was right, somehow. Nine hundred years had been more than enough time for the sole remaining human language, American English—as spoken in the Cluster and the Arm respectively—to diverge that much.

The long black cigarette holder was a jarring note, as were the shrewd and ancient eyes behind the glass, and the rising wisps of tobacco smoke. This frail and tiny woman, he reminded himself, at the age of seventeen, had somehow stolen a fully crewed starship from under the collective nose of the Powers. After finishing with the officers and conning the peasant ratings into going along with her, navigation textbook in hand, she had brought the Clusterian vessel, nearly single-handedly, from the outermost edge of the Galactic Arm, all the way to Luna.

And, like the big cheese she'd become since then, age had only sharpened her.

Not long afterward, she'd established herself, first as a widely read writer about the politics and living conditions in the prison-society she'd left, later as an accredited adjudicatory advocate, trying to prevent the same conditions from taking root here. Experimentalists and Durationites hated her. Even her own party, the so-called "Banishers," weren't terribly fond of her unwavering inclination toward consistent principles, no matter the political consequences.

She took a deep drag on her cigarette. "That is, indeed, what the data-file says, young man. But I remember you, as well, sitting there in that wheelchair, drawn and pale and smelling of cheap whiskey and of cheaper cigars."

Blackburn laughed. "You've just described every last ever-loving survivor of that mess." He turned his face from the screen. "But do you really remember me, or do you just say that to all the war heroes? What color are my eyes?"

She took the holder from her mouth, peered into the screen. "Blackened, exactly like both of mine, exactly like those of every individual in the Arm if you allow the tour you are assigned to protect to be interrupted by agents of our enemies."

Blackburn turned back to the screen. "Two people have died already, Madame Coordinator, and two more have come damned close. I don't have any idea who's doing it, although it has occurred to me I could just let your Powerist spy kill everybody until he's the only one left and I know who he is—provided he lets me live. It's getting to look like that kind of a situation."

They stared at each other in stubborn silence for a moment. It was Blackburn who gave in and spoke first.

"You know, Madame Coordinator, I had a longer talk with Edith Lenox than I wanted. Most of what we talked about was Durationism. It occurred to me then to wonder whether this isn't all a plot to discredit Arm Force Intelligence by sending, in all due modesty, their most incompetent operative on an impossible mission."

He extracted a cigar—all right, a cheap cigar—from his tunic pocket and lit it. The Coordinator took another pull on her cigarette, exhaled slowly, then gave a kind of whispered chuckle, which was the closest she ever came to a laugh.

"The Coordinated Arm," she answered at last, "is very short of being-power, Inspector, and I find myself under considerable political pressure not to 'waste' it on a 'mere' rock-and-roll tour." She peered at him appraisingly. "You possess a certain ruthless regard for the hard truth, young Nathaniel Blackburn, which I find very much to my liking in a representative of legitimate authority, despite your rather insubordinate manner of expressing it."

Blackburn blew a smoke ring.

"I'm a child, born and bred, of the Coordinated Arm, Anastasia. Insubordination is our most important product, and 'legitimate authority' a contradiction in terms. Also, I'm fed up, sick and tired of watching people die. If it were put to a vote, I'd have to be on the shutting-down-the-tour side."

The Coordinator frowned.

"It is not my intention to put anything to a vote, Captain-Inspector. The Coordinated Arm is a free polity, not a majoritarian democracy. Its inhabitants are neither citizens nor subjects. You must obey the dictates of your own judgment, as must each of those there with you. As must I. If everyone belonging with the *Fresh Blood* tour quits, I shall simply replace them, over and over again, until the purpose which I had in mind for it is achieved."

"Or until you run out of money—or people."

"I am aware that both are distinct possibilities, Captain-Inspector, I assure you. In the meantime, I will ask you please to attend to your own macramé, if that is the expression, and permit me to attend to mine. The *Fresh Blood* tour may be halted only upon my auth—upon my say-so, and I decline to give it."

"I understand. And I can go along with it," Blackburn answered after a moment.

Did she know about the coppery Turk's turban to be found within every force projector, and was her malapropism a not-so-subtle goad? Or was he simply getting too involved in politics and suffering occupational paranoia? He wasn't sure himself. Nor whether what he had suddenly decided to say was a joke or not.

"On one condition: that *you* tell me who the hell Paul was, and how he wound up dead."

The sudden startlement in Anastasia Wheeler's eyes wasn't a fraction less genuine than the fear he'd seen in Chelsie Bradford's. "Young man," she answered with a tight-lipped expression, "I have not the remotest idea what you are speaking of."

"Right," he answered lamely, "it figures."

Swell, Blackburn thought to himself, the fat ferret has dug up another someone who knows something about Dead Paul. And it was guilty knowledge, of that much he was certain. Another goddamned suspect. Only this time it was the lady who had hired him, his glorious Commander-in-Chief, the Coordinator of the Galactic Arm.

"You have a job to do," his newest suspect was saying. "Very well, then, do it. Is that clear, young man?"

Blackburn sighed, too weary and in too much pain to argue any further now, and nodded. "I'm afraid it is, Madame Coordinator, I'm afraid it is." He brightened. "Say, we're all having a wonderful time aboard the *Parkinson*. Wish you were here!"

She gave him her not-quite-chuckle once again. "I'd rather wager that you do, Captain-Inspector."

The screen went blank.

> *The world's round, Columbus said.*
> *He felt a little different when he sailed off the edge.*
> *(Learn something every day!)*
> *He felt a little different when he sailed off the edge.*

XV

Frog Strangler

The camera hovers high, a hundred meters or more, above wind-rippled reaches of a yellow prairie.

Along the not-quite-flat horizon to the north and east, the summer sky has a faintly greenish tinge. Far to the west, the sharp-edged peaks of a geologically young mountain range arise, their white-veined angularities deep blue and unreal in the haze of distance.

As far as the eye—the camera eye—can see, the prairie is deserted, empty, peaceful.

Without warning, the camera viewpoint stoops like a predatory bird, plummeting in a stomach-wrenching arc toward the plain below until, mere centimeters from the ground which seems to rush up to receive it, it levels out in the knee-high grass, pushing yellow stalks aside as it travels in a die-straight path toward the rolling skyline, sometimes almost tunneling through the summer-dry vegetation.

In a moment, there's an indistinct dark blur ahead.

It resolves into the worn, deep-treaded sole of an issue combat boot, upturned as its wearer lies on his belly. There is just enough time to recognize it, the small, nonregulation dagger tucked in the top where the pants blouse over it, and the camera passes, only to glide past, at a gradually increasing speed, the quiet form of yet another man, unshaven, dirty-faced and grim in his yellow-and-brown-striped coveralls, hunched on his elbows over the matte-finished gray-green bulk of a Clusterian two-handed force projector.

The camera passes quickly, picking up speed, leaving in the cloven grass-wake behind it, the tense, anticipatory forms of more and more Clusterian soldiers, ragged, weary, but clearly prepared to deliver up whatever is left of their lives ambushing some unwary interloper to the prairie lands they've recently won at such a terrible cost and are determined so desperately to hold.

As its speed increases, the camera rises slightly, the curve so gradual and graceful that the changes in its velocity and altitude go almost unnoticed until it stops, almost as if startled, a few dozen meters above the ground where the land, too, begins to rise gently, gathering itself into a long, round-topped hill.

From behind the hill there is a sound, a chord, a scratchy, wailing caterwaul which would terrify the dead.

It is followed by the cough of starting engines, a billowing of dust.

Over the rise, three gigantic hovercraft, painted the same mottled yellow-brown as the uniforms of the waiting soldiers, reach the hillcrest and begin to half slide, half trundle downward. Their forward movement is as relentless as the music which accompanies it. The music is as relentless as their forward movement. It is an ancient piece, Queen's "We Are the Champions."

The camouflage of the hovercraft, however close its colors are to the uniforms of the Clusterians, is in a distinctly different pattern, as is the clothing of the gunners, hunched in pockets behind windscreens, just below the topmost deck edges of the giant machines. Each vehicle is huge, its front and sides sloped steeply to repel boarders and deflect projectiles. A tornado roars from beneath its enveloping skirt. The projectors begin spitting death at the figures lying in the grassy valley.

They try their best to spit it back.

The outer pair of vehicles are escorts. Atop the center machine, protected by a knee-high slanting transparency, stands

*a young man clad only in camouflage fatigue pants and the
Arm Force footwear that goes with them. His naked torso
glistens with perspiration. His short-cropped hair shines
golden in the sunlight.*

*In his lean, long-fingered hands he holds the source of the
caterwauling, wailing, scratchy chord, amplified a thousand-
fold by the high-banked tiers of electronics at the rear of the
lumbering battle machine. It is a bandolar, its drum-head
body enameled the same color and pattern as his trousers. He
gestures, wielding the instrument like a weapon, which indeed
it is, accompanied by a black man playing electronic bass a
few steps behind him to the left. To his right, a husky blond
woman stirs a tempest with a portable keyboard slung from a
shoulder strap.*

*Trace-beams flare around them as the Clusterian force
projectors seek them out.*

They continue playing, heedless.

*The hovercraft sweep across the prairie, manmade light-
ning and thunder, smoke, and the stench of destruction in
their wake. Everywhere, men die, mostly among the unprotected Clusterians. Here, there are cries of agony and despair
from the long grass. There, an Arm Force gunner slumps
behind his shattered windscreen.*

*As the final notes of the music die, the hovercraft pass over
the horizon, leaving emptiness behind.*

Nathaniel Blackburn knocked on the stateroom door before
him. Inside, he could hear noises, a dull mechanical fumbling.

A louder clank.

After a brief wait, the door swung aside.

The combination of a brightly colored shirt in the ancient
pattern called "Aloha"—gold thread woven in and out of an
atrocious choice of shades and shapes—and a severe brass-
buttoned Coordinated Arm Force military kilt, was something
he'd never seen before. Or wanted to. The addition of a Uthabohn respirator mask, also decorated garishly, a sight the inspector had come to associate with the frozen, deadly
environment of the battle-planet Osnoh B'nubo—or, more
lately, patriotic teen-age music fans throughout the Arm—
made it . . . perfect.

He spoke first: "Captain-Inspector Nathaniel H. Blackburn—"

"—Coordinated Arm Force Intelligence," the other finished for him. The rich, twangy Uthabohn mangling of the langauge, which the inspector had anticipated—vowels shaped more like bananas than pears, glottal stops which hurt his own throat just to listen, dropped R's and H's—was even thicker than Blackburn had expected.

To the speaker, he nodded confirmation.

Despite—or possibly because of—his experiences on the planet of its origin, he felt somewhat uncomfortable addressing the mask before him. The thing was mostly transparent, its custom-molded, face-following contours highlighted with fine lines and whorls of golden carriage-striping, in grotesque caricature of the hypercom's encyclopedia illustrations of the ancient—and extinct—New Zealand Maori.

He extended a hand. "I didn't see you when I met the others."

A slender, string-callused appendage reached out, giving Blackburn's the briefest possible of touches. There was a reason for that, a very good reason, and Blackburn wasn't offended. The face behind the gilt-embellished mask lifted a just-visible single eyebrow. "P'raps because I wasn't there, eh, Captain-Inspector? Come in, then, and meet the mob. Step up—and do mind the inner door."

Now Blackburn saw—and immediately understood—the occasion for the brief delay. Inside the stateroom, a small metal-walled chamber had been installed over the original entrance, forming a sort of airlock. Regularly spaced flashes of red light flooded the partitioned-off space. He reached back to close the outer door—it sighed against tight-sealing gaskets —behind him.

Instantly there was a painful racket as high-powered electrostatic impellers in the built-up floor and ceiling tugged at his clothing. His ears complained, not only of the noise, but of a sudden drop in pressure. It was like being just inside the nozzle of a gigantic vacuum cleaner. In fact, the inspector realized, it *was* being just inside the nozzle of a gigantic vacuum cleaner.

The illumination in the chamber changed to a view-bleaching green-yellow—still punctuated by red danger flashes—rich with sanitizing ultraviolet. His host reached for a long-bristled implement hanging on the wall, handing it to

Blackburn, then taking another for himself. Both used the brushes, briskly slapping at their clothing.

Abruptly, the mind-filling racket died, chamber pressure rose to normal, Blackburn's eardrums stopped complaining, and, above the inner door a single small lamp turned green. His host opened it. "You'll pardon the ritual," the masked figure told him as they walked into the room beyond. "I'm told you know the reason."

Blackburn nodded. "Yes, I do. Hay fever squared. Another few months' lack of exposure to foreign proteins on your planet, and I'd be taking the same precautions. I was stationed on Osnoh B'nubo—assistant brigade-manager—crapped out in the Battle of Uthaboh, but survived the March to Lohua Fihr, all during which I worried a lot more about losing my immunities than enemy projector fire."

The Uthabohn figure reached up and removed his mask, revealing a broad, ironic grin. The pale face behind it was high-cheeked and thin, showing the carefully cultivated three-day stubble currently fashionable, all bones and tendons underneath tautly stretched skin. The blond hank above the face was wispily unruly on top, thinning a little in the front, roughly parted in the middle. At the sides he wore it skull-cap short. Entertainers of a generation earlier had looked like Rapunzel, the inspector thought to himself. Now this.

The eyes were something altogether alien, far more so than the brown and bovine organs of the Ewon, or, somehow, even those of the Ogat, forever hidden from view. Blackburn's own eyes traveled back to the grin, which he found not at all pleasant. Then again, the combat veteran reasoned, his own rueful half smile, at being reminded once again of the ruthless Clusterian decimation of the military and civilian population of that disputed human-Ewon colony planet, wouldn't likely have appeared very pleasant, either. Which is why he never bothered with one.

"Manners! Manners!" the outlandishly dressed individual before him exclaimed abruptly, spreading his thin arms in an embarrassed shrug. "Where the bloody hell have mine got off to? I'm Dack Stirkey, of course"—he waved a hand at two other figures Blackburn hadn't noticed until this moment— "Torus Strong"—the black man, relaxed and lounging on a sofa, nodded amiably—"and Astrid Ringer."

The woman stood behind the sofa with her hands behind her back. She nodded, too, but it was a nervous, subdued greeting, that of a peasant farmer toward a Cossack.

"Sorry," Stirkey continued, "I guess we've grown somewhat accustomed to being recognized by everyone without any introduction. Frightfully arrogant, of us, I'm afraid..." He paused. "And you, dear fellow"—he nodded toward Blackburn's injured leg—"you've been out of it quite a while in any case, haven't you?"

"Not long enough not to recognize *Frog Strangler,*" Blackburn answered, accepting Stirkey's gestured offer of a chair. "Just to refresh my memory, I took a look at your new video before I came to see you. Pretty grim stuff. I even knew who you were back on your home planet, before an album which went iridium before it was shipped, before the invasion, when the three of you were just getting started."

"Ah, yes," Torus Strong replied. His voice was deep and rich, accented exactly like Stirkey's. "Where would we be without *Breathing Vacuum,* our first, and so far only, masterpiece—which we were off on tour promoting at the time of the initial unpleasantness? Likely freezing our celebrated arses off in a Clusterian prison camp right now. Instead, we're making little movies to hearten the side and confuse the enemy. Silly, how these things work out, isn't it?"

Blackburn shook his head, a negative gesture of affirmation, and looked around the room. The airlock, its makeshift joints duct-taped and wrapped in wrinkled gold foil—or more accurately, the "allergen-lock"—took up a great deal of space in a stateroom which hadn't been very large to begin with. Furniture had been crowded up against the remaining three walls so that it was impossible to take more than two paces without having to step over or around something.

Strong occupied an end of a long couch, upholstered in metallic yellow vinyl, too big for the stateroom even before the lock had been installed. Stirkey flopped onto the other end and stretched his lean, slight-shouldered frame. Blackburn sat in one of a pair of high-backed comfortable chairs. There were also a couple of end tables and lamps.

Dozens of books—old-fashioned ones with covers and pages—and sheaves of paper lay everywhere, the latter mostly printed sheet music. Here and there, Blackburn saw a hand-written score with lyrics penciled in below the staves, chords marked over them in red. There were several musical instruments lying about in the clutter, among them the difficult-to-master bandolar, a twelve-string fretted banjo—although the lead singer seldom appeared on stage playing it. Clothing of every description had been tossed around haphazardly, as well, with the dried-out remains of several meals on trays taking up what space was left.

Stirkey grinned again. "It is a bit like being in a hospital, isn't it? One doesn't feel quite like tidying up oneself, and admitting the help's more trouble than it usually seems worth." For the briefest of moments, pain creased the young man's features, then it was gone, replaced by a smile, this time honest and open—although still ironic.

Strong added, with a glance at Astrid Ringer, "Makes enjoying female companionship a trifle awkward, too."

Ringer nodded. "I think it'd be a bloody marvelous idea to get our planet back."

Blackburn laughed, despite himself. "Yes," he answered, "it would. Especially since that appears to be the only place where you and yours can be comfortable—"

"—can walk around," Ringer interrupted, Stirkey again raising the single eyebrow in support, "in the open air without dying from any one of fifty-eleven allergic reactions, you mean."

"Yes," Strong offered. "You're far too polite, old fellow, to be much of a policeman. Is there some manner in which we may be allowed to return the favor?"

The investigator swallowed, braced himself, mentally took hold of his nose, and dived in. "You can tell me who Paul was, who wanted him dead, and how it was he died."

Torus Strong started violently.

Astrid Ringer let out a little moan, swayed, and had to support herself by leaning on the couch.

Dack Stirkey turned deathly pale.

Somehow, Blackburn thought, as he had with Anastasia Wheeler, he had scored again.

But how?

XVI

A Sleeper in the Works

Heads up! La la loh!
Though the trail is steep,
And the traffic is slow.
We moved ourselves out in a grim-lookin' row,
'Cause we heard someone say there was someplace to
*   go . . .*
La loh.

Nathaniel Blackburn thought hard.

What in the deep, dark, limitless hell had he wanted to learn from these people, anyway? He'd had the whole goddamned thing planned out before he came here. It had all seemed so simple—just do what the Coordinator had told him to, or else. (Although the "else" was becoming more and more attractive by the hour.) Now, having fired a shot in the dark— one that, with the exception of Anastasia Wheeler herself, had failed to hit the mark squarely every time he'd fired it before —and having heard somebody holler "Ouch!" he wasn't sure.

The problem was that he formed first impressions, good

and bad, all too quickly. And had a tough time shaking them afterward. He'd been discovering that he liked Dack Stirkey, Torus Strong, and perhaps even Astrid Ringer. The terrible experience the four of them shared—that all survivors and refugees of Osnoh B'nubo shared—made it that much easier to like them, and that much harder to do his job.

He concentrated: *Remember,* he told himself, *you don't like anybody involved in this idiotic mess. You don't like your boss—damn Anastasia Wheeler, girl Coordinator, anyway— you don't like the case, and you don't like the whole damned job in the first place. Make-work for a crippled and useless officer.*

"I certainly don't seem very well suited to it at that, do I?" he answered carefully, at last. "Being a policeman, I mean. As you said, I suppose almost anyone could do it better than I seem to be managing. Take Captain Ofabthosrah, for example. I'd say *Bohnous* Luswe is very good at what he does."

Stirkey seemed to have recovered. Again he raised the inquiring single eyebrow—Blackburn had practiced the same expression before a mirror for months before he'd gotten it right. Someone had told him—incorrectly, as it turned out— that it was a hereditary capability. Like wiggling one's ears. He'd mastered it anyway; there hadn't been much else to do in the hospital.

But, in exchange for whatever they could tell him, there was little he felt free to tell the Uthabohn group about what he was doing. And he desperately wanted to pursue this business about Paul—*if* he could do it without shutting off the people who had answers. It was, after all, the only lead he had.

But, as he had asked himself before, how?

After reluctantly launching his early-morning campaign of harassing hell out of Bandell Brackenridge, Blackburn had responded to an angry message from the captain.

The old Ewon had wanted to see him.

Now.

The detective had assumed—until he'd learned about the brutal murder of Edith Lenox—that he was on his way to a session of having his *glutei maximi* thoroughly masticated. As he was doing now with the three Uthabohns, on the way to the control-deck, he had reviewed, for the sake of defending himself from the captain, everything he knew. Everything he *thought* he knew. Now, since he was prepared anyway, he began reeling it off for the benefit of *Frog Strangler*.

"According to *Fresh Blood*'s keyboardist, Zibu Zytvod," he told the group, "Captain Ofabthosrah was originally an officer of the line. He's outraged, the story goes, about being wounded, stuck on an antiquated tub, out of combat."

With the captain, that would have been a direct question, intended to put the old being on the defensive, to elicit a reply, preferably at the top of whatever it was the Ewon used for lungs. Blackburn had found that truth is much more often hollered—or offered in a whisper—than spoken in a normal tone. But now, what he'd said about the captain was just another goddamned alleged fact.

Stirkey, however, laughed bitterly. "Too flaming right, mate!" He glanced around at his companions. "And doesn't *that* sound too bleeding familiar?"

There were answering nods, it appeared more out of guilt or duty than agreement, from both. Too weary of this mess to sort out which it was or what it meant, Blackburn shook his head.

"There's more. He's said to resent deeply what he regards as Chelsie Bradford's hypocrisy concerning the conduct of the War Against the Powers, a resentment I gather is augmented by the enemy's well-known attitude toward nonhumans. He's told me himself he hates dithering of any kind, whether it's ethical in nature or pragmatic. Whatever it is a being feels, it ought to be gotten on with."

In fact, during the subsequent meeting in Chelsie Bradford's stateroom, before it had been ended by the hype call from the Coordinator, the captain, attempting to terminate what he obviously regarded as Blackburn's dithering, had ordered the investigator to tell him everything he was up to. For a number of reasons—not the least of which that the captain himself was as much a suspect as anyone else—Blackburn couldn't. The rest of their conversation had been inconclusive —*you will, I won't, you will*—and even less pleasant.

Maybe that was why he'd been enjoying this visit with the Uthabohn delegation—until Dead Paul intruded. At least they all had something in common—as terrible as that something might be—and on that account, if no other, understood one another.

Strong nodded. "And you'd greatly appreciate our dishing you any of the dirt we may have collected about the Captain or Chelsie, is that it? And you're not going to ask us where we were the night of so-and-so, at such-and-such a time, when Victor Baldwin was getting himself defenestrated without benefit of *fenestra*?"

"You know," Stirkey offered, "I've a theory. I don't want to horn in on your job, old fellow, but I wonder if all this trouble isn't being caused by some less obvious group. Not the Powers, nor even their little friends the Experimentalists . . ."

"Somebody like the Durationites?" Blackburn asked.

Stirkey smiled. "Close, very, very close. How about—" He glanced briefly at his two friends. "What the bloody hell is it that they call themselves?"

"Mothers," Strong began, "Against Freedom—"

"M.A.F.I.A.," Blackburn supplied.

"The very ones," said Stirkey. "I'm not exactly intimately familiar with them—if anyone can be said to be—or their kind. In truth, I was quite shocked when I first heard about them. Live as close to the Cluster as we Uthabohns do—with a bad example close to hand—you come to value something like free speech."

"And," Strong added, "you get to be extremely watchful against any threat to same."

"Whatever the excuses," Astrid Ringer spoke up at long last, "they may care to offer."

Blackburn laughed. "And you actually think that M.A.F.I.A. might be committing sabotage—treason, technically—murdering people in order to stop the tour of a band—"

"Two bands!" Stirkey insisted. "Pardon me for interrupting, but being known for the quality of one's enemies is quite as important as being known for the quality of one's friends. Besides, credit where credit's due, I always say."

"All right, then," Blackburn conceded with an involuntary grin, "two bands whose music they disapprove of?"

"See here, Inspector"—Strong raised a finger and wiggled it at Blackburn—"anyone who'd seek to turn their moral or esthetic disapproval into brute force—law—well, what's the difference? Murder, sabotage, and treason are names for crimes we do ourselves. Whereas the other's a crime we hire policemen to do for us."

"Policemen like me?"

Stirkey shrugged. "If the shoe's flat, wear it."

"You always say," Blackburn suggested.

Dack Stirkey shrugged again. "If you must insist, dear fellow, if you must insist."

Blackburn laughed. "No, not really." He wasn't even going to ask them about Paul again, until he thought the time was right. "All right, first things first, then. Do you know whether it's true that Chelsie Bradford's anti-war?"

"Aren't we all, old man," Strong offered quietly, "aren't we all?" Most Uthabohns Blackburn had met had the habit of repeating their rhetorical questions.

"Inspector, please understand that there isn't much we get a chance to see or hear firsthand," Astrid Ringer said, still standing; her voice was cracked and feeble, she still looked just about ready to collapse. "Cooped up in here like this—"

Stirkey grinned. "Quite true, quite true. But I can tell you a little story, if you like."

"Sure," said Blackburn, "I like stories well enough."

"Can't say fairer than that. If you're well and truly a fan of ours, then you're aware that Torus here's a chap of Australian Aborigine extraction—darling Astrid's the husky, Valkyrie type so decorative on our album cover."

At the moment, Astrid Ringer looked neither husky nor particularly decorative. She looked small and frightened. But Blackburn nodded understanding.

"The bald fact of the matter is that we're all of the Australian persuasion—descended from Australians, that is—as are most of the human types of Osnoh B'nubo. What was left, one gathers, of a rather standoffish contingent here on Luna when the balloon, as we say so delicately back home, was dropped a millennium ago by their more powerful—and clumsy—enemies and allies."

Stirkey rose, went to a sideboard, brought back a small golden flask and a handful of thimble-sized gold-rimmed glasses. He poured, offered one to each of his companions, then a fourth to Blackburn, who accepted without interrupting.

"Now you'd think," Stirkey continued, "having had our

planet taken from us by the evil Clusterian Powers, that the
better part of the Uthabohn population would be solidly behind the war effort of the Coordinated Arm, wouldn't you?"

The inspector shrugged. He knew Uthabohn politics—
fully as complex as any he had heard of anywhere—pretty
well, but was interested in hearing another viewpoint.

"But—even overlooking historical progenitors decidedly
unenthusiastic about warfare and alliances—where individual
interests and opinions are concerned, things are seldom that
simple," Stirkey offered. "Take, for example, my old cobber,
Torus."

He turned a hand toward his partner, who raised both eyebrows, but offered no other comment.

"Here we are, the mighty and peerless *Frog Strangler*,
archetypal Uthabohn refugees, trundling along, or planning
to, at several multiples of lightspeed through civilized space,
at the late Edith Lenox's insistence, and for propaganda purposes. And doing quite nicely at it, if I do say so as oughtn't."

"But every silver lining," Blackburn nodded, taking a sip
of the Uthabohn liquor, "has a cloud."

"Too bloody right"—Stirkey paused, as if considering what
to say next—"for *la* Lenox's purposes, at least, our group
may turn out more hindrance than help. You see, my old mate
Strong belongs—quite loudly, I'm afraid, and if you didn't
have it from me, then you'd hear it from him eventually—he
belongs to an Uthabohn exile group who believe their interests
quite separate from the rest of the Arm."

"Too bloody right is *right!*" said Strong.

"Yes, I know the group," Blackburn answered, now addressing the black man more than Stirkey. "There may even be
considerable justice in their position, however unpopular they
are at present. Hell, if I'd stayed on your planet, I might have
joined it myself. They think that the Arm alliance got you into
this mess."

Strong looked disgusted. "It's worse than that, Captain-
Inspector, according to certain propaganda—"

Somehow Blackburn knew he spoke of Lenox.

"—we may even see helping the Powers as means of in-
suring Uthabohn independence in future!"

Blackburn wasn't surprised. "So you could be the spy I'm
supposed to be looking for—or, miffed by the counterpropa-

ganda, simply the righteous handmaiden of justice?"

Strong laughed.

Stirkey shook his head. "Could be *suspected*. That's all that worries me. I know this fellow, you see? He's no bleeding murderer. And there's always the future of the band to consider. We're all going to be as rich as bloody Croesus after the war, and why compromise that?" He paused to pour himself another drink before changing the subject. "Adding insult to injury, perhaps, there's Astrid, here. Her family came to Uthaboh as Clusterian émigrés."

Knowing what was coming, Astrid Ringer had paled at the latest mention of her name. Now she blushed and fixed her eyes on the carpet behind the sofa. So *that* was what was eating the woman. It certainly accounted for her cowed response to what even Anastasia had termed "legitimate authority." Blackburn chuckled. "Some of my best friends—including the Coordinator herself—are Clusterians."

"Yes, well if you know that," Stirkey insisted, "then surely it's occurred to you by now that she—our own dear Astrid, I mean—could be reasonably suspected as a sleeper agent, villainously attempting to crimp the tour a touch, eh?"

A brief-lived but hideous image fluttered by behind Blackburn's eyes of broken starships spiraling into the incandescent hearts of suns. "Listen," he forced himself to reply evenly, "between all the various parties who might be trying to sabotage this tour, and a second group who wants it canceled because of the activities of the first group—or groups—it's a wonder it's going on at all."

And that, thought Blackburn, was the result of nothing more than the iron will of a little old Clusterian lady who believed that "he who eez mozt conziztent vinz" and would not let herself be swayed from her course by any threat or obstacle.

"Oh, well," he lifted his tiny glass and what was left of the amber liquid within it. "What the bloody hell. Here's to indomitable spirit—annoying and inconvenient as it may be to lesser mortals of all species—and to its foremost practitioner, the Galactic Coordinator herself, *the* Anastasia Wheeler." He tipped his glass back and emptied it. "Where, as you said earlier of your mighty and peerless first and so far only masterpiece, would we be without her?"

"Where, indeed?"

Regardless of any irony the darker of the two men might have intended with the phrase, both Torus Strong and Dack Stirkey quickly followed his example.

Astrid Ringer didn't join them in the toast.

Astrid Ringer's glass was already empty.

> *Heads up! La la loh!*
> *Though the trail is windin',*
> *The traffic so slow.*
> *We worked ourselves hard in a hardworkin' row,*
> *'Cause we heard someone talkin' 'bout someplace to*
> *go . . .*
> *La loh.*

PART FOUR
12 NOV 2996

It's true there are no atheists in foxholes—
at least damned few. An individual too
smart to swallow an omniscient, omnipotent
Santa Claus is usually hard to talk into
going somewhere to be shot at by an enemy
somebody else made for him.

—Captain-Inspector Nathaniel H. Blackburn

XVII

The Dove of War

Standing alone by myself isn't what it ought to be.
Walking alone in the dark isn't half enough for me.
I have learned that, in the end
Life's no good without a friend.
And being alone, on your own, ain't the same as being
free.

Another "morning."

Blackburn thought it was too bad they had to spoil the first good weather they'd had the entire trip so far—the last Lunar weather of any kind they'd see until the tour was over.

Against that meteorological contingency, four sleek and predatory-looking interceptors, scrambled by the Nectaris City Tactical Wing as previously agreed, caught up with the *Benjamin Parkinson* in the clear skies above the mostly uninhabited Mare. Generating an unbearable racket, they "landed," wheels screaming, one by one, slamming against hastily beefed-up arrestercables on the narrow runway atop the starship's hull. There, swarmed over like a queen by worker bees, each was refueled, recharged, its instruments carefully calibrated against those of the larger craft. This last was important when so valuable a life was about to be dangled in their midst by a single delicate thread.

For his part, and despite his conversation with Anastasia Wheeler, Blackburn couldn't believe it was being done at all, not after what had happened yesterday to Edith Lenox. But, against advice from the inspector which, toward the end, had bordered on obscenity and personal abuse, they were going ahead with the video recording, anyway. Mix politics, he thought, and show business, and what have you got? He couldn't think of an answer, some metaphor or simile (he'd forgotten which it was he needed) that suitably implied disconnection from reality.

Chelsie Bradford stood, white-faced and silent in the gaping hatchway at the war vessel's stern, her photogenic form and finery wrapped in an issue camouflage blanket while final arrangements for the stunt were being made. A thousand meters below, the camera plane, a pre-war ducted-fan Armstrong, jockeyed into position. Additional angles would be provided by the fighter pilots, whose force-projector cameras had been supplied with high-quality stereo medium.

Even all three members of the opening act, *Frog Strangler*, had emerged from their protective seclusion to watch the taping. It would be something to remember, something to tell your great-grandkids about. And maybe the stewards would have a chance to clean their hypoallergenic rat's nest up a little. They stood now toward the back of the bay, incongruous and nearly unidentifiable in their lightweight clothing—the gale roaring through the starship would seem a light summer breeze to them, Blackburn knew—and their outlandish filter masks.

The director—Bandell Brackenridge, of all people, Blackburn thought—would ride in a transparent blister temporarily extruded beneath the nose of the *Benjamin Parkinson*. At present, he was here in the bay fussing with hardware and personnel while the detective looked on grimly. If Blackburn hadn't had to make special arrangements of his own, he'd have insisted on riding up forward with the band leader, the muzzle of his little Ingersoll tucked into Brackenridge's ear, making sure *he* wasn't the one trying to fix up an accident for Chelsie. Nobody had a convincing alibi where Edith Lenox was concerned. She'd been murdered before breakfast and it hadn't seemed to spoil anybody's appetite.

"Okay, baby..."

Brackenridge shouted against the wind as the mottled blanket whipped at the singer's ankles. His mouth moved again, but Blackburn couldn't make out what he was saying. Neither, apparently, could Chelsie, or anybody else. The band leader gave up with a disgusted expression and fell back on exaggerated hand gestures, his gangly limbs and long torso making him look even more insectile than usual. The slipstream, even at the casual hundred klicks an hour the *Benjamin Parkinson* was maintaining—the lowest at which the Tactical Wing could still control their fighters—lashed at his long hair, whipping it into his eyes, which were streaming with tears. He cupped his long-fingered hands about his mouth.

"Do this right the first time, and it's off for all of us, into the Wild Black Yonder!" He pointed a long thumb upward, through the starship's bulk, to the unseen sky overhead, and presumably toward the Centaurus System, which would be their first interstellar concert stop. "I'm going up front, now —break a leg!"

Chelsie nodded, fear and the effort of overcoming it painted thick over her already pale face. She'd just been told —after a lengthy argument between Blackburn and Ofabthosrah—the full, grisly truth about the most recent murder. With a dangerous stunt about to be recorded, the *bohnous* hadn't wanted to distract the girl. Suspicious of the Ewon's uncharacteristic solicitude, the inspector had maintained she had a right to know the truth about the risk she was about to take.

Now he wasn't sure.

Anchored firmly to the titanium decking, well inside the hurricane-filled chamber, the cable drum, a meter in diameter, was beinged by a couple of Arm Force Ogat, who didn't look much happier or more confident than Chelsie did. They wore weighted combat netting, were strapped by their manipulatorbases to the deck, and were attempting various mental exercises to deflate their gas-swollen canopies. Blackburn could hear them muttering meditative mnemonics. But, with their species, the fight-or-flight reflexes took an inflationary direction that was suppressed only with a much greater effort than these two ratings were apparently capable of generating. They bobbed at their tethers, fighting to stay put.

The starship gave a delicate shudder as the last of the fighter craft, re-energized and minutely readjusted, racketed its way off the end of narrow landing strip overhead, thunder rolling in its fuel-scented wake. The idiocy, Blackburn thought, was about to begin in earnest. Failing to convince anybody else, he had tried to talk Chelsie herself out of the stunt, but even an otherwise dubious Ofabthosrah had had to agree it would make a spectacular video, theoretically shortening the war, and in any event assuring that the lead track on the album currently in production, *The Dove of War*, would dominate the entertainment business for weeks.

Now the inspector stood by Chelsie's side, with another human, an Arm Force rating, flanking her. She took a deep breath, another, smiled weakly at Blackburn, nodded toward the nonhumans straining at the drum. She closed her eyes. The playback started, music pouring from the P.A. system. Stripping off the blanket, her blazing white outfit, ankle-length pantaloons with a billowing cape, flared. She adjusted the harness beneath it, hanging from its boom overhead . . .

She stepped off.

> *Some people say being loved ain't the only way to be.*
> *That may be so, but what's left doesn't mean too much*
> *   to me.*
> *So if you are lonely, too,*
> *I will leave it up to you,*
> *'Cause being alone, on your own, ain't the same as*
> *   being free.*

Blackburn whipped his eyes to the monitor to watch her being lowered into position. She'd been well-instructed or had had some sky-diving practice, for she turned upon the cable-end swivel without much effort, faced into the wind, and spread her arms, transforming her cape into the graceful wings of the human dove she was supposed to be.

Down ten meters.

Fifty.

A hundred.

Five hundred.

Three of the tiny fighters banked, screaming into the giant starship's path, preparing to rendezvous with their remaining companion around the singer. The air behind their blackened tailpipes shimmered, seeming to melt and crumple with their high-temperature backwash. His teeth already gritted, Blackburn clenched his fists. In addition to every other hazard she was facing, a single misstep, the slightest error, would incinerate Chelsie Bradford in an instant. Hadn't anybody in this insane outfit ever heard of special effects?

The pair of Ogat at the winch looked as if they were in as much pain as Blackburn. Despite the best of intentions their canopies were still taut and bouyant with the anticipation of disaster. Blackburn didn't blame them. Even collected on the drum, the monofilament upon which Chelsie's life—literally—depended, was almost invisible. It passed from there, forty meters aft to a pulley wheel on a fragile-looking spar above the doorway, and from that, straight downward.

Blackburn shuddered, forced his attention away from his helpless, acrophobic fascination with the hype monitor. *Watch the cable,* he repeated, over and over again, to himself, *watch the cable.* If everything went well, he could see everything else that was happening, later, on the hype—complete with music, when it was a big hit. If, thanks to his not keeping an eye on the dangerous machinations up here, something went wrong, well, it wouldn't matter.

A bird-of-prey shadow slammed across the open hatchway, followed by a brown-green mottled streak. There followed, a fraction of a second later, the deafening roar of a banking fighter's straining engines—the last ship to be processed upstairs—as it dived, looping for its pass at Chelsie. Blackburn winced. He hoped those fly-boys at the controls were all pop-music fans. The rakish individual he'd seen in that brief instant had actually grinned at him, all typical fighter-pilot confidence and calm, displaying the Ewonese tongues-up sign.

Frog Stranger—Dack Stirkey, Torus Strong, and Astrid Ringer—overcame their collective fear of the yawning, roaring hatchway, and wandered forward to join him at his nerve-wracking watch, just as Sabina Neville stepped through a doorway forward of the winch, and hurried over beside Blackburn, her own eyes glued to the screen. She wore a bright yellow jumpsuit that didn't flatter her much where it spread wider across her hips than it would have on Chelsie. She put her arms around herself, shivering. Blackburn noticed he still had the Arm Force–issue blanket he'd taken from

Chelsie. He wrapped it around Sabina, who, nodding grati-
tude, went right back to the monitor.

One Ogat cable-drum operator bobbed at the other,
wrapped his manipulator around a lever, and pulled. Machinery responded. Blackburn didn't notice the hand he'd
raised to his waist, turned palm outward, ready on the reversed butt of his Ingersoll, until later.

The drum slowed, groaning to a stop.

Risking a brief glance at the hype, Blackburn saw Chelsie,
as visualized by the hovering Armstrong's cameras trained
upon her, her slender arms describing slow, wide arcs as she
flew formation with the fighters on either side of her. Somehow during the thousand-meter elevator ride, she'd lost the
frightened look. Instead, she wore the same ecstatic expression Blackburn had seen at her concerts.

> *Some independence is overrated.*
> *The case for loving is understated.*
> *And being alone, on your own, ain't the same as*
>   *being . . .*
> *Standing alone, by yourself, ain't the same as being . . .*
> *Walking alone in the dark—ain't the same as being*
>   *free.*

He shook his head. Whether it was the real thing, or she
was simply the most professional performer he'd ever seen, he
wouldn't know until later, if ever—

The ancient starship gave a clumsy, lurching roll, scattering
Blackburn's speculations from him in shattered fragments—
alarms, red flashes, sirens, bells—the monofilament Chelsie
hung on angled steeply where it intersected the hatchway lip.
Sabina grabbed him as the *Parkinson* wallowed again. He
shoved her away roughly, watching the Ogat at the cable
drum, grimly fighting their controls.

At the very edge of the hype-screen, another aircraft,
painted bright red and labeled in white lettering, LUNAR EN-
QUIRER, tore across the starship's path. Blackburn could see
the glinting of a dozen lenses in the intruder's windows.

The *Benjamin Parkinson*'s voice circuit, previously occupied with the playback, now filled, first with cursing, then
with a torrent of radio-relayed excuses and demands. Up forward, Brackenridge in his bubble, then *Bohnous* Ofabthosrah

on the bridge, ordered the press plane to sheer off. From the plane there came garbled threats about freedom of the press and the "people's right to know."

Instead of any verbal contribution to the argument from the Tactical Wing, Blackburn heard a sudden mechanical cough. In the corner of his eye, he caught more movement on the monitor. The fighters escorting Chelsie on the left side held their position on her. Somehow she maintained both attitude and expression.

Chelsie's outermost right-hand escort—the Ewon who'd given him the go-to-hell grin—rolled over, ducking out of formation in pursuit of the newsship. When the red press plane saw the fighter coming, it let go with its afterburners, accelerating. The fighter pilot replied by firing his nose projectors.

A ruby tracer-beam connected the two aircraft for a brief instant. The audio pickups carried the sound of punished metal. Light flared on the red plane's tail, followed by smoke.

Lots of smoke.

The *Lunar Enquirer* spun downward, missing the ducted-fan Armstrong, the authorized camera plane, by a scant few meters, impacting with the already-cratered desert below. A long moment later, those aboard the *Benjamin Parkinson* heard the crash. It was too goddamned bad, Blackburn found himself thinking, that the fighter pilot hadn't managed to dump it right on the roof of M.A.F.I.A. headquarters.

Its circuits suddenly clear, the starship was automatically filled with music once more. The fighter pilot took up his position again, a single meter off Chelsie's outstretched right index finger. The *Benjamin Parkinson* stabilized.

Bandell Brackenridge, his circuit-relayed voice unsteady now with delayed reaction, gave an order. The Ogat at the drum moved as if they were one being. The winch, probably as old as the ship herself, groaned with the load—a kilometer of cable along with the lesser but more precious weight at its end—and began to turn. Monofilament began to stack up on the drum, but slowly, torturously slowly.

When, after what seemed an eternity, the singer became visible, hanging in open space past the hatch lip, two dozen shouting, whistling, cheering men, Ogat and Ewonese were there to help her in, give her another blanket, detach the harness, lead her away.

Still draped in the military blanket Blackburn had given her, Sabina Neville somehow got swept up in it, too. Catching glimpses of the brightly painted masks of Stirkey, Strong, and Ringer, Blackburn had to scramble to catch up.

There was an ocean of babble surging all around them. Somebody, perhaps it was Brackenridge, via intertalkie, said something about "cranking the Tactical Wing's interception of the *Enquirer* snoop-plane through an image processor, blotting out the identifying markings, and using the unplanned excitement in the video."

"Serve the bastards right," someone else laughed, "the goddamned *Lunar Enquirer*'s been doing exactly the same kind of thing to everybody else for decades!"

Hanging back from the crowd, Blackburn shook his head. Why couldn't the whole video have been done on an image processor in the first place, removing all the risk? As he stepped through the inside hangar door—the huge outer doors were grinding closed, the ship picking up speed again for the real beginning of its journey to the stars—he turned, saluting the two guys on the drum.

They grinned, waving back, rather like the fighter pilot had. Would they have grinned, Blackburn wondered half an hour later, if they had known that yet another victim, female and fragile, a pretty smile on her face when they had seen her last, was already lying dead a few meters away, her singing stopped forever by a ten centimeter steel blade?

XVIII

The Walrus

"It's an ancient assassin's stunt," Nathaniel Blackburn informed the hypercom screen in his cabin. Music filled the tiny stateroom, something about *They're gonna put me in the movies.* "Corny, but invariably effective: glide up to the prospect in a crowd. Let a guardless dagger, usually a cheap, anonymous, stamped sheet-metal throwing knife—the 'handle' half a meter of adhesive tape—drop from your sleeve into the palm of your hand. Thrust it into the victim's kidney—"

"Higher than most people think it ought to be"—the figure in the screen nodded her slick-surfaced gray-black head, grinning because she had no other facial expression—"if I recall my lessons in human anatomy, but larger, too, making it a better target."

"Right. Who's telling this," the investigator asked, counterfeiting annoyance, "you or me, Mallie? Then shove good and hard with the heel of your hand—"

"Or whatever appendage you happen to possess," unintimidated, she interrupted once again.

"If any." The detective's scowl transformed itself into its

own malicious grin. "—until the entire weapon, rudimentary handle and all, disappears into the body cavity."

Mallie nodded. "Collapse—shock, blood loss—would be instantaneous."

"Yes," Blackburn agreed. "And those around the victim, unable to see either the wound, or the weapon sealing it, mistake the event for a stroke or heart attack."

"And while they're busy learning better," offered the porpoise, "you make yourself scarce." She sighed dramatically, a purely human affectation she'd had to learn somewhere and practice privately. Bubbles drifted from her blowhole toward the top of the screen. "It all seems so very quick and easy, doesn't it?"

"It always is, Mallie," answered the inspector. "Killing is the easiest thing in the universe."

And so it had been for whoever had taken the life of Sabina Neville, curled up now in the same military blanket Blackburn had given her, left behind by the flood of beings which had swept her along to a rendezvous with death. As if to mock them, the stereo behind Mallie's image was crooning, "All you need is love!"

"The worst of it," Blackburn told his part-time secretary— and indeed, he knew better than most anyone that there were many things much worse than dying—"is that, just as poor Sabina always had to be 'the other one' in life—"

"'Doomed to be forever eclipsed by lovely Chelsie Bradford's brilliant and rising star'?"

"You've been reading those fan magazines again, haven't you?"

His words were mild, but now Blackburn suppressed real annoyance. These talks he had with Mallie were often productive. She understood him as no human did, somehow seemed to bring out the thinker in him, banish the habitual moper he'd become since Osnoh B'nubo. Instead of reacting as crossly as he felt, he nodded. This was the last chance he'd have for a cetacean word of cheer for some time.

"Yes, she very likely died for a similar ignominious reason, mistaken for the younger woman."

"I understand," Mallie answered. "Both blond, wrapped in camouflage. The crowding, confusion."

He chuckled. "And besides, as you're too polite to say, all human beings look alike."

The porpoise retreated for a moment in uncharacteristic indignant silence. Blackburn in fact suspected she'd been about to make that very observation.

He'd retired to his cabin for a final "conference," ostensibly with his assistant back at the Altai Escarpment, before the ship threw up its shields and made for the Centaurus System. In truth, the conference he wanted was with the inside of his own head and the contents of his bottle of Mellow Meltdown. For a moment, before he'd uncapped the container, he'd tortured himself with it, gazing down at the liquid inside, listening to it slop and gurgle against the plastic walls, testing his own character—what there was left of it—while he attempted to untangle the mess that this fund-raising tour had become.

At last, he'd pushed buttons instead of opening bottles, and gotten Mallie on the hype.

Then he'd opened the bottle.

"Well, Boss, accepting everybody's initial assumption, that the Clusterian Powers are sabotaging the tour as an act of war, your task is relatively simple—"

"To define, if not to accomplish." This time it was Blackburn who'd interrupted. "As the late Sabina Neville put it so succinctly: 'find the spy.'"

"Who can be eliminated?" The porpoise was warming to the subject now. Blackburn thought she enjoyed these conversations as much as he did. He'd have been surprised if anyone had suggested to him that the one bright spot in his life was occupied by a seven-foot rubbery gray marine mammal who weighed three times what he did. "Is there anyone who couldn't possibly be doing these things?"

"Xevroid Kypud, for one," he answered. "Zibu Zytvod, for another, and Luswe Ofabthosrah. Considering the Powers' uncharitable attitude toward sentient nonhumans, that is. Of course it's always possible the captain's become deranged by the war, by his injury, or by the loss of his sister/daughter."

"I guess it's also possible that either one of the Ogat concerned plays the ponies." Mallie grinned. She never did anything else. "Or their cultural equivalent (whatever that is—I haven't even finished figuring out you humans yet), and needs the money. Everybody needs money. But ... well, you tell me, Boss: would either of them go to work for an outfit which is openly running extermination programs for their species on half a dozen planets in the Occupied Arm?"

"Nothing's impossible where individual intelligent beings are concerned. People can talk themselves into anything. But many fewer things are *probable*, or even likely."

In the background, Blackburn was vaguely aware of someone singing about loving someone else when they were sixty-four. Moctesuma (who was about that age, he guessed) on the other hand, would do anything for money—at least that's what Lenox had told him. Of course her own Durationites had started this war, and were as politically untrustworthy as Lenox herself had proven to be personally. It was too damned bad she was dead. He had suddenly thought of a whole lot of questions he'd like to have asked her—for example, about possible connections between the *Lunar Enquirer*'s aircraft and the Durationite-owned corporation that ran the news service itself. Had the intrusion been a matter of conspiracy or simple stupidity? Too bad. She'd made such a swell suspect.

He said as much to Mallie. "In fact, you don't even need to drag the Powers into it at all. With Lenox around, an old-fashioned political desire to discredit the current administration is all the motive any detective could ask for. Politics is a murderous business at any time, and on occasion, the drapings fall askew, letting you have a look at the real ugliness squirming around underneath."

"Don't give me a bad time about my magazines until you lay off those old detective stories, Boss. Your prose is getting purple, and you're getting cynical."

"Or illuminated." This time Blackburn sighed, although he was unaware of it and would have denied it. "In any case, Edith Lenox is dead, and this is pointless—or is it?" He stopped and thought. "I never much liked the spy theory, anyway."

"Who else might have private reasons for sabotaging the tour?"

He thought about it. "Kypud: his 'art' is supposedly being overlooked for Chelsie's popular appeal."

"Would someone kill for a reason like that?"

"I knew somebody on Osnoh B'nubo who was killed for his last pair of dry socks." Blackburn was silent, then added, "What was it they said in I-School? *A consistent motive may be implied by each of a series of apparently unrelated acts. Properly interpreted, this should eventually demonstrate who committed them.* Sounds good in a textbook, but I left that home in a trunk. What does it mean, now?"

"A bomb killed Baldwin," Mallie offered. "What if it was intended for someone else?"

A typical cetacean leap, Blackburn thought. Some areas of a porpoise's mind worked ten times faster than a human's. "What brings you to a conclusion like that?"

"I don't know, Boss. When nothing works, rearrange things at random."

"I see. Someone else like who?"

"Chelsie Bradford. She's the central figure of the tour. A stage, later proven tampered with, collapsed, nearly killing her."

"And a sabotaged mike injured Zytvod at the moment it was handed to Chelsie. You know, I've never much liked the way Scotty Moctesuma slid past my questions about the sling he was wearing. Could have been another of these 'accidents.'"

"But," Mallie asked, "if he was a victim, intended or otherwise, why would he deny—"

"Same reason some people deny the possibility they could get mugged or burglarized," he answered. "Unpleasant to contemplate, and it implies certain burdensome responsiblities—like providing for your own physical security. I suppose our murderer might have believed Chelsie would be riding in Moctesuma's hovercraft."

"Yes, and Sabina Neville was openly murdered in a companionway...." This time she let the implication hang. At least, Blackburn thought, it hadn't taken him more than a moment to realize she'd been mistaken for Chelsie, wrapped in that blanket. He tried to remember who'd seen the younger woman dressed that way.

"We're on to something here. Maybe everything, every accident and outright killing has only been made to look like sabotage, and actually has been aimed at Chelsie!"

"Yes, Boss. But by who?"

"Whom," he answered reflexively. He told Mallie about meeting *Frog Strangler*'s Dack Stirkey and the rest of the opening group. He'd been intending to continue with them after the videotaping, until the subsequent tragedy diverted him.

"I noticed," he added, "maybe during the videotaping, although I was busy, and didn't realize it until later, that there's something funny about Stirkey's filter mask."

"Like what, Boss?"

"Like I overheard Torus Strong gloating that it's become a fad among the Arm's youth to wear imitation versions of them. You can buy them in every five-and-dime from Luna to the edge of the Occupied Arm. But they're not real, functioning Uthabohn filter masks. They're imitations, suited only for costume-wear."

"And?"

"And the mask Stirkey wore at the taping was also a fake. More expensive, but a phony nonetheless. Another goddamned meaningless mystery—that probably won't mean anything even when it's solved. Just like this 'Paul is dead' business."

"'Paul is dead'? Where did you hear that old—"

Blackburn's heart began to hammer. "You're telling me that you know what it means?"

"Of course I do, Boss. Why do you ask?"

Blackburn waited a few moments while his pulse ground back down to normal. "Because I want to know. Somebody left me a note to that effect when I first came aboard. I've asked everybody about it, but there isn't any Paul on this barge, and—"

"And the news is both stale and false," Mallie informed him. "Boss, this is strictly archaeology. Do you recognize what I've been playing on the stereo?" As the *Tursiops truncatus* turned the gain up with a nod of her head, he could hear, "Listen, do you want to know a secret? Do you promise not to tell?"

"I don't know," Blackburn answered, "just some classical junk."

"That 'classical junk,'" replied the porpoise, contempt dripping from every syllable, "is a pre-Blowup group—*the* pre-Blowup group—called the Beatles."

"Oh, yeah," he brightened. "I've heard of them."

"Hooray for education. One of those Beatles was a fellow named Paul. Paul McCartney. Fifty or sixty years before the Blowup, a rumor got started that he had died in a traffic accident, and been replaced by a double. Conspiracy theories of all kinds were very popular in those days, and this was just one of them."

"I imagine Mr. McCartney was rather annoyed by it."

"I imagine so," the porpoise nodded; the volume dropped again. "You think Stirkey is a double?"

Blackburn put up a hand, indicating that he wanted to do something before he gave her an answer. Pushing buttons, he split the screen, called up an archive file, searched through it for a moment, until he hit on what he'd been looking for.

"Listen to this," he said unnecessarily, since the porpoise could read what was on the right half of the screen as well as he could. "This is Dack Stirkey quoted in a magazine interview just before the invasion of Osnoh B'nubo:

"*'Art exists to serve no purpose, certainly not to be gawked at, drooled upon, fawned over, or bartered for like a head of cabbage, by the vulgar crowd. That, in fact, is the end of art, whose purest expression is never experienced by anyone but its creator. And if only that intrusion were unnecessary as well!'*

"And the interviewer—this is *Razor Blade,* a magazine which offers no respect to anybody—says '*Yeah? Well, don't mind me, Mr.* Artiste, *I'm just being vulgar, but how come you're doing what you're doing, letting the crowd gawk, drool, and fawn all over your art? Let alone barter.*' And Stirkey answers, '*For the lowliest, most obscene, and least worthy of reasons, old chum. To continue eating.*'"

Mallie was silent for a few moments. He'd learned in the past that some human ideas—and nonideas—took longer for the pragmatic predator in her to process than others. Then: "Interesting—bullshit, but interesting. But what does it prove? It's like that greeting of yours that gave me a headache, how did it go?"

Blackburn laughed. "'You're much more like you are now than you were when I knew you before,' a sentence designed long ago to contain nothing of semantic value. It doesn't prove anything at all except that I don't think the Dack Stirkey I talked to—and rather liked—would say something like that. I mean about art. It feels wrong—how's that for logic and the rules of evidence?"

He paused.

"You know, Mallie, Uthaboh's pretty damned important to the war effort, at least in terms of propaganda, if not strategically. And there's a respectable statistical mortality rate among Uthabohns who try to live out here in the rest of the Arm. Of course, that's what put me onto him in the first place: if that

filter mask of his is phony, then he's either a phony himself—
however likeable—or a corpse. And he seemed pretty lively
for a corpse to me."

"I see," the porpoise answered. "If the genuine Stirkey
died, say of massive allergic trauma, and had been replaced
by a double, then maybe there's something after all to that
nonsemantic sentence of yours. Stirkey's bound to be a lot
more like himself now than he was when he was dead. It
could be that Edith Lenox believed that the truth would damage morale, and was trying to cover up."

"Correct. And that *does* sound like *her*. It's what she'd do.
The only question is, does this mean anything with relation to
the murder case, or is it just a red herring?"

"Mmmm. Sounds delicious to me, Boss, although I prefer
mine raw, or at least in olive oil."

He ignored her. Mallie hadn't ever *seen* a herring, let alone
eaten one. He couldn't lean on Lenox, and that was too bad.
Then again, Blackburn thought, maybe she didn't enter into it
at all. If Stirkey wasn't Uthabohn, maybe he was the spy.

He opened his mouth to share that thought with her, when
he heard a noise. "Oops, I've got to go now," he told the
porpoise. "Someone rapping at my chamber door. Interstellar
rates are cheaper than ship-to-surface. I'll call you from the
Centaurus System."

Whoever it was knocked again. He rang off, rose, and,
unconsciously placing a hand on the reversed grip of his pistol, limped toward the door. But his mind was somewhere
else.

Paul is dead.

Find the spy.

XIX

From Ogatravo with Love

The Ogat travel light.

Blackburn had forgotten exactly how light, until he caught up with Kypud in Sabina's quarters. He'd wanted to see the Ogat as soon as possible after the videotaping and the latest murder. Some people were inclined to speak more freely when they were in shock, although he often felt guilty for exploiting that fact.

And then felt guilty for feeling guilty.

Instead, Scotty Moctesuma had shown up at his cabin, interrupting his call to Mallie. He'd gotten into a conversation with *Fresh Blood*'s manager, and was still thinking about it as, belatedly, he reached the dead woman's door.

"Okay," he'd told the rock group's manager as he'd admitted him in to the tiny stateroom. Armed with what he'd learned from Mallie, he was getting more and more impatient. "I'm glad you're here. I'm through fooling around with you people. I want to hear from you about two things and only two things. First, who's Paul?"

Now he'd see how much knowing who the original Paul had been was going to help him.

The older man had sniffed at the room's atmosphere and made a face. Now he blinked. "Paul who?"

It wasn't going to help at all, apparently. "Second—" Blackburn had a thought, and changed the subject. "Why is it that everybody I talk to denies knowing about him, but nobody seems very surprised that he wound up dead?"

"Who," asked Moctesuma, "Paul?"

Blackburn eyed him suspiciously. "I thought you just told me you didn't know him!"

Moctesuma took a step backward, confusion on his ruddy face. "I don't. I was only being polite."

"Yeah, and turning this conversation into a vaudeville routine." The detective sat down on the edge of his bunk to take his weight off his bad foot. He didn't offer Moctesuma a seat. "Third, about these seals of privacy you people—"

"I thought," Moctesuma answered, the confused look changing to a frown, "you said 'two things and only two things.'"

Blackburn shrugged. "Well, rank hath its peculiarities. Answer the question."

Confusion again: "What question? You didn't ask me a question."

"About the seals . . ."

Moctesuma spread his hands, all previous expressions replaced by one of exasperation. Inwardly, Blackburn chuckled, thinking he ought to send the older man a bill for the workout.

"I can't do anything about them, Inspector, as much as I might like to personally, just for the sake of friendly cooperation. Chelsie and Bandell are the celebrities. Why don't you ask them? I can't guarantee they'll go along with you. In fact, I can almost promise you they won't, not even to solve a murder—"

"*Three* murders."

"Not even to solve three murders." The manager shook his head. "I can't order them to or anything like that. I work for *them*, remember? I appreciate their problems in a way you can't begin to. They're recognized wherever they go. Newspeople consider them public property. Without a seal of privacy on their lives, they'd be hounded—"

Blackburn raised both hands, palms outward. "Okay, okay. I'll take your word for it. Let's leave Chelsie and Bandell out of it for a moment—and believe me, I *will* ask them. Especially Bandell. With prejudice. How about somebody else?"

That changed things. For some reason, Moctesuma seemed cheered by that prospect. "Like who?"

Blackburn grinned an unpleasant grin. "Like you."

"Oh."

Moctesuma's cheer had evaporated as quickly as it had condensed. He thrust his hands in his pockets, looked down at the mildewed carpet, and mumbled, "What do you want to know about me? I was born in Pournelle, just east of Campbell, Backside. I'm sixty-two years old. I was educated at Buckley Prep and Sagan-Winkle Memorial University. I am not now, nor have I ever been married—too busy making great stars as much greater as I can. Anything else?"

"How about lifting your own privacy seals—for the sake of friendly cooperation? For example, is it true you're the only beneficiary in Chelsie's will?"

A disgusted expression: "That story again. Honestly, there are moments when I'm actually glad that Lenox woman is— yes, it's true. Aside from her brother, Chelsie hasn't any family, and she's been like a daughter to me. But her career is only beginning. Even on a strictly monetary basis—and believe me, that isn't all there is to it, not at all—she's much more valuable to me, as she is to everybody else, alive. Aside from that, I can't tell you anymore, Inspector, really I can't. It would set a baleful precedent. I assure you, there's nothing in my past I'm ashamed of. No more, perhaps than any average person. But it would be like accepting a job at less than union scale, bad for everybody, union or otherwise. Anything else I can do for you?"

Blackburn had answered impolitely, warning Moctesuma that the subject wasn't closed and that he'd see him again later in the day. He'd then followed the agent/manager out the door and found his way to Sabina's stateroom . . .

Fresh Blood's nonhuman rhythm bandolarist floated just above the stateroom's yellow sofa, his single, dangling tentacle busy packing up that object which usually gets translated into English as "suitcase" from the Ogatik. But that was the only resemblance it bore to the human artifact of the same name.

Sabina's Gilbert and Sullivan posters still decorated the walls, but they looked dog-eared and shabby, somehow. The

colorfully dressed people in the pictures, historic casts of
The Mikado, Trial by Jury, and *The Pirates of Penzance,*
seemed to be sneering at him, in the light of what he'd let
happen to their mistress. On the hype, some overweight and
overstudied tenor was yodeling, "A wandering minstrel I, a
thing of thread and patches, of ballads, songs and snatches,
and—"

"Packing up your thread and patches?" Blackburn inquired,
leaning on the doorframe.

"What?"

If he'd been human, the male Ogat would have whirled to
confront the detective. Sometimes Ogat seemed to have eyes
in the backs of their flotation canopies. Other times, they
seemed to the detective even easier to sneak up on than human
beings. Perhaps, Blackburn thought, it was more a matter of
mental than of physical focus. As it was, Kypud drifted ceil-
ingward, curling his manipulator tightly and protectively beneath his canopy, demonstrating signs which, Blackburn
knew, indicated sudden reaction to unpleasant surprise among
his species.

"The door was open," the human explained. "I didn't mean
to startle you. Planning on taking a trip?"

The peculiar object in which the Ogat had been placing his
belongings consisted of a coarse mesh bag—Blackburn was
always reminded of the word "snood" when he saw one, but
only an individual with his perverse taste for mid-twentieth-
century films would have known what that meant—attached
to a flashlight-sized magnesium canister. The Ogat were se-
verely limited by strength and bodily construction in what they
could carry with them. At least by human standards.

On the other hand, the oxen-sized Ewon, very late invent-
ing unnecessary—to them—conveniences such as wheelbar-
rows and backpacks, might have formed the same impression
of *H. sapiens,* and simply been too polite so far to give it
voice.

In their own civilization, the Ogat had generally created
artifacts described by non-Ogatik sentients as "spidery,"
"filmy," "spindly," or "filamentous." As well as he knew the
species, Blackburn didn't know the function of three quarters
of the objects Kypud was putting in his bag. Likely they were
the equivalent of his toothbrush, toothpaste, comb, and nail

clippers. To the detective, it looked like a hobbyist's discarded pile of styrofoam and string cheese.

"Yes, Captain-Inspector," the Ogat answered, getting his involuntary buoyancy under control and drifting downward toward the couch, "I'm going somewhere . . ."

You couldn't tell—no one ever could—exactly in which direction an Ogat was looking. Radial symmetry, it was called. But something about the musician's tone or posture the detective had unconsciously picked up during years of association with the oddly shaped nonhumans caused Blackburn to gaze toward the cabin's porthole.

Outside, the black, velvety, star-punctuated void could be discerned through a bright, colorful, hazy aurora of secondary radiation—waste-energy—deadly to any unprotected sentient it might come in contact with. It was leakage from the *Parkinson*'s old-fashioned, inefficient inertial shielding. Between the ship's hull and the ill-fitting field, a narrow layer of atmosphere had been trapped and fluoresced violently, adding to the coruscation and the color.

Back in place a meter above the sofa once again, the Ogat stretched his tentacle, picked up some belonging to add to the pile in the bag, then suddenly stopped what he was doing, made a noncommittal sound, and drifted a bit closer to the human.

"Perhaps an explanation is in order, after all. I've taken our conversation to heart—the first conversation you and I ever had. About killing Clusterians. I've been on the hype all morning—enlisting in the Arm Force."

He tugged at the drawstring of his bag, closing it up, then touched a knurled ring on the attached canister. There was a hissing, and from one end of the cylinder, there appeared a brightly colored membrane which swelled and plumped out spherically until it dragged the "suitcase" from the couch and held it at an altitude, about two meters from the floor, where it could be towed conveniently by its equally buoyant owner. It was an ancient invention, the Ogatik equivalent of the wheel, and it seemed to take up most of the space in the suite's front room.

Reflex moved Blackburn's hand toward the synthetic handle of his force projector, the policeman's instinct to halt what may have been a fleeing felon. But a contrary sense about

Xevroid Kypud and what had happened to Sabina Neville, stopped the hand before it was halfway there. Blackburn felt like an officious idiot. That's what comes, he thought, of *any* amount of political power.

Then self-discipline and painfully earned experience took over, steadying the hand in its course until his fingers were between his body and the handle of the reverse-holstered weapon. He had a job to do—otherwise, he wouldn't have the power now, and the associated problems—and maybe this was the individual responsible for it.

"Kypud—Xev—stop. You know goddamned good and well I can't let you do that. I'm sorry."

The Ogat halted, bobbing at the doorsill, giving his suitcase a little touch with his tentacle to slow its momentum. Whether he saw the gun, ready to be drawn, and whether he cared, Blackburn couldn't have said with any certainty.

"Why—oh, yes." Absently, he drifted back toward the room's center. "I don't know why, but for some reason that hadn't occurred to me before this moment. I can't go. You can't let me go. I'm still a suspect in a murder case."

Blackburn nodded. "And I'm afraid you've made a committment you can't keep. I'll have the Coordinator's office straighten it out with Arm Force recruitment. I wish I could tell you when this is going to be over with, but I can't. I'm way out of my depth, here, I'm afraid, and going down for the third time."

"As bad as that?"

"Worse. I think Anastasia and her friends have bitten off more than I can chew."

"That's quite a confession." The Ogat was apparently surprised. "If I were the cynical type—as Sabina was for both of us—I'd suspect it was a ploy. Don't some fictional detectives pretend to be stupid, just to throw suspects off-balance?"

"I suppose they do at that," Blackburn admitted with a lopsided grin, "but I assure you my own stupidity's the genuine article. Although it seems damned strange to be in a situation where I have to prove it. There are other fictional detectives, you know, who pretend to be dishonest and corruptible—couldn't we play with that one for a while? There's certainly more dignity to it."

He picked out a chair, limped to it, and sat down. His foot had begun to hurt again.

"And a hell of a lot more profit," he finished with a sigh of relief. "Of course I'm only telling you all this because the shrinks at the Arm Force hospital told me that if I repressed it, I'd end up with ulcers or some kind of weird fetish."

"*Kibdryz!*" The reference Kypud made, Blackburn knew, was to the excrement of an Ogatik draft animal. Kypud floated to the end of the sofa nearest Blackburn, locked his tentacle about the armrest, the equivalent of sitting down. "Okay, Inspector, I'll play along. What do I have to do to get out of here?"

"You can help me clear this mess up. Don't you want to get whoever killed Miss Neville?"

"You know," the Ogat lifted his manipulator, then let it drop listlessly, "I'm greatly surprised to discover that I don't give a damn about that. In fact, there aren't any words, in English or Ogatik, to tell you how *much* I don't give a damn."

Almost unconsciously, Kypud rose as he spoke, exactly as a preoccupied man might pace, then drifted toward the porthole. Blackburn watched him, kept his peace, and listened.

"Inspector, the universe existed for twenty billion years before Sabina was born. In all that time, there was no one else even remotely like her. If it goes on for another twenty billion, there'll never be anybody like her again. That's trite, but it's what I *do* give a damn about. I can't change what happened. Catching some criminal, killing him, or beating him up, or locking him away won't change it. He can't do any worse to Sabina, or me, than he already has."

Blackburn nodded. "I see. Well, Kypud, *I* care about catching him and killing him, or beating him up, or locking him away. If I were more professional about it, I suppose I'd have a different preference among those three options, but I'm not and I don't. I also care about whoever he's planning to murder next. Don't you? What *can* I offer you, so you'll help? What do you want?"

Again, there was that sense of turning, of refocusing attention—although no visible movement accompanied it. Xevroid Kypud simply redirected his consciousness from the stateroom's porthole, back to Blackburn. And Blackburn somehow knew it.

"Aside from getting off this ship? I'd like very much not to be alive, Inspector—don't look at me that way, I'm not saying what you think, that I want to kill myself. Or even that I want to die, particularly. Consider it an exercise in avoiding ulcers and fetishes. I just want to *not be*. Go to sleep some evening and never wake up. Peace. I don't think it's quite the same as suicide. Am I making sense?"

"I know the feeling."

Blackburn's answer had been subdued, inwardly directed. He'd spent half his waking hours since Osnoh B'nubo in exactly that condition, the other half trying to remember when life had been more than just a matter of avoiding pain. He didn't understand, sometimes, just what it was that kept him going. Certainly not some mythical "will to live" that people talked or wrote about—mostly wrote about—and which he was certain in his own mind didn't exist. He just woke up every morning, and went on. Desire—to live or otherwise—didn't enter into it.

For some people, he thought, war can be a handy thing indeed. It lets suicides out of the dilemma which their essential cowardice—their inability to withstand the real world—created for them in the first place. He'd often considered the matter, especially during the long, frozen trek to Lohua Fihr.

There hadn't been much else to do.

That was how wars got started, he'd finally decided. Politicians—"statesmen"—terminally disgusted with themselves deep inside, didn't want to go on living. In their frantic need to put an end to their own miserable existences, they didn't give a rat's ass which (or how many) innocent lives—peculiar individuals who *did* want to go on living—they took with them to oblivion.

"If you're sincerely determined to get yourself killed, Xev," he answered at last, "there isn't a hell of a lot I can do to stop you. Even if I were inclined that way. Which I'm not. Sure, I can help get you off this ship, and you can let the Clusterians take care of the dirty work. You think Sabina would want that?"

The Ogat drifted back to his position over the arm of the sofa. "Sabina can't want anything, Inspector. Sabina is dead. What do you want for getting me off the ship?"

Knowing the time had come, Blackburn leaned forward in his chair. "From you, my friend, just as from everybody else, I need to know things. And the very first of them is whatever secret you and Miss Neville had been keeping between—"

A flip of his tentacle betraying his impatience, Kypud interrupted: "Look, Captain-Inspector, there are a few things I'm missing, here, things I want to take with me—always provided you decide to let me go." He rose from the couch arm—no one would have called it "drifting" now—and made for the cabin door. "Let's continue this on the way to the storeroom and back, what do you say?"

Without an answering word, Blackburn shrugged. Perhaps the time hadn't come, after all. He was learning what policemen and psychiatrists always learn eventually, that the supply of evasive tactics individuals rely on is endless. He leaned on his cane, levered himself to his feet, pushed the luggage-balloon aside at the stateroom door, and followed the floating Ogat down the corridor.

"Secret," Kypud remarked when they had traveled past several doors and across a connecting companionway. He was surprising Blackburn all over again by bringing up the subject himself. "You don't mean about our personal relationship. That certainly wasn't any secret. Why do you think I was packing up in Sabina's room instead of in the quarters they assigned me—and which I never used?"

"That's right." Blackburn nodded. Having trouble keeping up, he leaned into his cane harder. "I don't mean about your relationship. The day I met you, you were startled for a moment when you thought Sabina had given away your *real* secret."

"This is the stupid detective speaking"—the same tone from a human being would have been accompanied by raised eyebrows—"out of his depth and going down for the third time?"

Blackburn grinned over pain-gritted teeth. "I just see things and remember what I see. Putting them together in a pattern that makes sense is something else entirely."

The Ogat stopped and laughed. Blackburn was grateful for the rest. "Your modesty underwhelms me, Inspector. But you know, I think I'm going to tell you our 'secret,' after all. It has no bearing on your case. I was planning to let it die with me. But I guess I'd like to tell somebody, and I think you can— yes, I know about the promises you can't make—I think you can be trusted with it."

He resumed his progress down the corridor, this time setting a pace which didn't tax the detective's rapidly diminishing resources. "Sabina used to feel like this," he explained, "like I do now. She had moments of terrible depression. I got her through them. Now here I am, and where is she when I need her?"

Blackburn didn't answer. He knew it was a common reaction to the death of a loved one, that people experienced it, felt guilty about it, and then got over it.

"Never mind," the Ogat answered his own question. "Our secret concerns the first thing you asked her about, Chelsie taking her place in the band. She couldn't have felt more awful about it. As awful as a person can feel. When it became clear that's what was happening—to make things even worse, she couldn't help liking Chelsie, not blaming her, any more than anyone else could—that, on top of her miserable marriage to Bandell and the divorce, very nearly overwhelmed her."

Kypud slowed again, his entire attention focused on Blackburn. "That's when Sabina and I first got together, Captain-Inspector. Right after I found her lying in a bathtub full of warm water. She'd loaded up on *vedyzhiete*, opened up the veins inside her elbows, and was resigning from life with a smile on her face."

There wasn't anything to say to that. Blackburn slowly shook his head in sympathy.

Kypud went on. "I saved her life, Captain-Inspector, and although she loved me for it—never tried killing herself again—I don't think she ever forgave me for it, either."

They had arrived at the same storeroom where Blackburn had had his chat with Chelsie Bradford. The detective turned the dog and swung the heavy metal door aside.

Inside, they found a dying Ogat.

XX

Worst Foot Forward

Nathaniel Blackburn stood in the doorway of the storeroom beside Xevroid Kypud.

Multicolored artificial lightnings flared in upon the pair through the small, rounded window of the darkened room, pulsing like a neon sign outside a cheap hotel. Occasionally —far less often than any similar phenomenon transpired in the atmosphere of Luna—the brief-lived blue-white flash of a vagrant micrometeor being incinerated in the starship's protective fields could be observed.

Blackburn wasn't interested in waiting to observe phenomena. With a growl, he slapped at the old-fashioned switch plate beside the doorframe. Light of a different, kinder sort sprang into being. He stepped inside, ignoring his own pain to crouch down—he planted his cane firmly and slid both hands down its length to do it—beside the slumped, deflated figure of Zibu Zytvod. The Ogat lay, obviously injured, his body halfway under the bottom storage shelf.

"I'll be dogged," the wounded Ogat greeted the detective. He moved only slightly. His voice was hardly more than a whisper. "I sorta wondered if anybody was gonna happen along 'fore I cashed in. Dyin's a hard thing t'be doin' alone. Nice t'see you, Captain-Inspector. That Xev behind you, or the Welcomin' Angel?"

The investigator swiveled his head, "Get out of here and find an intertalkie"—Kypud was gone before Blackburn had finished the sentence—"fast!"

To the older Ogat: "Take it easy, Zib, help's on the way. Don't move or try to talk."

The words were hard to get out. They went against everything the investigator really wanted to say, things like "What the hell happened?" and "Who did this to you?"

Zytvod managed a little chuckle. "You don't mean that. You need t'know who bushwhacked me. 'Fraid I let m'self get snuck up on again, dadblast the luck! Come in here for a new keycap—G above middle C—an' somebody poked his appendage in, turned out the lights, an' backshot me. Hell of a thing."

Incongruously, Blackburn again found himself wondering who had taught this Ogat English. Zytvod's translucent canopy lay spread across the floor, limp and emptied of its hydrogen/helium mixture, perforated in at least two places. The ragged edges around the puncture wounds were rapidly becoming dry and brittle. It took more than deflation to incapacitate an Ogat, he knew. On Ogatravo, it had, in times past, been considered a humane—make that "ogate"—way of punishing criminals. Zytvod's injuries must be more serious than that, but there was little showing of the syrupy golden liquid the species used for blood.

The detective was reminded, as he had often been during his ordeal on Osnoh B'nubo, that, deprived of what normally appeared to be the bulk of their bodies—what was, in fact, simply a flimsy, gas-filled membrane—the Ogat resembled large snakes more than anything else he could think of. Large, muscular snakes, still fully capable of self-defense. A moment passed, then he realized that this meant, whoever it was who'd attacked Zytvod, it hadn't been an Ogat.

"Take it easy," the detective repeated inanely. "There'll be time to tell me everything once the medics—"

"Ain't no time left for me, Inspector, none at all, an' you know it. Got something I gotta tell you, an' it won't wait. See if you don't think I'm right." He took a deep, agony-wracked breath. *"I'm* the Clusterian spy you been lookin' for. That's right, nobody but little old me. From Occupied Ogatravo, actually, but I been workin' for the Powers, right along."

Shock sang through the detective's body. So much for this theory that a nonhuman wouldn't work for the racist Powers. Despite himself, he whispered, "But why—?"

The Ogat groaned, stirred slightly as if trying to find a more comfortable position. It probably wasn't easy, Blackburn thought, for one of the creatures, used to flaoting all its life, to be lying on a hard and gritty floor. He took his cloak off, bunched it up, then couldn't decide what part of Zytvod to put it under.

"That's better . . . more under the top, there."

Zytvod was silent for a heart-stopping moment, then: "Why'd I turn m'coat, is what you're askin', especially for those bastards? Why, it couldn't be a simpler proposition, kiddo. The goddamned Experimentalists—the Clusterian Powers been turnin' some of what they're stealin' over to 'em—they got my mate, Kobo, our seed-children, an' grandkids. I play ball with 'em, or else."

Another long pause. Blackburn wasn't certain that he'd be able to tell, for all that he had thought he knew this species, if Zytvod slipped away. The only dead Ogat he'd ever seen—on Osnoh B'nubo—there had been no question about.

Zytvod found strength again. "So y'see, given the choice between savin' my own family or the whole danged Coordinated Arm, I been playin' ball with 'em. As incompetent a job as I can get away with, naturally. But they expect that, allow for it, watch me pretty danged close, an' slackin' ain't been easy at all."

Blackburn wanted very much to pat the old Ogat, to comfort him somehow in what might be his final minutes. However, especially considering what he'd done to his own foot on Osnoh B'nubo, he was reluctant to touch the wounded nonhuman.

Instead, he spoke as gently as he could. "That's enough, Zib. You don't need to say any more. I understand, anybody would. No one would ever blame you for—"

"Shuddup, boy, lemme talk. Ain't got time t'waste, restin' up. There's somethin' else I gotta tell you, a paira somethin' elses. The first is that I'm confessin' to bein' a spy—but I ain't confessin' t'nothin' else. I didn't knock Vic Baldwin off, nor Sabina, God rest the both of 'em, nor even that Lenox critter."

"All right, then who—"

His manipulator clutched feebly at Blackburn's tunic. "I dunno who's doin' those things, Inspector, but like I told you day before yesterday, it ain't me. Lookit, this here's m'dyin' respiratory reflex, you understand? That makes it official, so you gotta believe me. After I check out I don't want nobody thinkin' I'd ever try t'hurt Chelsie. Hell, I love her just like everybody else does."

"I believe you," Blackburn told him, and he did.

The clutching tentacle relaxed. "I'm here t'tell you that's a hell of a relief."

He took a ragged breath.

"Okay, then, more unfinished business. Y'hang around bein' a spy long enough, y'learn things whether y'planned on learnin' 'em or not. Listen, Inspector, you wanna catch yourself a danged killer, maybe you oughta check into that little 'accident' Scotty had, just before the tour started. There's more t'that than meets the optical receptor. Pay some special attention t'Bandell. I dunno how he's connected. Scotty dropped a bundle quietin' it down—'course he's done that kinda thing before . . . but I think mighta been another—"

The elderly Ogat began coughing, a weird, shrill series of wracking near-ultrasonic vibrations which hurt Blackburn's ears—or perhaps his nervous system.

This time he did touch Zytvod.

"That's enough, now, Zib, you hear me? I'll check into it. And don't worry, nobody will ever think it was you who tried to hurt Chelsie, I'll personally see—"

Zytvod didn't respond.

He had quit moving entirely.

Blackburn's increasingly desperate attempts to arouse him met with no success. In that moment, Coordinated Arm Force Captain-Inspector Nathaniel Blackburn, decorated combat veteran and certified war hero, committed his own act of treason, determining never to tell anyone what Zibu Zytvod had told him. In the detective's opinion, between his family and the Arm, the little Ogat keyboardist and technician dying on the floor before his eyes, perhaps already dead, had made the right decision. It was exactly the same decision he'd have made if he'd been lucky enough to have a family himself.

As he was trying a final time to rouse Zytvod, Xevroid Kypud arrived behind a pair of husky Arm Force medics, one human, one Ewon, who shouldered the detective aside.

"You'd best give us some elbow room, Captain-Inspector," the human medic told him. "Go on, get yourself back to passenger country. There's nothing left you can do here."

Suppressing pain both physical and spiritual, Blackburn slowly pushed himself to his feet with his cane. Moving just outside the storeroom, he found himself blinking back tears, surprised—even, in an odd way, pleased—that after everything he'd seen and done in life, that he was still capable of them.

"Then you're telling me," he said to the medic inside, "that I just took his dying declaration." Testimony at the moment of death was invariably afforded a special status in the Arm's adjudicative system, as was the testimony of those who—

"Captain-Inspector," the medic answered, annoyance at the distraction coloring his voice, "I'm telling you he's gonna be just fine—provided you stay the hell out of our way and let us do our job." The human looked to his Ewonese companion, already laboring over the fallen Ogat, for confirmation. He added, in a softer voice, "They may look fragile as cotton candy, but these babies is hard to kill."

Blackburn had to suppress an hysterical giggle.

Following Kypud, he turned in thoughtful silence in the direction of Sabina Neville's stateroom. Neither spoke for a long while. Trying to absorb what had just happened, he realized, as he hobbled along behind the buoyantly bobbing nonhuman, that he'd been left once again with no clear motive for the *Fresh Blood* killings (as he'd begun thinking of them), no consistent *modus operandi*—the killer's methods so far had included bombing, stabbing, force-projection, and electrocution—and fewer and fewer surviving suspects. Unless he could change the course of events, this case was going to solve itself in the drastic manner he'd half-jokingly told Anastasia Wheeler it would.

Meanwhile, once again, he had nothing.

Nothing but four bodies—one of them, happily, a bit less dead than either he or the potential corpse had believed would be the case. Nothing but several incidents of varying degrees of violence, from practical jokes to murder, which continued to plague the *Fresh Blood* tour exactly as if he had never been sent to stop them. Nothing but bad advice: "*A consistent motive may be implied by each of a series of apparently unrelated acts. Properly interpreted—*"

Nothing but *kibdryz*.

A consistent motive may be implied by each of a series of apparently unrelated acts. It was—he realized with sudden inspiration—exactly as if several conflicting parties were working against him, possibly against each other, as well. Question was, did that inspiration constitute an improvement or just another complication?

Somewhere along the hallway, his leg began to throb as if it had never been treated. Blackburn inhaled, feeling the strength drain out of his body, set his jaw, leaned on his cane, and, without breaking stride, kept the same pace he'd begun with.

As soon as they got where they were going, the bandolarist twisted another ring on his suitcase canister—the device still floated by the door, taking up most of the space in the room —and the metalloids in the cylinder began reabsorbing the flotation gases. At once, there began to be more room in the cabin.

Blackburn found a chair, absently accepted the drink the Ogat offered him, and, without tasting it, closed his eyes, exhausted from the walk to the storeroom and back—and from what had come between. The thought of continuing this investigation . . .

"Well, Captain-Inspector," Kypud observed, "if you're nothing else, you're certainly persuasive."

"Me?" Blackburn's thoughtful mood was shattered. "What in the hell are you talking about?" He immediately regretted the irritated sharpness of his tone. Xevroid Kypud wasn't a bad fellow—always provided he wasn't a murderer.

"You. What you said. On the way to get the medics, I realized I'd made my mind up. Or rather you'd made it up for me. I don't want to quit the band, after all."

Blackburn nodded wearily, managing to say, with some sincerity, that he was glad to hear it.

"I thought you'd be," Kypud went on, "but I don't want to quit the tour, either. I want both of them to go on, the band and the tour, exactly as we discussed in our first conversation.

I want to go on fighting the Clusterian Powers with ideas instead of bullets—there'll be more of them left, that way, to buy our records after the war's over. I think I really am more valuable here than I would be in the Arm Force. Can you still fix it with the recruiters?"

Blackburn shook his head. "It might not be necessary, Kypud. Hell, all they want is warm bodies of any species, capable of lining up the sights and pulling the trigger. I may just take your place. I'm beginning to believe it's the only kind of work I'm suited for: ditch-digging—with a gun, instead of a shovel."

Kypud chuckled. "The Dumb Dick act again? It really doesn't suit you, you know. But go right ahead, Captain-Inspector. Use whatever methods feel right to you. They certainly seem to work. Meanwhile, I guess I'll start unpack—"

The hype started shrilling, a signal meant for catastrophies.

Blackburn glanced at Kypud, who somehow indicated the detective should answer the thing. Blackburn levered himself upward with his cane, stepped across the room, slammed a hand onto the squelch. The image of a crewbeing filled the screen.

"Inspector Blackburn? We got a call here on the bridge. Passenger trying to find you. Emergency. Frame 555, Suite 23. You want I should tell 'em you're coming?"

Blackburn didn't reply to the question.

He didn't hear it.

He was on his way—yet another violent incident filling his already overtaxed imagination—to Chelsie Bradford's stateroom.

XXI

Blaues Gras

He ran.

Vibrating with the mind-shattering racket of the ship's emergency klaxons, the gray-green walls flew past him in a blur. The agony in his bad leg, each time his artificial heel slammed down on the deck-plating, burned upward into his hip.

Yet another attempt was being made on Chelsie Bradford's life. And it was at this moment that he realized that, whatever else, he couldn't let that happen, because he—

Pain and motion were a single, evil, throbbing entity to him, its life measured out second by second in the thudding, irregular heartbeats of his alternating strides: one long distance-eating leap that felt to him like flying; one short, crippled lurch which terminated in a lance of agony being driven upward from his ankle toward his thigh. The entity screamed at him like a machine in need of lubrication. That was too many metaphors, he realized with dim irony.

The scream was silent.

Blackburn's feeling for Chelsie was, he knew—had

always known—quite hopeless. He had never touched her. Alone, he had spoken to her only once, briefly at that. Had he imagined, perhaps without admitting it to himself, that she saw something in him? Escape, perhaps? At least she seemed to come out of her trance a bit when he was around. Yet he dared not hope, and the strain of not permitting himself to hope had become as unbearable as . . . as unbearable as . . .

He ran.

Another long, another short. Pain pounded up the limb. But there was real screaming, as well. He ran as if to escape the entity pursuing him, and yet, of course, he never could. The telltales on his prosthetic—flaring an angry red beneath his stocking, told him what he already knew. If this went on much longer, he'd lose the leg—exactly as they'd warned him he would—and for good. Even his good knee, popping and twinging with each stride, threatened to give up trying to bear more than its share of the burden.

Corridor walls blurred past him. Doors to staterooms. Doors to storerooms. His breath was a series of ragged, irregular gasps. His uniform, soaked with perspiration, restricted movement, retained heat as he overtaxed his already exhausted body.

He ran.

He judged his progress through the twisted maze that was a starship by the pulses of his pain, and by the numbers of the wire-armored lighting fixtures spaced at regular intervals on the corridor ceiling, until it seemed to him that he had been running like this forever. Stencil-labeled corners came and went, some taken in a breathless, sideways-skidding moment of peril—if he were to fall, he would lose time, and he might never be able to get up again—others he ignored.

Startled human faces were ovals surrounding a triad of darker O-shaped orifices. To Blackburn they looked like pale coconuts, somehow surprised into life, exactly like the pursuing beast of pain and motion immediately behind him and within him. Blue-skinned Ewonese sailors lumbered out of his way. The frail Ogat among the crew shrieked and floated upward to the ceiling, out of his path.

He missed the cross-connecting corridor. He had to turn back, heart pounding, vision clouded with sweat and fatigue. Leaning on the wall, he rapped the door.

"Who's there?" came a voice.

"Who the hell," he gasped, "do you think?"

"Inspector Blackburn?" The voice was Bandell Brackenridge's, filled with fear or tension.

"That's right, what's going on?"

"Why don't you come in and see?"

Blackburn turned the dog and swung the door aside. Brackenridge stood with the toe of his right foot pointing at the detective and his left foot perpendicular to it, about his shoulders' width behind. His knees were slightly bent, his right elbow as well, so that his hand, curled and relaxed, nearly touched his shoulder. His left forearm lay parallel to his waist, that hand equally relaxed, but capable of becoming a fist—or a blade—in an instant.

Before Blackburn could react, an invisibly swift snap-kick had snatched the cane from his hand, whirled it across the room where it hit the wall with a crash and fell to the floor. Brackenridge followed with a high, sweeping kick aimed at Blackburn's temple.

Blackburn ducked, stopped the kick in midair with an upraised palm, seized the foot before it could retract, twisted the ankle it was attached to, and *shoved*.

Grinning, Brackenridge danced backward and recovered, but by the time he was ready to attack again, Blackburn's Ingersoll force-projector, tucked safely back at the detective's waist, was out and aimed at the musician's solar plexus.

"Sorry." Blackburn raised his free hand, palm outward. *"Gun-do* beats *tae kwon do* every time."

Brackenridge wasn't even breathing hard. Blackburn still hadn't recovered from the running.

"Okay, okay, a truce," the other replied, raising his hands. "I just wanted to prove a point. And I'd still give odds that I could take that piece away from you before you could pull the trigger." He shrugged. "But we'll leave it at this."

It would have required, the detective thought, more self-discipline than he himself possessed, to accept that roughing up down in the hangar office. They were depths, apparently, to Bandell Brackenridge, that he hadn't anticipated. Heart still pounding, Blackburn nodded. "It suits me. Consider your point taken."

Slowly at first, so that the man still holding the pistol could observe every move, Brackenridge crossed the room, then flung himself into an armchair. "Okay, then, ask your questions now. And I'll answer them. I even have some information to volunteer."

He leaned forward, and fury contracted his thin features for the briefest of moments. "But listen, Blackburn, if you ever lay a hand on me again, be prepared to kill or be killed."

Blackburn shook his head, put his gun away, and limped over to retrieve his cane. "Where's Chelsie?"

"Not here. I had Scotty get her out. He thinks I'm just going to beat you up." He glanced at the hand which had stopped his sweeping kick so casually, at the now-holstered pistol which had appeared as if by magic. "Fat chance of that. In any case, there wasn't room enough for this demonstration in my own cabin, and I wasn't sure you'd come. It's all right, though, she's okay."

"Then why the big emergency?"

"Emerg—oh—that's what the noise was about. Shit, I didn't tell the bridge there was an emergency. I told the captain's flunky I needed to see you, that it was very important. I might even have said 'urgent,' but people I know say that about their hair appointments. God, they're getting jumpy around here."

Too disgusted for words—and too exhausted—Blackburn simply nodded. "Then I take it—and I can't say I blame you —that you were holding out on me down in the hangar office."

"Why not? If I've heard you tell one lie, I've heard *about* your telling a dozen."

Blackburn nodded again. "Tactical lies, Bandell, part of the job description. I draw the line at telling strategic lies. What made you decide to lie to me?"

"I had my reasons. Now I'm going to tell you about them. But first, tell me how you liked my little stunt with the fire extinguisher the morning you came aboard."

Do we have to play a game where you look back a year
And make me pay the price that you paid then?
Now life can make you happy love, or give you pain, my
*   dear,*
If you want to make the same mistake again . . .

Blackburn felt disgust welling up inside again, this time with himself. He'd pegged Brackenridge for the extinguisher bit the first moment he'd laid eyes on him, then dismissed it as an aspect of his first-impressions habit. From now on, he was going to pay a lot more attention to what his guts had to tell him.

"You're not much of a detective, you know that? I was afraid they'd send some hack who'd just go through the motions. So I rigged the extinguisher. I wanted to keep your interest, let you know there was a real live killer aboard, not some bureaucrat's statistical abstraction." He grinned. "Can you dig it, man?"

"Which is why you left me the 'Paul is dead' note. That had me going for quite a while."

"No points. Anybody could have guessed that after I confessed about the extinguisher."

"I don't want any points." Xevroid Kypud's speculations about detection by self-deprecation returned suddenly to Blackburn, along with miscellaneous thoughts about tactical lies. What had been, with him, a defensive habit was about to become a *method*. "I'm not only not much of a detective, *man*, I'm no kind of detective at all. I majored in Business Administration and was a glorified stock clerk for a middle-sized Nectaris corporation when I enlisted. For a solid year I did exactly the same kind of work for the Volunteers—when I wasn't ducking enemy force-projection and projecting a little force right back."

"Then how come you wound up—?"

"I've always been curious about that, myself." He took out a cigar and lit it. "I cleared up a little misappropriation mess, mostly by dumb accident and dumber luck, a sort of military embezzlement problem. And as a reward, they promoted me and stuck me in Arm Force Intelligence! Hell, if the rest of Arm Force Intelligence know their jobs the way I know mine, the Coordinated Arm is doomed."

> They say you hurt the one you love, but that was never true.
> You only seem to hurt the one that loves you, yes you do . . .
> You only seem to hurt the one that loves you.

"I see what you mean." Brackenridge shook his head sorrowfully. "That's why I wanted to see you. I rigged the extinguisher, left you the note—in Clusterian, so it would fit in with all that spy stuff—hoping they'd keep you interested, maybe even help you. But I'm beginning to think I'm just confusing you."

"Better than you realize." Blackburn drew on his cigar, thinking hard. "But I'm not altogether incompetent. I'll give you a free detective lesson, like they gave me in school, and if I'm wrong, you can laugh, and I might not even shoot you. You wanted to be sure I'd collect the right miscreant. There's a war on, and you were worried I'd find out about your Experimentalist background."

"Experimentalist?" He did laugh then, but there was no trace of the bored, whining hipster in his voice. Blackburn didn't shoot him. "Shit, what do you expect? That was in college. I don't make any deep dark secret of it. Lots of people know about it. Lots of people fool around with Experimentalism in college. And I was somewhere between Stage Three and Stage Four at the time."

Blackburn blew smoke at the ceiling and raised his eyebrows. "Stage Three and Stage Four?"

"Yeah," the musician answered. "My own personal, private way of keeping track. I've been through all the seven stages of patriotism, Inspector. Grew up with Daddy's thrilling war stories of the glorious struggle against evil Clusterians. Loved the Arm and everything it stood for because—self-evidently, of course—nothing could possibly be better. That's Stage One, see?"

"And Stage Two?" Blackburn asked.

"I grew up a little, started learning things. A little history, a little politics, a lot about human nature. Things they'd really rather you didn't learn. So Stage Two is still loving your country—and wanting to make it better."

He let it hang. Finally, Blackburn surrendered. "Okay, we've gone this far. How about Stage Three?"

"It comes with growing up some more: making your country better so you can maybe start loving it again." Brackenridge shrugged. "That usually doesn't last very long. The line's pretty fuzzy between that and Stage Four—being willing to destroy your country, so something better can be built.

Something that'll turn out to be like you thought your country
was before you grew up."

> Now we can spend our lives confirming someone's old
>   clichés,
> Or use them learning something fresh and new.
> We have so little time, my love, so many precious days,
> And what we do with them is up to you . . .
>
> They say you hurt the one you love, but, baby, that ain't
>   true.
> You only seem to hurt the one that loves you, yes you
>   do . . .
> You only seem to hurt the one that loves you.

Blackburn had heard it said that everyone had at least one
book inside them which might be worth reading. He didn't
know about books. In his experience, everybody—from businessmen to bag ladies—had a theory about something, which
they all longed secretly to be dragged up on a soapbox, by
popular demand, to elucidate. Make that businessmen and bag
ladies and bandolarists.

"And Stage Five?" he heard himself asking.

"Destroying your country because that's what justice demands. Because it *deserves* to be destroyed. And from there,
you get to Stage Six—destroying it for the sheer sake of destruction. Because that's the only goddamned joy they've left
you."

Blackburn shook his head, outwardly disapproving. Inwardly, he wondered which stage he himself had gotten to. It
seemed to vary, depending on how much he'd been remembering the war lately, how much his leg troubled him, and
how many drinks he'd had.

"But there's something else," he suggested, finding himself
curious now, "beyond that? You did say there were 'seven
stages of patriotism,' didn't you?"

"Sure, man. Like now I just don't give a shit."

Blackburn grunted. "Okay, Experimentalism's out as a
useful motive for anything. Then how about another demonstration of my admittedly modest detecting powers: Scotty
Moctesuma was almost killed at the beginning of the tour, in a

car accident. It was you who made the clumsy, unsuccessful attempt on his life."

Brackenridge sat up. "I'm impressed at last!"

"No great feat of reasoning involved, Bandell. Since he tried to cover it up—whereas he called me in immediately when Baldwin was killed—I'd even guess it's something personal. It hasn't got anything to do with the other murders, or anything else that's happened—the way that Baldwin, Lenox, Sabina, Zytvod, Chelsie, possibly even one member of *Frog Strangler,* each seem, at one time or another, to have been the target for some madman, madmen, or madwomen unknown. This feels different. Are you going to tell me about it? Start with why."

"That's easy." Brackenridge sat, his elbows on his thighs, hands crossed over each other between his knees, and he looked down at the carpet. "I hated his fucking guts."

Blackburn controlled his eyebrows. "And?"

Brackenridge looked up. "No 'and' to it. It's easy hating Scotty's guts, anyone can do it." He paused, as if considering, then: "There's a 'because,' though."

"Because?"

"Look, Inspector"—he spread his hands—"do you mind if I tell you a little story?"

"Why the hell not?" Blackburn ground his cigar out in an ashtray. "Everybody's doing it, including Whatshisname, Paul, I mean the counterfeit Dack Stirkey. I'm getting to expect it. My day wouldn't be complete without it. Go right ahead."

Brackenridge sat for a long while, as if collecting his thoughts. Finally, he began. "Okay, this story starts twenty-three years ago. An ambitious would-be promoter seduced a young, aspiring country-western singer. Her name was Cordelia Anhaenger-Hike. Her family could trace themselves back to the West German scientists, assigned on Luna, who built the starship used in the original Banishment. The promoter promised her a career, a recording contract . . ."

Blackburn turned a hand over. "I suppose that's the usual line in this business."

"He used her," Brackenridge continued without answering, "and then he dumped her."

Blackburn shrugged. "It's ugly, but it happens."

"It happens, all right." Brackenridge scowled. "All the time. She was pregnant. That happens, too. So she married the home-town war-hero-next-door, who'd always wanted her, let him think it was his baby, and gave birth to a son in 2974."

"And," the detective suggested, "they lived happily ever—"

"Cordelia Anhaenger-Hike led a short life, Inspector. A despairing life brightened only by a talent she saw developing in her son. She died in 2988, the same year that the son, wanting to begin the career his mother had always wanted for him, signed on with a man who'd become the biggest talent agent in the Arm."

"None other than . . . Scotty Moctesuma. No points for that one, either, I suppose. Or for the revelation that Cordelia was your mother. Unknown to the listening public, and *almost* everyone else, you're Scotty Moctesuma's son."

> *Forget the time that I hurt you, the time that you hurt me.*
> *It couldn't happen any other way.*
> *No, the only time that matters is the time we still can't see.*
> *The time to touch tomorrow is today . . .*

Bandell nodded. "*Fresh Blood* was created. It wasn't a country band, as Mother might have wished. But it was a band, one I made sure was influenced by the music she loved, and, in a way, died for."

"And what happened afterward is history."

"Pretty sorry history. In 2992, I married Sabina, who'd come to the band when we formed it. The first two years weren't bad, I swear to God, but they passed. I'd been pretty naive until then, thanks to my mother's sadder-but-wiser up-bringing. And my father's, whose name, by the way, was Hugh. Then I learned about the demands Scotty had made on Sabina as a condition of her employment. I tried not to let it get to me. So did she when she found out I knew. But it spoiled things. That, my drinking, her drug-taking. It destroyed our marriage."

"Then Chelsie came along."

Brackenridge exhaled. "Chelsie joined the band in 2994, two years ago. Scotty began neglecting my career, those of

Xev, Sabina, everybody else, for hers. Last year, my father—Hugh Brackenridge, the man I thought was my father—got pretty sick."

The musician stood, hands in pockets, and faced Blackburn. "His struggle against the Clusterians caught up with him: radiation-induced cancer. He'd never mentioned it to Mother, but he'd known the truth about her and Scotty all along. He loved her. Things worked out so she eventually loved him back. He even loved me, amazing as that seems. Enough to tell me the truth on his deathbed. It wasn't until later I found out that Scotty had known I was his son, right from the beginning."

"And that," Blackburn offered carefully, "you desired the same woman: Chelsie turned down 'romantic' overtures from both of you."

A rueful expression distorted Brackenridge's face. "I went haywire when that happened. Dad—Hugh Brackenridge—was a hovercraft mechanic. I played in his shop as a boy. So I fixed the impellers on Scotty's rent car—what did you call it, clumsy and unsuccessful? You're no detective, but you've got a gift with words. I failed and got caught at it, but Scotty forgave me. There was a sort of reconciliation."

Blackburn shook his head. "One question. How come you didn't just tell me this in the beginning, instead of all the crap with the fire extinguisher and—"

A distressed look crossed Brackenridge's face. "It was my life—my mother's too." He smiled a crooked smile. "We're all public property in this business. You learn to protect your privacy until it's a reflex. I won't say we didn't ask for it. But I figured you needed to know about Scotty. It was weird for a while. I think Sabina had it figured out, but no one else."

> They say you hurt the one you love, but this, I know, is
>   true (yes I do).
> You can't hurt anyone that doesn't love you (am I get-
>   ting through?) . . .
> You can't hurt anyone that doesn't love you.

XXII

Und Grüne Himmel

"Hello, hype-room?"

Impatient, the investigator stared into the screen. He'd hurried, not quite as fast as his legs could carry him—he'd been through that once already today and didn't want to repeat it for at least a couple of years—back to his own quarters after finishing his revealing conversation with Bandell Brackenridge.

The bastard son of Scotty Moctesuma.

Immediately on arriving, he'd rummaged through his gray soft-sided bag, extracted his bottle of Mellow Meltdown, unscrewed the top—and then, as a solid image had begun forming before his eyes, transmitted from the communications section of the bridge, set the bottle down on the bunkside table and forgotten it.

"This is Captain-Inspector Nathaniel Horatius Blackburn, Coordinated Arm Force Intelligence," he told that image now. "Urgent and confidential. I'm a passenger in Stateroom—"

He looked around his little cabin, shook his head, and suppressed the sarcastic tone which he'd begun to feel creeping into his voice in the space of that last word.

"—in Stateroom 96, Frame 753. I repeat, urgent and confidential. Take all available security precautions. How soon can you get me on the Luna downlink?"

The three-dimensional image in the hype-room, that of a very young, very light blue Ewon—robin's egg was the shade it would have been called a thousand years ago, before all the robins had stopped laying eggs—gabbled at him frantically.

"Yes, Ensign, I know how much it costs. This is official business. I tell you for the third time, urgent and confidential. Coordinator's priority Alpha Three—"

The Ewon interrupted again, wanting to argue. Technically, ship-to-surface communications were a lot of hassle (the ensign used another word, a scrubbed-up, socially acceptable cognate of the captain's favorite, *fonthdun),* distances and velocities making connections tenuous, difficult to maintain. Blackburn had decided it was worth the trouble and expense, damn the *fonthdun,* full speed ahead.

At least he hoped it was. Working for the duly constituted authorities wasn't what it had been in its heyday before the Blowup, but he had no way of knowing that, short of having paid more attention than he had in his history of economics classes.

"Look, Ensign, you want to pay for a second call yourself, to check that out with the Grand Duchess? Talk to your captain, or have him—good. I'm glad to hear we agree about something at last. I guess we won't disturb him, then. Tell the Lunaside station operator that I'm calling my own office, ALTai 5-2525."

Outside his "stateroom," through the tiny porthole, Blackburn could see the *Parkinson's* inertial fields flare a brilliant green, momentarily washing out the starry blackness. Different colors at different times—there didn't seem to be any rhyme or reason to it—whatever the gods of quantum physics liked at the moment.

Meanwhile, he served different gods—or they'd end up serving him, medium rare. When this was finally over—if it ever was—his expense account would be gone over with a finer scrutiny than anything the villainous and semilegendary IRS had ever imagined. What occupied Blackburn's mind now, however, was that he needed to talk with Mallie. There was work for both of them to do. And for the first time since this whole thing had begun, he felt like a real detective.

Bandell Brackenridge had been both correct and incorrect at the same time. In itself, his confession—if that's what it could be called—hadn't been of much objective use to the detective, except that it had jogged his memory of an earlier conversation, one he'd been pretty dissatisfied with at the time. It had also shifted his attention toward someone else's past.

Several someone elses.

And that had led to another thought. Perhaps there *was* a way to get around privacy seals, after all. An easy way. Like all good ideas, it seemed so obvious now that, rather than enjoying having thought of it, he was chagrined he hadn't thought of it earlier. Oh well, the point was that maybe he could learn something useful from the kind of information no one ever thought to—

"Hello, Mallie?"

"Boss? Is that you?"

It was nighttime in the Altai Escarpment area. Exactly as he'd known it would, his office machinery had relayed his long long-distance call to his secretary's home, a split-level tank of artificial ocean water in the Polybius suburbs, east of the downtown business district. All of the surprise that the porpoise couldn't show on her face was present in her voice. He was a little surprised, too. After arguing with the ensign on the bridge, he'd expected snow and static. This connection was as crisp as if he'd been calling from next door.

"Sorry to get you up," he told her. "I thought fish never slept . . . Yeah, I know you're not a fish. I just wanted you to be sure it's me. It's me, all right, calling from Cisplutonian space on the Coordinator's dollar. Listen, Mallie . . ."

As quickly as he could, he filled his sleepy assistant in on what had happened since he'd last talked to her, what he'd learned from Bandell Brackenridge and others. As usual, she listened to him patiently, gathering her wits, a thread of silvery bubbles drifting upward from her blowhole toward the top of the screen.

"Something has troubled me, nagged me almost from the beginning of this assignment, Mallie, and, having had one brilliant idea already—which I'll tell you about at great length in a minute—I also think I just figured out what the trouble is. If I'd seen it sooner, I might have saved some lives. There's a glaring contradiction represented by the murders of Victor Baldwin and Edith Lenox."

"But, Boss," Mallie demanded, "how can something like two murders be contradictory?"

He wanted to jump up and down. He'd asked that question of himself a hundred times before conceiving of an answer that made sense. He hadn't felt this much excitement since— since—and, recognizing what he was feeling, he felt the feeling die. That happened to him a lot these days, and it was worse, he thought sometimes, than the occasional nightmares, the constant fatigue, or even the pain.

"It all depends," he sighed, "on why they get committed in the first place. It's what I told you before. What they told me in Intelligence School: *'A consistent motive may be implied by each of a series of apparently unrelated acts. Properly interpreted, this should eventually demonstrate who committed them.'*"

She swished her flukes impatiently. "Great, Boss, but what does it mean?"

"It didn't mean a damned thing," he answered, "and that's what I should have noticed. Any motives I could imagine for killing Lenox were canceled out by any motives that made sense of killing Baldwin. Look: you have a guy who's vital to an enterprise because he smooths the way between two difficult idiots, right?"

She nodded her head. "That would be Victor Baldwin."

"Right. So, if you're interested in sabotaging an enterprise, the first thing you do is get rid of the peacemaker, right?" He struck his left palm with his right fist. "But then, just for the hell of it, you get rid of one of the difficult idiots and undo what your first murder accomplished? It just doesn't make sense."

Very quietly: "That's what I said, Boss."

Blackburn threw up his hands. "So sue me for violation of copyright. I was beginning to think I had more than one murderer, working at cross-purposes to one another. But that violates another law, which I'm henceforth going to call 'Blackburn's Razor': don't multiply your murderers beyond the necessities of parsimony. I'd abandoned the political sabotage theory and was concentrating on purely personal motives. It never occurred to me that I should abandon that, too, and look for some third reason for killing all these people."

"Which is?"

He shrugged. "I'm not sure yet, precisely, but it's why I called you. I don't have a lead, but I have an idea of how to get one. It's what I want you to help me figure out."

"At these rates?" With these words, she very nearly generated a facial expression. "How?"

"I want you to check deeply into the backgrounds of Victor Baldwin, Edith Lenox, and Scotty Moctesuma. Right now. Tonight. We'll look for things outside the context of the *Fresh Blood* tour that any two of them might have in common—"

"But, Boss," she protested, "the seals—"

"I prefer porpoises," he leered. "That's my other brilliant idea. Don't bother with anything under purchased privacy. Concentrate on things people are usually proud of, things they want in résumés, brochures, things they'd like to see in print or on the hype. We'll talk about it first. I'll stay on the line. There should be some kind of minimal files in the Coordinator's office, too. Wake everybody up—Anastasia the Terrible herself—if you have to. I'm trusting to luck, and to the undeniable intelligence of my personal part-time secretary."

"Boss, you flatter me."

He nodded. "That's because I can't afford to pay you overtime."

Mallie began checking.

An hour went by.

Two hours.

At Blackburn's direction, and while he waited impatiently, she began with a universal key-word search of hypercom newsfiles, going on to print magazines, and finally with security checks ordered by the Coordinator in preparation for the tour.

With publicist Victor Baldwin, they hit a dead end: no connection was apparent between the man and Moctesuma going back more than the few years they'd both worked for *Fresh Blood*. None at all could be found between Baldwin and Lenox before the tour.

More time ticked away.

Expensive time.

Finally: "Here's something, I think, Boss. It says here that Edith Lenox attended four years at Sagan-Winkle Memorial

University. Isn't that the same—"

"Ha!" Blackburn crowed. "The same Durationite-oriented college where Scotty Moctesuma went, after going to Buckley Prep. Did she happen to go to Buckley Prep, too?"

"No, Boss, I don't even think it's coed. There's a two-year overlap in the period they each spent at Sagan-Winkle. We could start looking around for friends they had in common, classes, extracurricular activities, professors, and so on. But I think I've got a better lead. Sagan-Winkle's where Moctesuma was, among other things, first a staffer, then, it says here, 'the outspoken editor' of the student hype-net publication. Care to see some samples?"

"No. But send them up anyway."

Thus another two hours came and went.

Together, and at mounting ship-to-surface hype rates, which had been astronomical to begin with, they skimmed Scotty Moctesuma's early, impassioned writings: essays, editorials, feature pieces, even the italicized replies he made to letters to the editor.

The pattern was clear. Unlike most individuals, worn down by the unrelenting pressure of embarrassment at the hands of moderate professors and peers—during a period of four years, in addition to covering campus events and news stories of general interest to the Arm, he'd attended conventions, demonstrations, pressure group meetings, workshops, retreats, and "discussion clubs"—the young Durationite had grown more radical with each issue of the publication.

By the time Blackburn and Mallie had gotten through it all, the detective told her, "You know, I hate to admit it, but I think I'm almost proud of Scotty Moctesuma, in a weird sort of way."

"Yes, Boss, I know exactly what you mean. If for nothing else, then as a young fellow who stuck to his guns—whatever that peculiar expression means."

"Yeah, and despite the fact that I'm still tempted to vomit over the man's ideas."

Mallie laughed. "Brackenridge was right, Boss, you do have a way with words."

At long last they came to the bottom of the young Moctesuma's file. Writing in his senior year, he'd done a final column for the university hype-net.

I have become disgusted with the militant moderation and unprincipled gradualism I perceive growing like a malignant fungus within contemporary Durationism. Consequently, I have tendered my resignation as editor, effective immediately, and I renounce the Durationite Faction—which hasn't even the stomach to call itself a party. I intend to drop all personal connection with the Durationites, and concentrate, instead, on a career in business.

All *visible* personal connection. There was still the matter of that red-enameled news plane, the *Lunar Enquirer*, the one shot down by the Tactical Wing, the one that could have gotten Chelsie killed, the one owned by a Durationite news service.

Too many coincidences.

It was Blackburn's hunch that Moctesuma, the campus radical, rather than mellowing with the years, convinced that his faction had deserted him, not the other way around, had remained a lifelong dedicated Durationite. At this point the record didn't peter out abruptly—there were letters to the editor in a dozen publications, even a five-thousand-word article for an independent service—but what remained was sparse. It was as if he hadn't made his mind up all at once. Disillusioned by cobelievers to whom the Cause was no more than a hobby, he'd severed all ties with the public group, and gone underground for some purpose of his own.

And maybe, Blackburn thought, he knew that purpose now. If he did, then he knew why Baldwin had been murdered. Now he could even guess why Edith Lenox had died, and what it was that made her death consistent with Baldwin's instead of contradictory.

And, if he knew all of those things, he thought, then he knew who the killer had to be.

XXIII

The Prepared Mind

"Scotty, it's common knowledge that the Durationites want to demonstrate that voluntary measures don't work during crises. War is the ultimate crisis—'the health of the State.' They'd be happy to see the tour fail. A dedicated Durationite—you, for example—might be willing to *help* it fail, even if it meant sacrificing his own interests."

Leaning on his cane, Nathaniel Blackburn stood in the middle of Moctesuma's stateroom, not taking trouble to conceal the force-projector he'd drawn as soon as he'd stepped inside. He held it against his thigh, muzzle pointing at the floor. For his part, the pink-faced manager hadn't bothered to affect surprise.

Moctesuma laughed, "It would be no great harm to offer hypothetical answers to your surmises." He walked across the room, sat in an armchair, leaned back, and crossed his legs. "If we remember they're hypothetical, without application to the real world."

"All right." Blackburn felt a sort of tired disgust. "Why did you—"

Moctesuma put up a hand. "Hypothetical, remember, Inspector?"

"Have it your way. Why would someone like Lenox, just as an example, have to die? Wasn't she—wouldn't she have been on your side—assuming that you killed her?"

"On the contrary," Moctesuma answered, "if a soft-spined moderate threatened to interfere with legitimate actions committed in the name of the Cause—actions which, in her weakness and confusion, she had come to regard as immoral and treasonous—she might very well have had to be put out of the way."

"The grammar's a little convoluted," Blackburn nodded, "but I see."

"Of course," added Moctesuma, "that would have been pure self-defense—a necessary but narrowly self-interested act. Not productive to the Cause, at all."

"Killing Baldwin, on the other hand," Blackburn suggested, "who took the bumps out of everything for everybody—that would have been clever, subtle, *and* productive."

"'Would *have been*,' Inspector," Moctesuma smiled. "Grammar, at this juncture, though convoluted, is critical. 'Would have been' clever, subtle, and productive. Just as acknowledging such a compliment would *be* stupid, clumsy, and suicidal."

Blackburn tried again: "'Would have been'—provided he was the target. I wonder—hypothetically—if Chelsie wasn't supposed to meet somebody in that chamber. Baldwin did her a favor, ran the errand for her. Or maybe someone told him they'd seen his missing briefcase, the briefcase someone else had 'borrowed' to build a bomb in."

Moctesuma shook his head, refusing to reply.

"I guess we'll never know. The real key to the tour," Blackburn offered, "would be Chelsie. When two, maybe three attempts at sabotage failed to kill her, one might go on trying, mightn't one? Sabina died in a dim companionway for no better reason than that she'd been mistaken for Chelsie, wrapped against the cold in the same blanket Chelsie had worn. But why Zytvod? More stupidity and clumsiness?"

Moctesuma shrugged. "I've no idea, Inspector. I thought this was your hypothetical tale."

"C'mon, Scotty, be a sport. Give me an educated guess."

"Mmmm . . ." The man closed his eyes, wrinkling his brow

in concentration. "How about this: spy that he was, perhaps Zib knew too much—or might have come to know too much in the future—and was telling too much of it to a certain Inspector of Arm Force Intelligence."

"That clears things up." Blackburn couldn't conceal his satisfaction. Judging from his expression, Moctesuma seemed to understand the slip he'd made a fraction of a second after he'd made it. The detective raised his Ingersoll to center it on the older man's midsection. "Tell me, if all of this is so god-damned hypothetical—*then how the hell did you know that Zibu Zytvod is a spy?*"

"*Don't!*"

The scream came from the door to the companionway. It was Chelsie Bradford's voice. Blackburn didn't glance that direction or let the muzzle of his pistol waver.

Looking toward the door, Moctesuma spread his plump hands. "Call the captain, my dear. Tell him to bring some crewbeings. I believe the good Inspector's mind was shattered by his war experiences. 'Shell shock,' they used to call it, 'combat fatigue,' or 'delayed stress.' He's come unhinged and needs help."

Blackburn took up trigger-slack. The pistol's sighting-laser painted a brilliant carmine dot on Moctesuma's solar plexus. Still he didn't look away, but he could tell from her voice that Chelsie had crossed the threshold and was approaching.

"It's no good." The girl's voice sounded wearier than it had the first time Blackburn had heard it. "I've been at the door for quite a while, Scotty. I just don't want you shot."

Blackburn could see her now, in the corner of his eye. With a pale, shattered expression, she turned toward him. "Please don't hurt him, Inspector—"

"Nate," he found himself correcting her inanely, "at least call me Nate—and go ahead. Call the captain."

Ignoring his words, she stepped closer. "I know he hurt a lot of people, Nate. He tried to hurt me. But please don't hurt him back. Two wrongs don't make a—"

Moving like a younger man, Moctesuma was out of his chair, behind Chelsie before Blackburn could pull the trigger. One of the daggers he carried in his boot materialized in his hand. He pressed it against her throat until a scarlet droplet formed at its tip.

"I'll have the gun now," Moctesuma said, extending his other hand from behind the girl. "But first, throw your cane over there, through the bedroom door."

The laser spot went out. The cane clattered against the doorframe as it passed by, and disappeared. Beaten, Blackburn sighed, let the force-projector's muzzle drop, reversed the butt, handed the weapon to the other man, who ordered him to empty the contents of his sporran, kilt, tunic, and pockets into the chair. Keeping the gun on the detective, Moctesuma lifted a foot and resheathed his dagger.

"This has all been very pleasant," Moctesuma sneered— Blackburn could see where Brackenridge had come by the expression—"but I'm afraid all good things come to an end." He wound the stubby fingers of his free hand into the pale golden hair at the back of Chelsie's neck. "My dear, you've been like a daughter to me—"

"Yeah," Blackburn interrupted. "Look at the way he treated his own son!"

Without replying, Moctesuma twisted Chelsie's hair in his hand until the girl gasped and sank halfway to her knees in agony. The muzzle of the force-projector swung from Blackburn's midsection until it was pressed against the side of Chelsie's face.

"As I was saying, I'm very fond of you, my dear, and no less fond of my own well-being. But there comes a time when sacrifices are necessary. Even of the things we're fondest of." He shook his head. "What sort of sacrifice would it be, otherwise?"

The question didn't require answering. Rummaging through Blackburn's belongings, Moctesuma waved the pistol toward the stateroom door. "Inspector, let us agree from the outset: you'll precede me us down the corridor. Should you attempt to overcome me or escape, she'll die that much sooner —in more pain—than I've planned."

Shoulders sagging, Blackburn took a couple of steps, then paused at the door, leaning on the jamb. "Why does she have to die, Moctesuma? You've wrecked the tour. This"—he waved a hand, indicating what had taken place in the past fifteen minutes—"ought to finish it off. Let her go. Take a lifeslip from one of the—"

Moctesuma didn't speak for a moment, as if tempted by

Blackburn's suggestion. "No, I'm afraid that won't do. Sabotaging the lifeslips was the first thing I accomplished upon boarding this vessel. And there's another difficulty..." He paused again, as if choosing words with great care. "You see, this tour, conceived for the purpose of raising money for the Arm's war effort—at which it has succeeded altogether too well for my tastes—has had an unexpected side effect."

Blackburn raised his eyebrows, hoping the man wouldn't notice he was stalling for time.

Moctesuma grinned, shaking his head. "Yes, I'll explain—even if it buys you a few extra minutes. In the end they'll prove valueless in staying your execution. But I'm no more anxious to die than you, and that, I fear, is what's required."

He unwound his fingers from Chelsie's hair. Taking her arm with one hand—Blackburn's pistol was in the other—Moctesuma rolled his eyes back, as if struggling to clear his mind.

"The Coordinator"—he fixed his eyes on Blackburn again—"saw to it that these concerts were beamcast to Powerist-occupied systems, from unmanned orbiters placed near enough to eliminate light-lag delay. Recordings were transported by scoutship. Before you ask, I don't know how she hit on such a plan. Some intuition perhaps even she couldn't explain. She's a Clusterian, she ought to know what will work."

Standing in the doorway, Blackburn remained silent, ignoring the pain in his unsupported leg, thinking hard as he tried to listen for something that might help.

Moctesuma continued, "By whatever means such things are measured, our own Chelsie is shortening the war, all by herself." He shook his head. "Something she manages to convey..."

Blackburn's laugh startled everyone including himself, almost causing Moctesuma to pull the trigger. "Why do I always understand these things *after* they're explained? That's why Anastasia wouldn't let me cancel the tour. It's also why you Durationites can't afford to let it continue. Talk about private means proving superior!"

Moctesuma's tolerant expression turned to anger. "Not *we* Durationites, you fool, *me!* Those pusillanimous parlor prattlers could never work up the nerve to do what I have! They don't see the danger I saw years ago, that the Coordinated Arm may fail to throw off its lazy peacetime indiscipline and reorganize—all because of a . . . a fluke! Look at the bungled job with the news plane—"

Moctesuma stopped, his pink face swollen, veins standing out on his forehead. Blackburn kept his peace, knowing that the wrong word could get both him and Chelsie killed.

"That's more than enough talk." Moctesuma shook his head as if to erase unpleasant thoughts. "It's past time we got moving. Go on, I'll tell you where."

Except that the detective had to lean against the wall every few steps, their passage down the corridor proved uneventful. Moctesuma kept the pistol concealed at the small of Chelsie's back, in a bloused fold of her dress. Both he and Blackburn, each braced in his own way for a distracting encounter with a crew member or passenger, were disappointed. They came to a door Blackburn recognized—once it had been opened and the contents of the room behind were unmistakable. It was the storeroom where he and Chelsie had had their only private talk.

Moctesuma closed the door behind them, stood with his back to it. "My dear, I want you to take that lamp—yes, that one will do—pull the cord from its base."

The girl tried, but wasn't strong enough. Under Moctesuma's watchful eye, Blackburn did the job for her.

"Thank you, Inspector. Now, Chelsie, I want you to tie the Inspector's hands behind his back. Make it a good job. I'll be checking up on you, once you're finished."

He watched her as she complied, telling her not to finish the square knot she'd started. He spotted a roll of duct tape on a shelf, shoved toward the rear by a bandolar case. He ordered Blackburn to lie down, Chelsie to tape his legs together above the knees.

"I wouldn't wish to let you slip out of your prosthetic, out of the bonds, and thus escape."

Blackburn shook his head. "It doesn't come off, Moctesuma. It's not designed to."

"Well," Moctesuma smiled, "we won't have to worry, then, about whether you're telling the truth, will we?"

He produced handcuffs he'd taken from Blackburn's sporran. "Now we'll take care of you, my dear." At his demand, she taped her own ankles, as she had Blackburn's legs. Holding the gun on her, Moctesuma cuffed first one wrist behind her back, then the other, squeezing the serrated jaws of each cuff until she winced with pain.

Moctesuma bent over Blackburn, who was lying face-down on the floor. "You know, sir," the older man said, pointing the muzzle of the confiscated weapon at the back of Blackburn's head, "I'm not quite the fool you take me for."

He bunched his muscles, raised an arm, drove it down, striking Blackburn on the tailbone with the pistol. Pain exploded through the younger man's body. Before Blackburn could recover, Moctesuma seized the ends of the cord, then pulled them away from each other.

"I, too, know the trick," Moctesuma gloated as the finished the knot, "of tensing the wrists to assure a loose bond. Now you won't squirm out when I'm not watching."

He rose. "I'm going now to assure that this vessel spirals into that sun." He indicated the brightest star of the Centaurus System, toward which the *Parkinson* was traveling. "It will be concluded that the Clusterians have struck again. It seems the quickest, kindest way to end this tour. If I've been successful, I'll return here. We shall spend our last few moments together."

He was gone.

"Are you all right?" Chelsie asked when the door had closed behind Moctesuma's back.

Blackburn groaned. "Glad somebody thought to ask." The pain where he'd been struck was worse than his leg had ever been. "I wonder how it'll be to wear a prosthetic on my— how about you?"

She nodded, blinking back tears.

"See if you can roll over here. We can't afford to waste a moment. I've got a little job you can do."

When Chelsie lay beside him—facing away, but closer than she had ever been, touching him for the first time—he ignored the faint, natural perfume of her hair. "I've got a spare handcuff key behind a little tag on the underside of my belt."

It was an old cop's trick, taught him by an old cop—a military peacekeeper at Intelligence School—designed to get a man out if he'd been locked up with his own cuffs, an embarrassing phenomenon which occurred, by criminal intent or idiotic accident, more often than most officers admitted. The extra key lay concealed at the small of Blackburn's back, where his hands would have been (and were now) had he been

manacled with his own cuffs. He'd just never figured on being
tied up while someone else was restrained by the cuffs.

"Careful with the buckle," he warned the girl. "It's a concealed knife."

With her hands behind her where she couldn't see, she did
nick her fingers on the razor-sharp edges of the buckle. Chelsie unfastened Blackburn's belt, worked it through the kilt
loops until she found the pocket with the key.

"Don't drop it!" He gave directions until she managed to
locate the tiny L-shaped metal splinter in the proper place on
the left cuff. A good thing, Blackburn thought, Moctesuma
wasn't as smart as he believed—and hadn't been trained by
that hairy old sergeant. If he'd oriented the cuffs the other
way, so that the lock faced toward the elbow, rather than the
thumb—and pushed the double-locking pin with the little ex-
trusion on the edge of the key—Chelsie's job might have been
impossible. As it was, it just *seemed* hopeless until the key
snicked home.

Gentle pressure, and her arms were free.

She used the dagger-blade to cut the tape on her legs and
on Blackburn's, but the detective cautioned against cutting the
old-fashioned electrical zip-cord binding his wrists.

"We're going to need that, I hope."

He smoothed the tape against his bare thighs. Already
worn out from one kind of pain or another, he was unwilling
to face pulling it off—and with it, a great deal of hair. Chelsie
wore stockings. The job would have been less painful for her,
but he advised her to leave the tape in place. It might be
desirable as camouflage.

As soon as she untied him, Blackburn leaned on a shelf,
levered himself upward, limped to the door. Moctesuma,
doubtless prepared for the contingency before he'd come
aboard, had managed to lock it, despite decades of painted-
over corrosion which had left the stateroom locks unworkable.
"Chance," the detective told the singer as much for his own
benefit as hers, "favors the prepared mind. I was prepared,
too, with my wee penknife and key. Now we'll see who
chance favors most."

He glanced out the porthole, where the colorful and deadly
inertial fields danced. He'd heard that a man could survive in
the atmosphere trapped between them and the hull of a ship.
He considered this as an avenue of escape, then dismissed it

as he measured the width of his shoulders against that of the tiny window.

Next, he examined the three-meter length of zip-cord, found the plug intact, searched for the old-fashioned outlet it was made for, one of which he located near the door. Seizing an abandoned coat hanger from the floor, he handed it to Chelsie.

"Break this—bend it back and forth—into a pair of straight, six-inch lengths."

He frowned.

"I'm sure I saw a broom here somewhere."

XXIV
The Most Dangerous Weapon

Nathaniel Blackburn had seen something like a broom, but it turned out to be a mop.

While Chelsie followed his instructions with the coat hanger, he took the homely implement—he was certain from the smell, if nothing else, it was a relic of the First Skirmish —forced it under one leg of the shelving, and broke it off close to the head. He was pleased to see a long crack in the handle, across its diameter and back toward the rounded end —he hadn't looked forward to sawing the slot he needed with his buckle knife, which would have been awkward and uncomfortable. He used it instead to trim insulation from the broken zip-cord ends and scrape enamel from the two short, stiff lengths of hanger wire the girl handed him.

"This would be easier with a pair of pliers," he told her. "Of course the whole thing would be easier with a one-ton force-projector and a Special Forces unit, wouldn't it?"

Chelsie remained silent.

Humor in uniform, he thought.

Wrapping the frayed ends of the parted cord around the bases of the hanger wire pieces, Blackburn used his knife again, this time as a wedge, widening the crack in the mop handle. He forced the copper-wrapped steel in as far as he could, then pulled the knife out, leaving a flimsy two-pronged spear with an electric cord dangling from its head. A length of duct tape secured the prongs.

What was that two-liner he'd been hearing, ever since that trilogy of pre-Blowup space-operas had been going the rounds?

"Why," he asked Chelsie as he worked the material tightly around the wires, "is duct tape like the Force?"

Looking confused, she shook her head. Maybe she hadn't seen any of the movies.

"Because it has a light side"—he pointed first to the adhesive coating—"and a dark side"—then to the silvery-gray outer layer—"and it binds the entire universe together."

This time she grinned.

He gave them both a passing grade again.

At last there wasn't any more he could do. "We won't have time to test this. And if Moctesuma's plans include sabotaging the powerplant, along with whatever other mischief he's up to, then I guess we'll be back to relying on my knife."

He plugged his contraption in.

The lights chose that moment to flicker and go out.

In another few seconds, however, the emergency power system seemed to take hold. The single lightbulb came back on, to about half-strength. Despite himself, Blackburn held his breath. Another power dip, another flicker—another missed heartbeat—and it was as bright in the little room as it had been before.

Blackburn looked at his makeshift weapon. It was of an unfamiliar length. He was going to be hampered by the cord which attached it to the wall. He hadn't yet puzzled out what tactics would be appropriate—if Moctesuma had survived whatever had made the lights flicker—nor was there time left for such considerations.

"Lie down where you were," he told Chelsie, handing her his knife. She concealed it beneath her thigh without being prompted. As an afterthought, careful to avoid touching the electrified prongs, he reached up with the unadorned end of the mop-handle, smashed the light fixture through a space in its protective grill. Placing the weapon beside him, he followed the girl's example, trying to lie about where he'd have wound up if he'd struggled to turn over.

After what seemed hours, there came a fumbling at the door.

It swung open, revealing the silhouette of Moctesuma. Even in the backlight from the corridor—his face illuminated by the vessel's inertial fields shimmering through the porthole —Blackburn could see how disheveled the man was. His clothes were torn, spattered with crimson, green, and gold, mixing in shades the detective had become all too familiar with on Osnoh B'nubo.

"What's going on in here?"

In his hand, replacing Blackburn's force-projector, was Ofabthosrah's L.A.R. 2000, seven times as powerful as the little Ingersoll. Between his apparent struggles up forward, the power failure, and a bulb he didn't know was broken, Moctesuma, peering into the darkened storeroom, was confused just long enough.

"What have you been—"

Blackburn *lunged,* thrusting the mop handle at Moctesuma before the older man could raise his stolen weapon. The stiff wires sank into his belly until they were stopped by their taped bases.·

Moctesuma froze, a look of agony contorting his face. Blackburn was surprised to hear no hum, no crackle, and smell no burning meat.

The lights flickered and dimmed again.

With a little moan, Moctesuma fell back off the points of Blackburn's spear and into the corridor. Stunned, but neither dead nor incapacitated, he somehow held on to the captain's weapon, struggling now to bring it to bear on the detective, who'd risen with his first thrust and was moving to strike again. Blackburn stabbed down desperately, as if taking a dangerous fish in shallow water.

The projector *cracked,* a ton of energy slamming into the doorframe over Blackburn's head. The frame buckled under the assault, showering the detective with hot paint chips and ricocheting secondary radiation. Pins and needles danced in his scalp and shoulders. Chelsie, close behind, gasped and ducked back into the storeroom.

Blackburn's second thrust went wide, grounding between Moctesuma's arm and the side of his body. Moctesuma rolled aside and scrambled to his feet. Grinning, he thrust the pistol toward Blackburn just as Blackburn raised his pole for a third thrust.

Contact!

Tender flesh scorched and shriveled on the inside of Moctesuma's arm where the wires tore through his sleeve. Growling through his teeth, Blackburn advanced and thrust again—jerking the cord out of the wall inside the storeroom.

A desperate Moctesuma lunged forward, slamming the heavy military pistol into Blackburn's head. He lost hold of it in the process, and ran. Blackburn toppled to his knees. His temple screamed in harmony with his battered back and leg.

Head reeling, he leaned forward on one hand, scooped up the projector—its gauge warned that it was close to exhausted; Moctesuma must have used it up forward a lot—thrust it into his waistband. He turned and climbed, hand over hand, until he was erect again. If he paused to think about it he'd collapse again.

Instead, he charged, pursuing the older man down the corridor.

On and on they ran, the younger man slowly gaining on the older. At one long, straight stretch of corridor, Blackburn knelt and held the heavy pistol up. Trying to control his ragged breathing and the shaking of his overtaxed body, he lined the laser dot up on Moctesuma's dwindling back. An Ogat was suddenly in the way, coming out of a cross-corridor. The rating's translucent canopy lit scarlet with the aiming beam. She looked back at its source, and screamed.

Disgusted, Blackburn dragged himself to his feet and ran onward, after Moctesuma.

The chase ended at the main starboard airlock. Blackburn caught up with Moctesuma just as the older man was discovering that there wasn't anywhere else to run. Moctesuma stooped, drew both push-daggers from his boot tops. Standing with his back against the hastily repaired wall, he brandished them defiantly at Blackburn.

On the backswing, one dagger tip caught the thermoplastic and ripped its way through. Moctesuma's arm followed it, disappearing through a widening hole, then his shoulders, then his torso.

He screamed.

Without letting go of the pistol, Blackburn ran forward, seized one of the man's feet. If the *Parkinson* had been in orbit, without its fields in operation, both men would have been sucked out the opening as automatic bulkheads slammed, sealing off the rest of the ship. As it was, some pressure was maintained by the residual atmosphere trapped outside the hull by the fields.

His boot slipped off in Blackburn's hands.

"Help me!"

Moctesuma had managed to get a purchase on something on the outside of the ship. His feet slid through the ruptured thermopatch, but Blackburn could hear him breathing, just beyond. The detective tore at the plastic in order to—

Moctesuma slashed at Blackburn, opening a deep, welling gash from the detective's elbow to his wrist. Anesthetized by rage, Blackburn snarled, retreated, pushed the force-projector through the hole and pulled the trigger. Then, slapping the plastic aside, he followed the L.A.R.'s muzzle through the opening.

Up to his waist in the opening, Blackburn could see where Moctesuma lay against the hull two or three meters away, clinging to the housing of one of the ship's sensors. Atmosphere, trapped between the curved hull and the brilliant, dangerous shield-envelope, coruscated pulsed spill-over from the generators. Blood dripped down Blackburn's forearm, splashing off the hull toward the man. It joined the stains on Moctesuma's shirt where he'd been wire-stabbed.

"Get in here, you fool!" the detective shouted against the hissing and crackling of the fields. The air outside felt strange, electric and exhilarating. Blackburn's hair stood straight away from his scalp. "You're not going to die! I'm not going to let you! You're going to pay restitution the rest of your life!"

"Come and get me, boy!"

Hampered by his crippled leg, Blackburn climbed through the hole in the ship's side and out onto the hull, into open space. The air was thin there, the light shifted and flared. He hadn't yet gotten his bearings when Moctesuma was upon him again, arms flailing, blades rising and falling.

One of them struck Blackburn along his ribs.

Another sank into his thigh.

Seizing Moctesuma by the shirt, he raised the captain's pistol and pulled the trigger. Moctesuma dodged the shot and raked a blade across the already heavily bleeding wound on

Blackburn's arm. There couldn't be much power left in the gun.

Blackburn thrust the pistol at Moctesuma's nose and pulled the trigger again.

This time he didn't miss.

The man's face sank inward at the center, collapsing like a rubber mask being inverted from the inside. He opened the bloody ruins of his mouth to scream, emitted not a sound, and lost his hold on Blackburn and the hull. As if jerked off his feet by invisible strings, he was hurled into the coruscating shields while Blackburn dived for the sensor housing and held on by a finger.

He watched as a brutal, conscienceless murderer flashed briefly like a firefly, exploded into scarlet mist with a dull, hideous pop, and vanished, totally consumed.

I want your full attention, while I give the impression
That I'm the type who knows what's going on.
So here's a declaration, without equivocation.
I'll take these words and carve them into stone . . .

> *I think I love you . . .*
> *I really mean I know I think I love you . . .*
> *And I think I know that you love me . . .*
> *I guess I meant to say I hope you love me . . .*
> *Anyway, I thought you'd like to know (like to know).*
> *Anyway I hope you want to know.*

You need no explanation. I mean no hesitation.
My feelings and my words tend to get in each other's way.
There's really no confusion. It's merely an illusion.
You'll understand exactly, when I say . . .

> *I think I love you . . .*
> *I really mean I know I think I love you . . .*
> *And I think I know that you love me . . .*
> *I guess I meant to say I hope you love me . . .*
> *Anyway, I thought you'd like to know (like to know).*
> *Anyway I hope you want to know.*

I guess it's partly that I've been so lonely for so long,
And on the way been burned a time or two (three, four, five) . . .
But more because I want you to be sharing in my song.
Be sure because it's really up to you . . .

> *I think I love you . . .*
> *I really mean I know I think I love you . . .*
> *And I think I know that you love me . . .*
> *I guess I meant to say I hope you love me . . .*
> *Anyway, I thought you'd like to know (like to know).*
> *Anyway I hope you want to know.*

XXV

The Day After

"Daybreak."

Another "night," an artificial period of quietude and darkness, contrived in interstellar space by men and manlike beings for the convenience of men and manlike beings, had come and gone.

Another "morning," just as artificial, was arriving.

Blackburn was awakened by his own recorded voice, the loneliest phenomenon, he'd often thought—in fact had thought every morning when it occurred—that could happen to a man. He never remembered that he'd thought the same thought every morning. Each time it occurred to him, the insight seemed new and freshly depressing.

Not remembering any better, at first, what had happened during the seemingly endless day before—that the *Fresh Blood* murders were over with—he ran a hand across his scalp and through his hair, as he ran a set of imaginary fingers through his mind to straighten out the sleep-tangles twelve hours had put into it.

When he did remember, he sat up.

Tough old Luswe Ofabthosrah had succumbed last night to

force-projector wounds inflicted by Moctesuma. Although the old Ewon's attempt, after the idiot had left him for dead, to steer the *Parkinson* away from Alpha Centauri, to save his ancient starship and everyone aboard her, had been successful. He'd expired at the controls. And he'd been right—it *had* been for the rest of his *fonthdun* life.

Blackburn was through, free to go, to catch another starship at the next planetary stop, a starship which would take him home, to Luna, to the Altai Escarpment. Somehow that thought failed to cheer him as much as he'd felt all along it ought to.

When he'd digested that much, his slowly focusing eyes took in the fact that there was a red light blinking on the hypercom console, indicating he had a communication from someone other than himself. He reached out an arm until he'd stretched so far there was no real point to remaining seated on the bunk—which he did anyway—and stabbed the button which would yield up the message.

"Captain," came the voice, and with it the grim implication that, since Ofabthosrah was dead, no confusion would result from granting Blackburn the military title he'd earned, "this is Bandell Brackenridge. I wonder if you'd join us, Miss Bradford and me, in the forward gun-room at eight thirty?"

Forgetting, as most people did, that the hype could tell him the time as well as any other instrument, Blackburn searched for his watch among the confusing rubble of his night table. He was still half asleep. After he'd showered, the night table wouldn't seem as cluttered. Nor would the rest of the world he lived in.

The watch said 0815.

Aching in a dozen places from the previous day's exertion —oddly enough, his bad leg didn't seem to be bothering him as much as usual—he made as quick a job as possible of the soap-and-water routine. He leaned toward the mirror, peering at the whites of his eyes. Those two shades of red and yellow looked terrible together. Deciding he could face the day, the first part of it anyway, without a shave, he did take a moment to jump-start his insides with a swallow of Mellow Meltdown, and was only five minutes late meeting Brackenridge and Chelsie, as requested, in the forward gun-room.

> *To know you've got things figured is to know you've*
> *figured wrong.*
> *To give it all to make things right ensures you won't*
> *belong.*
> *You try so hard to fool yourself that dreaming wears you*
> *down.*
> *Believing is for children, the truth is what I've found . . .*

The narrow, eerie, oddly shaped chamber, located in the very nose of the *Parkinson*, hadn't been used for its intended purpose since the First Skirmish, forty-three years before. Pierced by empty gun-ports, sealed with plastic as thick as his hand was wide, its walls were alive with peculiarly shaped spots of light, flitting around as the ship maneuvered into the multisunned Centaurus System.

Chelsie was there, all right, back straight, arms folded over her breast, staring out one of the ports. Around her slender throat she wore a pearl necklace at least a thousand years old. Another Recovered Artifact. Was this an example of an entertainer's affluence, or perhaps the tribute of some wealthy fan? And did they call them fans when they were wealthy, or afficianados?

Bandell Brackenridge was present, too, looking uncomfortable.

Blackburn had the impression that, now that the shooting, metaphorical or otherwise, was over, Brackenridge was there to prevent some kind of embarrassing or unpleasant scene which he, or possibly even Chelsie, had anticipated might take place.

They were probably right.

> *That life's a broken promise, there ain't no other kind.*
> *And all we ever love are shadows, made up in our*
> *minds.*
> *All we ever love are shadows, made up in our minds.*

The idea, he assumed, was to pat little Nathaniel Blackburn on the head and dismiss him with a minimum of fuss. The only relevant thing the detective could think of right now was a poem whose title he couldn't remember, something by Rudyard Kipling, about somebody or other named "Tommy

Atkins." At that, it was better than promising himself once again, as he had a dozen times since waking up and agreeing to this meeting, that he wasn't going to make an idiot of himself. Something insane inside him wondered briefly if Tommy had been any relation to Chet.

"I, er..."

Brackenridge was making a mess of things, right from the beginning. He should have realized that everybody concerned wanted this over with as badly as he did.

"We...that is, Chelsie—as her new manager, she asked me—she wants to thank you for everything—"

He handed Blackburn a small package, white paper wrapped up in lacy white ribbon.

"It was nothing," Blackburn interrupted. "Forget it. I'm certainly going to try."

Chelsie turned from the porthole, giving him a look he'd wonder about the rest of his life.

Brackenridge spread his arms in a questioning gesture. "But you solved the case," he protested, "and in only three days. Shouldn't we thank you for that?"

Blackburn shrugged. "It solved itself. And four people died."

"Five," Chelsie said, her lips hardly moving.

> The characters in picture books all seem more real to
>   me
> Than paper dolls who pass me by, pretending they can
>   see.
> The world's a hall of statues who push and pull and
>   shove,
> And mannequins and silhouettes are all you'll ever love.

He realized that, with all the intrusive questions he'd asked everybody else in the last three days, about themselves, about the business they were in, about her, all the personal, embarrassing, disgusting things he'd had his nose rubbed in, he'd never discovered anything concrete about Chelsie's feelings or opinions.

She may not have had any.

Maybe he'd gotten the impression that she...that his feelings for her were reciprocated in some way—maybe he'd just grabbed the wrong end of her capacity to hypnotize an audience. Maybe he'd just fallen in love with her goddamn music.

To the detective, it was as if she suddenly didn't seem to be a real person at all. With the single, insignificant exception—that day in the storeroom—he'd learned what little he knew of her only from the reports of others, as if she were a creation not of her own making, the way every sentient being is when you boil it down, but of everyone and anyone around her.

The discovery hurt him far worse than his leg ever had.

"I'm not counting Scotty Moctesuma," Blackburn answered—no mater what, he wasn't going to make an idiot of himself—"among the people I feel guilty about."

Perhaps there was some justice in the universe, the detective thought. Moctesuma had wound up stabbed, just like he'd done Sabina Neville, electrocuted like Zibu Zytvod. He'd been shot in the face like Lenox, had fallen as Chelsie had, had blown up like Baldwin, and had burned, just as he'd intended for the *Parkinson*. Blackburn shrugged off the thought with a shudder. It made him feel like an instrument, a puppet of some kind, and he'd had enough of that lately.

He added, "Five people? You might as well count whoever died aboard the goddamned *Lunar Enquirer*. Listen, I've got to be out of here in an hour. Anything else you need?"

Chelsie turned her back again, and stared out the window.

Blackburn wondered what she was looking at out there.

Or for.

He thought about Sabina, and what she'd paid for her brief, unsatisfactory career. Chelsie hadn't had to pay that particular price, he knew. But he also knew—somehow from the way she stood, looking out that goddamned window, that she'd paid her dues somewhere else, and in a different currency.

> For life's a twisted tunnel, through which we burrow
> blind.
> And all we ever love are shadows, made up in our
> minds,
> All we ever love are shadows, made up in our minds.

Nobody said anything. Blackburn got to his feet—his leg was hurting again—and, giving Chelsie Bradford a nod after glancing toward the package in his hand, left the room.

She'd remained an enigma from the beginning of their acquaintance to its end. He'd come to—yes, goddamn it, he'd come to love her. And maybe she'd even loved him, a little bit, for a little while. But her trance, the trap she lived in, was self-induced.

She lived only for her audience.

> *And life's an empty mailbox, where bills are all we find.*
> *And all we ever love are shadows, made up in our minds,*
> *All we ever love are shadows, made up in our minds.*

PART SIX
15 JUL 3008

Life is a Recovered Artifact. Each night we sink into the perilous darkness, grope through the dust and turmoil of disastrous conflict, emerging into the light each morning with treasure in our clutches—or trash.

—Captain-Inspector Nathaniel H. Blackburn

XXVI

Reprise

The music in my head is always playing.
It follows me, it's there when I arrive.
It's something that I do instead of praying.
*And sometimes I think it's the only thing that's keeping
    me alive.*
*Sometimes I think it's the only thing that's keeping me
    alive.*

Vibrating with the mind-shattering racket of the klaxons, the
gray-green walls flew past him in a blur. Pain and motion
were a single, evil, throbbing entity to him, its life measured
out in the heartbeats of his ·alternating strides: one long
distance-eating leap that felt to him like flying, one short,
crippled lunge which terminated in a lance of agony being
driven upward from his ankle toward his thigh.

Another long, another short.

He ran as if to escape the entity, and yet, of course, he
never could. He judged his progress through the twisted maze
that was a starship by the pulses of his pain, and by the
numbers of the wire-armored lighting fixtures spaced at regu-

lar intervals on the corridor ceiling, until it seemed to him that he had been running like this forever.

Stencil-labeled corners came and went, some taken in a breathless, sideways-skidding moment of peril—if he were to fall, he would lose time, and he might never be able to get up again—others he ignored. Startled human faces were ovals surrounding a triad of O-shaped orifices. To him they looked like pale coconuts, somehow surprised into life, exactly like the pursuing beast of pain and motion immediately behind him and within him. Ewonese sailors lumbered out of his way. The Ogat among the crew shrieked and floated upward from his path.

And yet, this time, this one last time, it didn't matter if they got out of his way, for they were ghosts, every one of them, if not long dead, then long gone from the companion-ways of the *Benjamin Parkinson*. The klaxons sounded only in his mind. He was alone inside the starship, he had it all to himself.

Chelsie Bradford was dead.

Mallie, too, mercifully and instantly killed in the only successful Clusterian Powerist raid on Luna, a final, desperate stab for murderous revenge, if for nothing else—certainly for no tactical or strategic purpose—in the last year of the war.

In here, inside the peeling gray labyrinth of the *Benjamin Parkinson*, it was cool, humid, a little musty-smelling. Just like his memories. Of all the places for a special magic to linger, it couldn't be anyplace but here.

Not for him.

Sun broiled the back of his neck as he emerged from the portside hatchway. The pain in his long-healed leg was equally a ghost, although sometimes a vengeful one. Over his left shoulder, not far from the jungle-fringed horizon, dead Earth shone with the internal, sickly light of a moldering phosphorescent skull, the same funeral-shrouded radioactive cauldron it had been for a thousand years. As it would be for another thousand and a hundred thousand after that.

Blackburn looked for the bomb patch on the *Parkinson*'s hull. He couldn't find it. The old starship had logged thousands of parsecs in the twelve years since he'd last been aboard. By now the patch was lost among many others like it. Far below, settled on its deflated skirt, the battered old Frontenac steamer waited for him loyally.

Chelsie Bradford was dead.

By now the speeches would be over with. The music, too. The dark rectangular hole they'd slowly lowered her pale body into, filled with damp Mare Imbrium dust. Camera shutters by the thousands had fallen silent, their peculiar, insane, insectile racket stilled. In Archimedes, center of the human entertainment industry since mankind had once again had time to think about such things, a million individuals—maybe as many as ten million—were turning their backs on that snowy mountain of flowers, turning their minds to matters of the present and of the future, as they relegated Chelsie to the past.

Which was, of course, exactly as it should be.

Life goes on.

Death doesn't.

Breathing hard—and exulting that he wasn't breathing as hard at thirty as he would have been at eighteen—he fetched up against the rail at the airlock walkway, suddenly interested in the weight he felt against his ribs. He reached into a jacket pocket and retrieved the flask—he could hear the liquid within gurgling against the thin-beaten silver walls, a genuine Recovered Artifact—he'd carried there since Chelsie had made it her parting gift to him.

"To love," he said aloud, unstoppering the container, "to long-lost, unrequited love."

He tipped it back. Somehow it didn't taste the way that Mellow Meltdown ought to. Nothing was the same as it had been anymore. He screwed the top back onto the flask and tossed it, still gurgling, into the dizzy-making depths.

Chelsie Bradford was dead.

But the music in his head, her music, would go on forever.

GLOSSARY

A

Aborigine: distinct tribe of hum., orig. indigenous to island-continent of Australia, some of whose descendents were among surviving hum. on Earth's moon, after Blowup.

adzudyzh: legendary Ogatik monster resembling giant flying porcupine; no evidence of actual historical existence.

Aeri: hum. settlement on Osnoh B'nubo, overrun during War Against Clust. Powers; starting point of famous "Long March" of hum. refugees, defeated mil. forces to Lohua Fihr.

aircraft carrier: spacecraft (or, pre-Blowup, oceanic surface vessel) used to transport, service, launch, recover atmospheric combat vehicles.

airlock: chamber aboard starships or similar vessels sealed against hostile environment, through which beings, equipment can be transferred without compromising integrity of onboard life-support.

allergen-lock: inform. coin. for device to separate differing environments in terms of content, in their atmosphere, of ambient foreign proteins which are poisonous to certain individuals, especially acclimated colonial inhabitants of Osnoh B'nubo; see "airlock."

"Aloha" shirt: hum. garment legendarily from chain of islands W. of Cent. Amer.; generally outlawed in Clust.

anti-Banishers: gen. political term for individuals, groups who, for var. reasons, oppose those responsible for Banishing Powerists to Cluster.

Apollo: project name for American program which first placed hum. on Earth's moon; after Blowup, gen. taken to mean Apollo 11, first spaceship to land on moon under that program.

Apollo Shrine: partially preserved historical landing site of Apollo 11 in SW Mare Tranquillitatus.

Arm: inform. term for that segment of "home" or "Milky Way" galaxy inhabited by hum. beings, also for loose confed. of hum., Ewon, Ogat living there.

Armadillo: informally known as "New Texas," Backside village in Mendeleev region noted for presence of Piper College.

Arm Force: volunteer mil. organization in Arm which, under var. temporary "Coordinators," fought two wars against Clust. Powers.

Arm Force Intelligence: information-gathering, covert operations unit of Coord. Arm Force.

Armstrong: city located near Apollo Shrine, named after first hum. to walk on Earth's moon.

arrester cables: devices for slowing aerospacecraft when it is landing on another, larger craft, or in similarly confined quarters.

B

background singer: also, "backup singer," in mus. group, vocalist in support or principal or "lead" singer.

Backside: unflattering term for that face of Luna permanently turned away from Earth; see "Nearside."

bandolar: 12-stringed fretted musical instrument resembling ancient "banjo," in common use among hum. pop. musical groups at time of War Against Clust. Powers.

Banishers: in hum. politics, anti-authoritarians who expelled opponents from Luna after Blowup; also, their philosophical descendents.

Banishment: in hum. history, expulsion of large numbers of authoritarians among surviving pop. from Luna after Blowup.

Banishment Day: October 23, widely and elaborately celebrated anniversary of Banishment.

bedroom farces: in var. media, form of lit. popular before Blowup, revived afterward both for export to nonhum. pop. of Arm, and for enjoyment by hum.; chief characteristic is humorous violations, reassertions of hum. sexual mores (often regarded as humorous in themselves by nonhum. pop. of Arm).

Big Footprint: inform. term for gen. region of Tranquillitatus' Apollo Shrine.

binary fission: method of biological reproduction in which single individual divides itself to become two; may be asexual or sexual in nature, with conjugation, exchange of genetic information preceding latter; method of biological reproduction among Ewon.

blood-type: one of number of differentiating immunity factors by which biological circulatory liquids, esp. hum. blood, may be identified.

blowhole: respiratory orifice of *T. truncatus*, q.v.

boarding-hatch: large airlock, usually principal entrance of starship.

bohnous: (Ewon., "center" or "mind"), term denoting gen. authority or responsibility; common English translation is "captain."

Bradford, Chelsie: popular singer during War Against Clust. Powers, sometimes credited with shortening conflict with her moving, persuasive performances beamcast into Clust. territories.

Breathing Vacuum: during War Against Clust. Powers, critically acclaimed first album of popular Uthabohn refugee musical group, *Frog Strangler*.

brigade manager: nominal second-in-command of Volunteer brigade during First Skirmish, War Against Clust. Powers; responsibilities usually less tactical, strategic than logistical in nature.

Browning 680: common mil., police force-projector at time of War Against Clust. Powers, model number denoting (as is common) nominal kinetic energy output in English foot-pounds; brand name, one trad. respected in weaponeering circles, has no meaningful connection with pre-Blowup company of same name.

C

C.A.F.: acronym for "Coord. Arm Force."

captain-inspector: C.A.F. rank, title ordinarily accorded to Arm Force Intelligence field operatives.

cardiovascular system: gen. term for that biological subsystem which circulates oxygen, nutrition, disease-immunity to individual cells of organism.

Centaurus System: stellar system nearest to that of Earth, consisting of three stars, numerous asteroid-size planets.

central hump: body or "torso" of Ewon, minus its legs or tentacles, consisting of major organs including brain.

Central Rim: inform. galactological term denoting middle portion of edge of hum.-occupied Arm of home galaxy.

Cluster: gen. term for dense collection of stars outside Galac. Rim to which authoritarian Lunar survivors of Blowup were Banished.

Clusterian: adjective referring to people, places, things from and within Cluster.

Clusterian Powers: rulers of Cluster; Clust. politics were volatile, albeit invariably authoritarian prior to conclusion of Coord. Arm's War Against Clust. Powers; historians are still engaged in sorting out, cataloging myriad forms, excesses.

companionway: corridor within starship.

Coordinated Arm: that portion of hum.-occupied sector of galaxy, along with var. nonhum. allies, who, accepting direction (but not authority) of Galac. Coord., fought against Clust. Powers.

Coordinated Arm Force: combined mil., defense organizations of Coord. Arm, consisting of thousands of groups of volunteers under loose direction of Galac. Coord.

Coordinator: nonauthoritarian term most gen. accepted for that individual chosen for, charged with direction of Arm's conflict against Clust. Powers.

copper: common term for coin of lowest denomination used by Coord. Arm.

D

dead as dirtside: slang term for lost cause or foregone conclusion, referring to Blowup in which vast majority of Earth's pop. was exterminated in widespread nuclear conflict.

detective stories: in var. media, form of lit. popular before Blowup, revived afterward both for export to nonhum. pop. of Arm, and for enjoyment by hum.; chief characteristic is "mystery," often murder, to be "solved" by protagonist; two main varieties exist (along with mixtures of varying degrees of success), "English" style, in which "clues," logical solution are paramount, and "American" style, in which realism, hum. factors are regarded as more important.

dorsal tympanum: upper, domed surface of Ogat's flotation canopy.

ducted-fan: obsolete propulsion system for air-, hovercraft.

Durationite: hum. political group which, for var. of reasons, desire more authority in hum. society, during First Skirmish, War Against Clust. Powers, worked to make office of Coord. permanent one.

*dylos***:** (Ewon., "sideways," "upright," or "edgeways"), nonperjorative Ewon. term for hum. beings.

E

Earth: planet on which human race evolved, rendered uninhabitable by nuclear warfare (Blowup) in 2023.

End (the): alternative term for Blowup.

Ewon: sentient native of planet Ewonatha.

Ewonese: common adjective applied to Ewon; general human name for languages of that species.

Experimentalist: in Coord. Arm, advocate of adoption of Clust. Powerist methods of social, political, econ. organization.

F

faosth: staple high-protein Ewon. food popular as well among hum., Ogat; source is small, blue, motile leguminous plant orig. herded in vast numbers by nomadic Ewon.

ferret: small predatory mammal native to Earth, rendered extinct in Blowup.

First Nectaris Volunteers: mil. group chiefly noted for "Long March" to Lohua Fihr on Osnoh B'nubo during Clust. invasion of that planet; one in ten survived.

First Skirmish: conflict following first contact between Coord. Arm and Clust. Powers.

fission: in biology, system of reproduction in which original individual splits to form two or more new organisms; may be asexual (as with various lower life forms) or, as with sexually undifferentiated Ewon, sexual and preceded by conjugation for exchange of genetic information.

floorplate: bottom surface of handle of force projector or pistol.

flotation canopy: gas-filled double membrane which constitutes majority of volume of Ogat.

force beam: energy output of force projector.

force projector: employing phenomenon discovered empirically and still little-understood device for generating and directing beam of pure kinetic energy; used for various purposes, including as weapon.

Fresh Blood: musical group popular at time of War Against Clust. Powers, best known for having introduced Chelsie Bradford.

Frog Strangler: during War Against Clust. Powers, popular Uthabohn refugee musical group.

Frontenac: name-brand of personal hovercraft popular shortly before War Against Clust. Powers.

fusion engine: power-generating and propulsion device employing now-obsolete principle of nuclear fusion in which two or more atoms are forced together, yielding new element, plus energy; principle on which stars operate.

G

Galactic Coordinator: nonauthoritarian term most gen. accepted for that individual chosen for, charged with direction of Arm's conflict against Clust. Powers.

galaxy: one of large collection of billions of stars, stellar systems, etc., of which Earth, Ogatravo, H'fothe em Ewonatha, are part.

gas-dirk: weapon consisting of sharpened, large-diameter hypodermic tube, compressed gas cartridge, designed so that thrust will penetrate opponent's body, delivering gas charge in single blast, disrupting gross morphology, biological function in manner similar to firearms "contact wound."

Gilbert and Sullivan: pre-Blowup (19th Cent.) creators of popular comic operettas.

Grand Duchess: popular nickname for Galac. Coord. Anastasia Wheeler.

H

hardcopy: printed output from information storage/retrieval or communication system.

harmonicorn: series of dozen or more brass trumpetlike musical instruments connected to common air-source, operated from keyboard by single player; not generally popular.

H.E.: acronym for "high explosives," term for class of powerful chemical tools, weapons.

heat-guns: device for softening, adhering, setting thermoplastics.

helium: inert elemental gas used in lighter-than-air vehicles, exotic welding, some nuclear powerplants (both fission and fusion), and required as dietary supplement in Ogat.

h'foni: small, elusive beast of Ewon. mythology.

H'fothe em Ewonatha: full, formal name for planet on which Ewon evolved; said to mean, in some contexts, "a swell place to be *from*."

high-plains: mountainous plateaux of Luna, esp. in N.E. Nearside, where semi-autonomous agricultural lifestyle has arisen, drawing its values from mostly legendary Amer. west (see "westerns").

Holmes, Sherlock: pre-Blowup (19th Cent.) "consulting detective" believed by some Revisionist historians to have been fictional; serious scholarship offers little support for this position.

hydrogen: elemental gas biologically generated by Ogat for flotation.

hype: named for carrier-wave capable of exceeding lightspeed, making interstellar communication possible, short for hypercom, principal means of communication, information storage/retrieval in Coord. Arm.

hype-print: see "hardcopy."

hypercom: gen. hum. term for Ogat. integrated communications technology capable of propagation above lightspeed; by extension, any related information storage/retrieval system.

hype-screen: ephemeral display area of hypercom device.

I

inertial shielding: field generated by starship to nullify those qualities of its mass which restrict its velocity to less than that of light.

Ingersoll 291: popular make of small low-powered pocket force-projector at time of War Against Clust. Powers, model number denoting (as is common) nominal kinetic energy output in English foot-pounds.

intertalkie: as opposed to hypercom, within building or vehicle, any purely internal communications system.

iridium: named for precious metal, status accorded recorded mus. performance which has sold more than one billion copies.

J

'jector: slang term for force-projector.

Joplin, Scott: pre-Blowup hum. composer of "ragtime" music chiefly popular among Ewon.

jumpseat: in vehicles of various kinds, informal, extra chair.

K

kevat: Ogatik food popular among hum., source is microscopic "air-plankton" indigenous to Ogatravo.

kilt: mode of human dress, worn by males, resembling woman's pleated skirt.

L

laser cells: small coherent light source used mostly for advertising.

Leach, Archibald: proper name of pre-Blowup media star popular among enthusiasts at time of revival during War Against Clust. Powers; see "bedroom farces," "detective stories."

Loch Ness monster: one of several legendary or mythical reptilian creatures, possibly dinosauroid, said to inhabit large lakes in Scotland, elsewhere on pre-Blowup Earth; scholars differ on question of actual existence.

Lohua Fihr: Ewonese settlement on Osnoh B'nubo.

Luna: common name for Earth's single natural satellite; after Blowup, principal dwelling place, home planet of sentient species *H. sap*.

***Lunar Enquirer*:** hum. news-gathering agency of questionable veracity at time of War Against Clust. Powers, later discovered to be front for Durationites.

M

manipulator: gen. term for natural appendages used by var. species to hold, carry, or alter objects.

Maori: distinct tribe of hum., orig. indigenous to islands of New Zealand, believed to be extinct since Blowup.

Mellow Meltdown: brand of alcohol-based intoxicant popular among common soldiers during War Against Clust. Powers.

***Mikado*:** set in pre-Blowup Japan, operetta by Victorian-era composers Gilbert and Sullivan.

Morrison, Marion Michael: proper name of pre-Blowup media star popular among enthusiasts at time of revival during War Against Clust. Powers; see "westerns," "detective stories."

N

Nearside: densely populated hemisphere of Luna which perpetually faces Earth, noted for presence of "seas" or "maria" (as opposed to lightly populated, geologically uniform "Backside", q.v.)

netting: gen. hum. term for style of bodily covering favored by Ogat.

Nolan-Travis cell: portable power source developed during War Against Clust. Powers, employed in manner similar to batteries, but in technical fact sort of antenna drawing energy from source (later learned to be parallel continua) then unknown.

nose-projectors: gen. term for aircraft-borne force-projectors.

O

Ogat: sentient species native to planet Ogatravo.

Ogtik: adjective used with ref. to Ogat.

Ogatravo: home planet of Ogat.

Oggie: nonperjorative term for Ogat sometimes used by hum. beings, especially hum. sexual partners of Ogat.

Osnoh B'nubo: planet colonized by both hum. and Ewon, occupied by Clust. forces during War Against Clust. Powers.

Outer Arm: that portion of hum.-populated Galac. Arm considered nearest Rim, thus, before First Skirmish, briefly again during War Against Clust. Powers, likeliest to be under Clust. domination.

P

permapanels: partitioning material used in shipboard construction during First Skirmish.

plains: extensive areas of flat or flattish geography, usually limited to temperate climates, covered in graminid plant species; specifically, those areas of Luna, both highlands and maria, where agrarian subculture, with its own traditions, folkways, arts, and mores, dominates.

Powerist: anyone favoring cause or policies of Clust. Powers; in gen., anyone believing central authority to be necessary or desirable in hum. (and by extension, sentient) affairs.

PR: acronym for "public realtions," considered to be lowest order of advertising, propaganda.

privacy seal: see "seal of privacy."

push-dagger: any hum. edged weapon with its handle affixed perpendicularly to midline of blade so that, with shank or tang protruding between fingers (usually first and second, or second and third), thrust may be delivered with same motion as blow of fist.

R

ragtime: form of syncopated music made famous by pre-Blowup composer Scott Joplin and still popular, especially among Ewon, during War Against Clust. Powers.

Rapunzel: ref. to pre-Blowup folk tale in which girl, imprisoned in tower, let down her improbably long hair in order to permit visitors to climb up.

rivet: Ogat. term for hum.; resemblance to English "rivet" is source of many bad attempts at humor.

S

seal of privacy: contractual arrangement under which individual's personal vital statistics were released by registrar only to explicitly authorized parties.

seed-parent: male or female Ogat. progenitor; Ogat reproduce sexually via nonsentient symbiotic species into which both sperm and egg are deposited, leaving both parents free to nurture, defend offspring.

shock-knife: thrust. or cut. weapon aug. by high volt. elec. differential applied to double blades separated by air-space.

skirt: perjorative slang term, with sexual connotation, for female hum.

smallsword: any one of number of muscle-powered edged weapons, indigenous to hum. culture, too large to be called knives, usually lightweight, slim in design, greatly favored by Ogat.

Sonofabitch: first hum. inhabited world of Centaurus System, actually small planetoid with extremely eccentric orbit, making prediction of position impossible, hence name given planetoid when finally rediscovered.

speech-synthesizer: any one of number of devices designed to facilitate speaking of one species' language by another.

spiracles: Ogat. respiratory orifices.

sponge-diving: obsolete maricultural activity indigenous to Earth, in which fibrous, plantlike animals were harvested for home and industrial use.

sporran: decorated leather pouch worn on belt, usually while wearing kilt.

suiting rooms: chamber aboard starship used for storing, donning protective clothing for extravehicular activity.

superpowers: obs. slang term for dominant nation-states on pre-Blowup Earth.

syncopated: term applied to music in which principle rhythm, accent of melody line, are out of phase; see "Joplin, Scott."

T

tartan: woven multicolored pattern, usually plaid, trad. to kilts, denoting clan affiliation; during War Against Clust. Powers, tartan denoted mil. organization.

taxation: obs. var. of slavery in which some or all of individual's productive capac. was claimed, on threat of injury, incarceration, or death, by central authority; usual justification was "vital" soc. services, such as "pub. works," support for indigent, or collectivized defense; in truth, provided livelihood for nonproductive oppressor-class.

tentacle: supple, boneless manipulatory or locomotory appendage; principal extremity of Ogat, Ewon.

theramin: electron. mus. inst., controlled by performer's body capacitance.

thermonukes: slang term for fusion-powered explosives.

thermopatch: expanse of thermosetting plastic used to effect temporary repairs to hull of starship or other pressurized enclosure.

thin-film synthesizer: electronic device only few molecules thick, used by one species to imitate speech of others, this light and compact form especially favored by Ogat.

Three Mile Island: legendary pre-Blowup "disaster" (in which no one died or was injured, nor any property damage done) depicted on Mellow Meltdown label.

tracer-beam: visible laser employed to show where force-projections are being beamed.

Tursiops truncatus: formal name for single species of sentient cetaceans which survived Blowup.

tympanum: in general, any thin organic membrane; in Ogat, underside of flotation canopy employed in generation of speech.

U

ultrasonic cleaner: any cleaning device which employs sound waves beyond range of human hearing, usually in liquid medium.

Uthaboh: name for general region of Osnoh B'nubo ceded by Ewonese and settled by hum.

V

vacuum-dancing: slang expression in use during War Against Clust. Powers for activity performed outside hull of spacecraft.

Valkyrie: female warriors in pre-Blowup operas by Richard Wagner, drawn from European legends.

vedyzhiete: euphoric originated by Ogat, in use by some hum. beings, usually absorbed through skin-contact.

ventral tympanum: lower, less-curved surface of Ogat's flotation canopy, containing, among other things, that species' organs of speech.

video: pictorial portion of hypercom entertainment; specifically, visual presentation which accompanies performance of popular music; term predates Blowup.

vinyl: obsolete synthetic material; gen. inform. term for var. physical media (whatever their actual nature) on which music is recorded.

VIP: "Very Important Person"; term predates Blowup.

voez: (Ogat., "seeds"), nitrogenous Ogat. staple crop, prepared in var. manners, which has found favor among hum., Ewon.

Vytpukav ad Regey: original Ogat. settlement on arctic planet Osnoh B'nubo (subsequently found not to that species' liking, sold to hum./Ewon. consortium); later, planet's largest spaceport, thus principal focus of attack which helped precip. War Against Clust. Powers.

W

westerns: in var. media, form of lit. popular before Blowup, revived afterward both for export to nonhum. pop. of Arm, and for enjoyment by hum.; chief characteristic is time-setting, usually during later colon. of western North America; two main varieties exist (along with mixtures of varying degrees of success), "action western" in which adventure, heroism, struggle between good, evil are paramount, and reactionary or revisionist "psychological" style, in which trad. virtues are called into question.

Wheeler, Anastasia: Galac. Coord. during War Against Clust. Powers, most noted for having been Clust. escapee, successfully contriving nonmil. victories, minimizing loss of life, liberty, property, for resigning at conclusion of war.

Wild Black Yonder: fanciful term, dating from War Against Clust. Powers, for interstellar space.